THE OPPOSITE OF NORMAL

A novel

Judy Mollen Walters

Also by Judy Mollen Walters

Child of Mine

Cover design by Sherwin Soy

The Opposite of Normal is a work of fiction. Any resemblance to actual events, locales, institutions, or real persons, living or dead, is entirely coincidental. Names, characters, places, and incidents are the products of the author's imagination or used fictitiously.

For more on the author, visit JudyMollenWalters.com.

This is for everyone who has ever doubted…and especially for those who never do.

Chapter 1

Hannah

Hannah waited to go to her jewelry box until she heard the slam of the garage door. Her heart hammered as she heard the car purr out of the garage door and snake onto the street. She lifted the lid and then listened again, but for what, she didn't know. Once the car was down the block, she was safe.

She slipped the small, thin, gold band on her ring finger and held it out in front of her, admiring. She startled when she saw the clock. She had to get going, or she would be late for school. She quickly ran a brush through her straight, fine black hair, and rubbed a bit of Juicy Fruity lip gloss over her mouth. She grabbed her backpack and hurried down the stairs, stopping briefly in the kitchen to grab a strawberry toaster pastry before heading out the door for the bus. Today would be a long day. She had Hebrew School right after regular school, and then an extra half hour with the cantor, preparing for her Bat Mitzvah. She was so sick of trope lessons. Who cared if she sang the melody just so? No one would even know if she did it right. No one but her father.

She took her usual seat, three quarters of the way down the bus, on the left. Kristin would get on in a couple of stops, and everyone knew they were best friends. No one would dare try to sit next to her in the two-seater and take Kristin's place. She took out her pocket mirror, just to make sure her hair hadn't gotten messed up when she'd run to catch the bus. It looked okay, but still, she smoothed down a few of the tangled pieces and then scowled at herself. She hated the slant of her eyelids, the brownness of her eyes that was nearly black, the fullness of her lips. And her skin was darker than everyone else's, not quite white enough, almost orange-y. She wanted to look like everyone else, and she never would. In New York, she had never worried about this stuff.

Kristin got on the bus just minutes later. Kristin looked like everyone else. She had blond wavy hair and sharp blue eyes and in the summer her skin freckled, which Kristin didn't like, but Hannah couldn't understand why. Freckles were so cute! She wished she needed to lather up with SPF 30, too. Hannah was so lucky that Kristin wanted to be her best friend. When Hannah's family had first moved here, no one wanted to be her friend. The end of fifth grade and most of sixth had been terribly lonely; she'd spent most of her days, evenings, and weekends on the computer with friends from the city. She'd wanted to go back so badly; she'd begged her father. But then, towards the end of sixth grade, Kristin, one of the most popular girls in the school, had sat down next to her on the bus one afternoon and they began to talk. Before she knew it, they were best friends.

"Do you have it?" Kristin asked now, glancing at Hannah's left hand.

"Of course!" Hannah flung her hand out in front of her, so Kristin could see. She loved wearing the ring, but she had to be careful. Every afternoon when she came home from school, she had to take it off and hide it in her jewelry box so her father wouldn't see, wouldn't ask, "What's that?" So she wouldn't have to explain. How could she explain, really?

She hid the ring in a secret compartment in the back of the box. Her grandmother had given the box to her when she turned ten, saying, "Now you're becoming a young lady and soon you'll be collecting some baubles." Hannah had smiled politely. She waited until after her grandmother had gone home to ask her mother were baubles were, anyway. "She just meant jewelry," her mother had told her. "You know, bracelets, rings, necklaces."

"But I don't have anything like that," Hannah had said.

"You will," her mother had told her, a glint in her eye. "You will."

And of course, like most other things, her mother had been right about that. Here she was nearly three years later and she had the special ring. And some other stuff. A couple of bangle bracelets, a couple of necklaces. She was really hoping Kristin would get her a "Best Friends Forever" necklace for her Bat Mitzvah. She knew just the one she wanted -- the one that looked like half a heart, the words broken down the middle. She'd wear one half and Kristin would wear the other. They'd never take them off.

But Kristin probably wouldn't even come to her Bat Mitzvah, that's what she'd said, anyway. Hannah was still hoping she would change her mind, that her parents would let her. Hannah had promised Kristin, it wasn't that she wanted to have a Bat Mitzvah; she *had* to. She had no choice. She was the rabbi's daughter. It was what she was expected to do. And she'd promised Kristin there would be a huge party afterward, with a DJ and games and dancing. And she'd invite that Jimmy McElroy even though she hated him. But Kristin loved him, so she would do it. She'd try to get Jimmy to dance with Kristin, and she'd make sure they were seated next to each other. She would do anything she could to get Kristin to come. How could she have a big party without her best friend there?

At lunch on the first day of school this year, Hannah and Kristin had been eating when Kristin had asked her to come over after school, but Hannah had had to say no. "I have my first Bat Mitzvah lesson after school today," she'd said miserably as she'd munched on the tuna sandwich she'd made hastily that morning before school. "I wish I didn't have to have a Bat Mitzvah. It's so stupid."

"You told me Hebrew School doesn't start until next week." Kristin was sipping Yoohoo. Hannah wanted Yoohoo but her father always forgot to get it at the store. Hannah was pretty sure he was forgetting on purpose.

"It doesn't. But Bat Mitzvah lessons are extra, once a week, every week until my Bat Mitzvah." Hannah sighed. It was going to be a long year.

"Every week? Why?"

"It's a lot of Hebrew. And you have to say it a certain way. I don't know…it's stupid. I don't even know what the words mean…they don't mean anything, actually. Not to me, at least."

"They must mean something if you're saying them." Kristin rolled her eyes, and Hannah felt her stomach rebel against her sandwich.

"No, they really don't. At least to me."

"So tell your father that. He wouldn't want you to do this if you didn't want to. In my church, no one gets baptized until they're ready to accept Jesus Christ as their savior, and my parents said that can take time; they haven't pressured me."

It just wasn't the same. But Hannah couldn't explain that to Kristin. And now, holding the ring out on her finger, she said to Kristin, "But you have to wear the ring."

"Not have to…want to," Kristin said, sticking her own hand out and putting it up against Hannah's so the rings were touching.

Hannah wasn't so sure about that, but she didn't want to upset her friend, so she didn't say anything. She didn't know what the truth was, not really, or even if she really cared. Because as much as the ring meant something to her, it didn't mean what it was supposed to mean. Well, it sort of did. But she didn't take it as seriously as Kristin and Kristin's parents did. To them, it was a symbol. To her, it was just a means to an end.

Chapter 2

Rabbi Mark Friedlander

Mark wrestled with the voice in his head all the way into work. He'd left Hannah to get the bus herself today. He much preferred to stay home with her mornings and drive her to school, and one of the good parts about his schedule was he sometimes could do that. But today he had a morning meeting with the president of the temple, and he had to be in by 8:30 to prepare.

The president, Anna Nachman, was a shrill woman, tiny but powerful. She stood at just four feet, eleven inches tall, and she wore her overly color processed hair plastered closely against her head. Mark had liked her the first year, well, part of the first year, anyway, but by the end of last year, by April or May, her shrillness had gotten to him. She was constantly calling him about this or that -- none of it ever seemed very important. And now, just months into his second full year at the temple, she was already making noise about how few new members he'd brought in -- in fact, she liked to point out regularly, their membership was declining. Somehow, she had concluded this was his fault.

He sighed. He'd taken this job for his kids, for a fresh start, to get out of the city, to get away from the memories. He thought living in a corner of Northwest New Jersey would be idyllic. He'd pictured rolling fields, a few quaint farms, a quiet life where they could start over. He wanted excellent public schools, so he could stop shelling out thousands every year for private, a tight knit, vibrant Jewish community that could help his kids through their healing process, some nice Stay-at-Home Moms who might take them under their wings. Instead, he'd gotten this.

He pulled into the synagogue lot. From the outside, the temple still looked impressive. It was a fairly large building, with a peaked roof and stained glass windows that had been endowed by a wealthy family who had made their money at M&M Mars, which was just in the next town over and seemed to employ nearly everyone at synagogue. The walkway was brick, also endowed by many of the wealthier families. Each brick was carved with a family name to celebrate a life event or a dedication to a loved one long gone. In Honor of Our Son Jacob's Bar Mitzvah, The Gronlund Family, March, 2002, he read as he walked up to the doorway. Baby Naming of our

Daughter, Rachel Phoebe, November, 2004, the Golds, another read. And on and on. He'd almost memorized all of them at this point.

Anna Nachman was waiting for him in his office. No one had the key to his private chamber besides him and his secretary, an older woman named Gladys who was slow in getting things done, often forgot to give him messages, and still didn't use email, but who worked cheap and had been with the temple for forty years. Anna had probably demanded the key from Gladys, who had probably protested very little about giving it over. He ran his hand through his hair and set a smile on his face as he entered the doorway.

"Anna! You're an early bird!" Indeed their appointment had been set for nine o'clock; it was only eight fifteen. Rabbi Friedlander had been hoping to fix himself a cup of coffee and review their agenda, to check his email and, perhaps, check the *Sunday Times Book Review* online before starting what was sure to be a long day. After Anna left, he would have hospital visitations, a Friday night sermon to write, and a lunch meeting, and then he still had to make sure there was dinner for Hannah between Hebrew school and her Bat Mitzvah lesson. The hospital visits were his favorites. He loved talking to his congregants, to offer them some small comfort while they healed. But he wouldn't be home until after seven tonight. Fortunately, his son Aaron was seventeen, and he drove and could take care of himself. Still, up until a couple of years ago, Aaron always came home to someone there, and Mark had wanted that to continue. That was another reason he'd taken this job. They had sworn if he lived close enough, some days he could probably run home in the afternoons for an hour or so, greet his children, check on how homework was going, have an early dinner with them, before coming back out for evening meetings and classes. But it hadn't worked out that way. He should have known; he'd run a synagogue before.

Anna was sitting in one of the visitor's seats on the opposite side of his desk. He could practically see her ribs through her too-sheer shirt, and her hair was puffed up so high today that he almost wanted to pat it down. He quickly walked over, gave her a peck on the cheek, and then settled down across from her. They chatted for a few minutes about her sons -- one was a sophomore in college now in Chicago, and Anna spent at least one weekend a month out there, checking on him. The other was a second year medical school student in Florida and while she was constantly bragging about "my son, the future doctor," Rabbi Mark sensed that she was less than thrilled about the fact that her older son was not only far away but insisted she not come to visit him once a month at medical school. He was too busy and had his own life. Anna didn't seem to have much to do outside of temple, and Mark guessed that was part of the problem.

"Mark, I'll get right to the point. Membership is down. We brought you in so it would go up." Anna looked straight at him, making him feel like he was eight again, not a forty-seven-year-old man with two kids of his own. "We were down ten percent last year. This year, that number's going to be even a little higher."

"I'm well aware, Anna. And -- I think there are many reasons for it. This economy, for one. The fact that so many Jews are moving out of this area to the closer-in suburbs is another – and those are just for starters." He had assumed that Northwest New Jersey, like most other parts of the state, would have a decent Jewish population, but he had found out soon after he had moved that the area he had picked was just the opposite – Jews were leaving for other suburbs, following each other to Short Hills and Westfield and other towns with quicker transport into the city.

"Those may be reasons, sure, but the fact is, we're down. And we can't afford this. So we -- the board -- need to give you notice. If the numbers don't come up a good ten percent this year, by the spring time, we won't be able to renew your contract. It's really as simple as that." Her voice grated on him with its heavy Brooklyn accent. Anna had left New York City twenty five years ago to raise her sons in "the country," as she called this place. But her voice still reflected a childhood among concrete buildings.

Mark pushed himself back, feeling as if he'd been hit by a great force. "You can't do that. If you want to remove me, I get a hearing by the board before you give me formal notice."

"We met last night." He couldn't believe this. Railroaded by the very people whose children he had been teaching, taking through Bar and Bat Mitzvah, marrying....

"I'm supposed to be present," he said now. "To plead my case." It would be almost impossible to find something else, at his age, a congregation in a nice town with good schools and reasonable pay. More and more over the years, he'd been hearing of colleagues taking temp rabbinical jobs or heading down south to small congregations, working part time at three or four at once, traveling rabbis. The kids -- well, Hannah, at least -- desperately needed stability. He couldn't afford to pick her up and move her, not now, midway through middle school.

But it wasn't as if he loved it here, himself. The congregation was indeed less financially stable and struggled more than they had let on at his interviews. The schools were good, but with very few Jews compared to what they had expected, he sensed the kids were uncomfortable. Still, he wasn't ready to pick up and move on. He believed his congregation could make it, if they listened to his ideas and the board members spent some time on recruitment and let him...

Anna waved an arm in front of him. "Mark?"

"I'm sorry."

"You went away for a minute." She said it accusingly, as though he'd deliberately left her.

"Sorry," he said again. "I was...thinking about what we should do. Look, I'll make every effort to recruit this year. Maybe we'll set up some more 'Coffee and Conversations' in the members' homes -- do a formal outreach to surrounding communities. We could, I don't know, offer Hebrew School at half price?" He winced as soon as he said it. He wasn't supposed to get involved in temple finances.

Anna stood up and smoothed out her skirt. It was way too short for a woman of her age and he was sure she knew it, but didn't care. "We'll talk about that, all of it. Today is just to let you know...to formally involve you in the situation. Look, Mark," and for a moment he thought he saw her eyes soften, as though she felt sorry for him, as though she wanted to help him, even though he knew that she didn't, that she'd been against his hiring two years ago and that the other board members had overruled her. She still resented that she hadn't gotten her way. Then her mouth hardened again. "You have a job to do, and we have a job to do. Your job is to be the rabbi. It's our job to run the temple. And we'll do that however we see fit." She turned on her heel then, and he watched her go before sitting down at his desk. He might as well get started on his Rosh Hashanah sermon. "Happy New Year," he grumbled to himself, and turned on his computer.

Chapter 3

Aaron

Aaron's legs dangled over the side of his bed as he stared at the Common App on his screen. He was sick of filling in worthless information, sick of the "supplements" most of the colleges required, sick of writing essays that sounded like someone else was writing them.

But it was a means to an end, he reminded himself, an exciting end. He couldn't wait to go to college. And his dad kept reminding him, too, when he grumbled about the work involved in applying to college. "You gotta get through the shit," his dad would tell him, and the first time he said it, Aaron had started. His dad had never cursed, not in front of him anyway, until his mom had died, and since then, the four letter words, the expletives, had fallen from his dad's mouth like foam from a waterfall. "It'll be worth it," his dad promised. And Aaron knew he was right. He was getting away from this small town, hopefully back into the city where he still had friends and could go to Columbia, his dream school, or if he didn't get in there, NYU -- or maybe to Boston, to BU or Tufts. Somewhere, anywhere, but here.

His dad had hoped he'd carry on the rabbinical tradition, and he wasn't subtle at hiding his feelings. In fact, he outright said, many times, "You'd make a fine rabbi." When he was little, six or seven or eight, yeah, he'd wanted to be just like his dad. He would go with him to the temple, help get out the Torahs -- he'd loved the holidays, the pomp and circumstance. He'd proudly started fasting on Yom Kippur when he was ten, when it wasn't even required yet, not until he was thirteen. This year when Yom Kippur came up in a few weeks, he wasn't even planning on fasting. "Stupid tradition," he'd told his dad a few weeks earlier, when they'd discussed it. He could see he'd upset his dad, but it was just how he felt. And become a rabbi? He'd long since abandoned that plan. He wasn't sure what he wanted to be but it wasn't going to be a rabbi, that was for sure. His dad said if he wasn't going to become a rabbi, he'd be a good doctor. "You can make good money and help people." To have a child become a doctor was every Jewish parent's wet dream.

The only person he ever felt comfortable with anymore was his girlfriend, Marti. It was short for Martha, and the first time she told him that, sitting under a tree in her backyard ripe with color last fall, he'd felt honored. Marti had lived here her whole life and never told anyone, had made her parents promise never to tell anyone that she was actually Martha. It was such an old fashioned name, and she hated it. She was named for her grandmother, her father's mother, who had passed away a long time ago. But they'd always called her Marti and people thought it was cool. He did, too.

They'd been dating over a year now, and she was the only thing he would miss in this town. She was a senior, too, but she wasn't going anywhere. Her parents didn't believe in college. They would rather she learn a trade and then have settle down with a husband, young, and have lots of kids. It was a shame, his father had said more than once, that a girl so bright would never be able to realize her potential. And indeed, Marti was smart. She had straight As and took all honors classes. She loved animals and had talked about wanting to become a vet. But she accepted her parents' will, she said, and she wanted to honor them, so she was going to beauty school next year and had decided she could open her own salon someday. And then she would have kids and stay home with them, like most of the women in her family did. She didn't need a college education for that, she'd said more than once.

She asked him sometimes if he would consider staying, go to Ramapo College, not far away, and live at home. "You could get your Bachelor's there," she would tell him, as they lay together in his house when no one was home. "And I'll get my cosmetology license in a year, start working... then I could support us while you finish college; we could get married. You'd probably get a full scholarship to Ramapo anyway. I don't need anything but you, you and a tiny house, with a picket fence, just like on TV. . ."

But this wasn't TV and when she talked about marriage, his heart started beating more rapidly and he felt like he was going to throw up. All girls talked about getting married, his best friend from New York told him when he'd admitted the whole discussion made him nervous, that the last thing he wanted to do was get married at eighteen or nineteen or twenty. His friend had reassured him. "They say it but they don't mean it."

Aaron wasn't too sure. Marti was always showing him wedding gowns she'd seen on the Internet, or talking about colors or who they'd invite. At first he hadn't taken it seriously. They were seventeen, after all. But when he saw that she truly had no intention of leaving town, when he saw how strict her parents were -- he was amazed that they'd figured out how to be alone at all with her parents constantly on watch -- when he saw how her older cousin had married at nineteen and they'd been so excited -- like this is what you were supposed to do at nineteen -- he got nervous. And for a while, he thought about breaking up with her. But Marti, with her thick golden curls waved down her back and her innocent, big blue eyes, Marti with her killer body, the solid D breasts, the curve of her waist, the softness of her skin, Marti, who listened to him so intently, who was always cheering him on, made him want to stay. And he wanted to stay. And go. All at the same time. He knew he loved her; he was *in* love with her. Then why did he sometimes feel like he couldn't wait to leave?

He sighed again and went back to his applications. He wanted to finish them by next month so they could go out early. He'd get out of this town, one way or another, and eventually he wouldn't be so hypnotized by Marti.

Chapter 4

Hannah

Hannah didn't remember to take off the ring after school. Usually she was good about it but today she was rushing to temple for Hebrew School. She scowled as she ran; Hebrew School started just fifteen minutes after school let out, and if she was late, the teacher would give her a look. The look that said, "Your father is the rabbi and you need to be on time. You can't embarrass him like this. You're supposed to be an example." It made the bile creep up in her throat.

There were ten kids in her Hebrew School class, and they were not only from her town – there were only two others from here – but from the surrounding area. It was so different than in New York, where she had gone to a Jewish Day School, and everyone had been Jewish. Everyone suffered together through the boring prayers and the tediousness of reading Hebrew until they were fluent. Everyone wanted to be Bar or Bat Mitzvahed, or if they didn't, they acted like they did because the parties were always huge and they got a lot of money. She'd gotten her Bat Mitzvah date when she was nine, before they'd left there, because they always got the dates four years early, at least, to book the best places for their receptions.

Here she got a date because she was the Rabbi's daughter. Her father had picked May 25, over Memorial Day Weekend, because more of their relatives would be able to come. He also picked it so they would have something happy to remember on that date, he said, instead of something sad.

It had nothing to do with her thirteenth birthday, like it was supposed to. At her old synagogue, her date had been in February, and her mom had worried about bad weather and relatives not being able to make it in. Still, she reminded herself when she got annoyed that May 25 was all wrong, they didn't even really know when her birthday was. It made her feel like such a freak. Everyone else knew their exact birth date.

Her "birth date" was really the date they'd found her, abandoned and cold in the snow of a China winter. She was in a basket in front of a church, a note written out in black ink, *Take care of her*, not even a name, as though she'd been too unimportant to bother with calling her something. She had been maybe a few days old.

The church had taken her in, of course. Then they'd sent her to an orphanage about four hours away. It was her destiny from the beginning to go America. In America, couples took in baby girls no one in China wanted, like her. Her mom had said it was like she was meant to be, for them, from the very beginning, and that her birth mother had suffered, knowing that she had to give up her perfect, beautiful baby daughter for a better life. What a courageous thing, her mother had said. To give up your baby. And her mother's eyes would well with tears. "I could never give up a baby," she said. "I can't imagine how hard that would be."

The thing was, Hannah had always thought, they didn't know why she was given up. Sure, maybe her mother had been forced by a husband who wanted a boy, but maybe her mother just didn't want any babies. Or maybe she had been a really ugly baby -- there were no pictures of her before the one they'd taken at the orphanage when she was about six months old -- the one they said they'd taken after she'd gotten strong enough to put her up for adoption in America. The one that was meant to lure in desperate couples.

And here was the other part that always gnawed at her. She wasn't really Jewish. She was Christian, or nothing, or whatever the people in China were. Did the orphanage know she was given to Jews? How would her birth mother feel if they knew she was Jewish? Would she even care? Did she even think about her?

She would never be able to find out. Her mom had said it would be nearly impossible. She remembered the time she'd asked. Her mom had been sick a long while by then, and she spent much of her time in the big reclining chair in front of the t.v., her bald head covered by a turban. Her mom laughed at that turban, said it was stylish and in fashion, but Hannah knew her mom had been hurt by being bald. That she hated it. Anyway, Hannah knew there wasn't that much time left, even though when she'd asked her dad, he'd promised her that her mom would be around for a long time, that the chemo was working. But he had turned his head away when he said it so she knew it wasn't the truth.

So she'd gone to her mom, curled up in her lap, tried not to put too much weight on her. "Mommy," she'd asked.

"What is it, Honey?" Hannah was nearly ten by then, but still tiny and stick thin.

"I was wondering...about China."

"What about it?" Her mom had said she could always talk to her about being adopted, about China, about anything she wanted. And she had believed her.

"About my....my...." she wanted to say real mother, but the other mother, her birth mother, felt so fake. So not real. And her mother would be hurt. And she didn't believe the China mother was her real mother anyway. Just this unknown woman, a generic Chinese woman, who had one day had a baby she hadn't wanted, had thrown that baby away, and that baby had become Hannah. Still, Hannah knew she had to ask. So she took a deep breath, like she was about to go swimming, and she asked, "birth mother. That...woman. Could I ever find her?"

Her mother made a face, a screwed up face that said she wasn't expecting this. Probably she hadn't been. Hannah bet her mother didn't even realize Hannah thought about it. A lot. But then her mother took a deep breath, too, and said, "I don't think so, Honey."

"Why not?"

"Because...because....do you know what anonymous means?"

Hannah thought that she kind of did, but still, she said, "I'm not sure."

"It's when someone makes it a point not to be found. That's what your birth mother did. She was like a...a magician. She did a magic trick. She brought you to a safe place, and then she disappeared." Her mother tilted her head, and Hannah knew she was making it up as she went along. "And she did that to protect you, so you could have a good life, with us."

Now Hannah raced into the Hebrew classroom, not even stopping at the water fountain, like she desperately wanted to do. She saw she was too late when she reached the doorway. Her teacher had already started going over the prayers they were learning. Everyone was quiet, heads down, concentrating. But then they all stared and looked up at her. The blush grew over her face and she hurried to a seat.

"You're late," Morah Sylvia said. Morah Sylvia wasn't like her Hebrew School teachers back in New York, who were young college students looking to make an extra buck, who put on cool music and played games with them. Morah Sylvia was about a hundred years old, or at least eighty, and she didn't like kids, of that Hannah was sure.

"I'm sorry, the bus..."

"No excuses, remember? Now turn to page seventy two." She flipped her book open and the teacher went on to harassing someone else. Hannah wished she could disappear like her birth mother -- away from this place, from this temple, where she was just a stranger, and not truly Jewish. Even the half-Jews in the class -- like Evan Rosenstreich, whose mother was Catholic and went to church, who gave him Christmas presents and Easter baskets, but who'd promised his dad they'd raise their children as Jews, were more Jewish than she was.

Molly, this girl from the next town over, sat next to Hannah. Molly was the only friend Hannah had in Hebrew School, and not even a friend, just someone she'd felt more comfortable with than the others. Now Hannah saw Molly glance at her finger. "You have a purity ring?" she whispered. "Why?" *Shit*, she thought, *I knew I was forgetting something*. But before Molly could answer, Morah Sylvia said, "Girls, you know we're silent during prayer time. Why are you talking? Hannah, do you need to go see your father?" Hannah's ears turned bright red, the blush creeping onto her face and up her cheeks. "No," she said silently. She pulled the ring off, stuck it in her backpack. She'd remember to get it later, hide it away again until tomorrow. If she didn't wear it to school, then Kristin wouldn't like her, and if Kristin didn't like her, no one else would either. Wearing the ring was what stood between being popular and being nothing.

Chapter 5

Mark

Mark stared at his computer screen, willing the words to come. But they wouldn't. Rosh Hashanah was only weeks away and still, he had nothing to talk about.

Sermons had always been the easy part of his job. Put him in front of a keyboard and he could have a thousand words down in an hour, and they'd be good words, too. He'd wanted to be a writer for a while, during college, before he'd met Julie. He imagined himself living in a tiny one bedroom apartment in New York, a view of the Empire State Building in front of him, typing away, his editor waiting eagerly for new pages. He'd majored in English and his professors had all said he showed promise.

But meeting Julie, that year after college, while they both worked at a Hebrew school, he, trying to figure out what his next move would be as he wrote a novel, which turned out to be way harder than he had ever imagined it would be, and she, working with the preschoolers part time while attending law school, changed everything. Julie loved everything Jewish. She loved lighting the Sabbath candles, she loved fasting on Yom Kippur, even, and somehow, she got him to attend services with her every Friday night as she introduced him to the beauty of the religion. He began to remember times as a child when he loved Judaism – how his mother lit the Sabbath candles and made a nice dinner every Friday night no matter what else was going on; his grandfather's Passover Seders, where he encouraged everyone to sing all the songs, no matter how bad they sounded, and his experience in Youth Group as a teen, when they would have synagogue sleep overs, staying up all night, debating social issues. Before he knew it, Julie had convinced him that he'd make a great rabbi, and since it paid better than being a writer would, and since he had fallen in love with Judaism, too, the two years they were dating -- though he sometimes now wondered if he'd fallen in love with Judaism, or whether he'd fallen so hard for Julie that she'd convinced him he had -- he applied to, and got into, the HUC -- Hebrew Union College -- where he would become a Reform Rabbi. Julie had been delighted -- no, delighted wasn't quite the right word -- she'd been ecstatic, and they married the summer before he started rabbinical school. She used to read all of his sermons, exclaiming over the metaphors, telling him how good he was. But now that she was gone he could barely put a sentence together. His sermons laid in his brain, hidden, not wanting to come out.

It was after six anyway. Hannah would be done with Hebrew school and coming down the hallway to his office. They had a meeting with the cantor in fifteen minutes to practice for her Bat Mitzvah. The melody had to be read just so. He'd forgotten to pick up dinner for his daughter -- again -- and she wouldn't want to wait another hour to eat. Maybe he could sneak out to McDonalds to get her a burger and fries? She might not be as mad that way. He could tell her to get started with the cantor without him.

He had no idea how he was going to pull off this Bat Mitzvah. Julie had done everything for Aaron's Bar Mitzvah. How did she pick the right venue? Decide on a theme? Aaron's theme had been track and field, seventh grade had been the year Aaron had fallen in love with the sport. What could a theme be for Hannah? What was she passionate about? He didn't really know. He'd only prepped his son for the Hebrew part, that was about it. Now it was up to him to pull off the whole thing. He should make something equally as nice for his daughter, more than equal. She'd been through so much, losing her mother at such a young age. Aaron was...at least he seemed to handle it better. He'd been fifteen when Julie died and while he had been upset, he'd seemed to bounce back more easily. And now he was applying to colleges, almost a man. Mark didn't have to worry about him.

He heard, rather than saw, Hannah enter the doorway, her thick backpack full of middle school textbooks seemingly weighing her down. She was petite anyway, and he noticed, not for the first time, that she was starting to develop. He had no idea how he was going to be able to handle bra shopping and period talk. He'd been thinking lately of asking one of the synagogue women to do it, but how would Hannah feel about that? She wasn't particularly close to anyone except a couple of girls at school, and those friendships were more recent. He ached for his daughter, who he feared was a misfit of the seventh grade, cursed with being the only Jew in her class as well as the only Asian.

"Hey, Honey," he said. "How was school, and Hebrew School?"

"Fine," she said, noncommittal. "I'm hungry. What's for dinner?"

He flinched. "I'm going to run to McDonalds while you start your lesson with Cantor Strauss."

"You forgot? Again?"

"Sorry, Sweetie. It was a busy day." He grabbed his car keys. "Same as usual?"

"I guess." She hung her head down over her phone, texting. He couldn't tell if that meant, I'm mad and ignoring you, or I don't care, whatever. Teens -- near teens in this case -- spoke their own language. And he wasn't good at deciphering it.

He led her down the hall to the cantor's office. At least the cantor, Robyn, was warm and engaging. He sometimes wondered if he should ask her to take Hannah under her wing, to develop that womanly conversation with her. But Robyn was so young...thirty or so, he guessed. Her experience with teenagers was limited to time she spent teaching them the melodies of the Hebrew prayers and working with the small teen choir club they held on Sundays. What would she know about a twelve year old on the verge of puberty, other than from her own experience going through it? Then again, that was all his wife had had to go on, too. But he'd never gotten the chance to find out what she would have done to help their daughter.

Chapter 6

Aaron

When Marti lay on top of Aaron naked, he completely forgot about his college applications, AP Physics, how he and his dad barely spoke, how much he missed his mom, and track. All he thought about was her skin against his, the smoothness of it, the softness, the way her back ended in a soft curve, and the way her boobs brushed against the hair on his chest.

Marti was supposed to be at church tonight, working on her fake *Wait Until You Say I Do* campaign. She'd come up with the idea on her own -- every Tuesday night, she had told her parents, she would be at church with six other girls, developing a campaign of pamphlets, posters, speeches, and other materials to convince other teens to remain pure until marriage. This gave them at least one night a week where they didn't have to worry; her parents thought she was safe at church.

But on Tuesday nights she was with him, in his bed, although sometimes in his dad's. He only had the same twin he'd had since he was three and just coming out of his crib, and now that he was six two and a hundred eighty pounds, he barely fit in it, never mind adding her. His dad had the queen he'd slept in with his mom, but he tried not to think about the bed's origins. He just wanted to be comfortable.

"You have to go soon," he told her as he glanced at the clock. It was seven thirty, and his dad and Hannah were always home by eight. They'd cut it close one too many times, Marti sliding on her Uggs and sneaking downstairs out the back door as his father pulled into the garage.

She purred, actually purred. He couldn't believe his luck. He was dating the hottest girl in the school, and even though his friends joked that he would never get in her pants, he had taken her virginity, something he knew he shouldn't be proud of, but was. They'd dated six months before she'd let him touch her chest -- an eternity. But soon after that one thing had led to another, and then they'd started doing it. He used condoms, sometimes, and other times she would say it was the safe time of the month. Marti had read about something she called Natural Family Planning -- some shit about counting the days of her cycle to know when it was okay and when it wasn't -- for nearly a year now, and they'd always been fine. At first he was nervous about it, but when she kept getting her period month after month and whispering in his ear, "I want to feel you inside me," he couldn't resist. So they'd stopped using condoms in June, and she'd been right. It was much better this way.

"Don't worry. Your dad gets home at 7:52 -- always 7:52 -- we have twenty minutes." She slipped her purity ring back on her finger. Her father had given it to her in some big church ceremony when she was twelve. Aaron hadn't even noticed it, at first, but her father had pointed it out to him when he had finally given his blessing for them to date. "You know what that is, Son?" he asked.

"A ring?" Aaron stuttered. Was this a trick question, he'd wondered. It was just a plain gold ring.

"It's a ring symbolizing Marti's commitment to remain pure until marriage."

Aaron had gulped. They hadn't had sex yet, not at that point, but they were getting close, and just that week, Aaron had traveled to the next town over to buy some condoms. He'd been thinking they would finally do it that weekend.

"Yes, sir," he'd said. What else could he say? After that, Marti had taken her ring off every time they fooled around. They'd never talked about it. He loved that she just knew to do that. Still, when she took it off and then put it back on, he thought about what he was doing, somehow more than he'd thought about it any other time. It was like her church, her parents, her religion...they were all in the room with that ring.

His dad hadn't had "the talk" with him, though he knew that Aaron was dating Marti. His dad said he liked Marti, but it didn't look right for Aaron to be dating a non-Jewish girl. "Dad, it's not like I'm marrying her," he'd said, rolling his eyes. And it was true. It was just -- he did love her -- a lot, and though he fully intended to go off to college, letting her know he would date other girls while he was there, he still sometimes wondered if ultimately he would come back to her. He didn't care that she wasn't Jewish, but he knew she would never leave. She'd stay in this little town in the middle of nowhere and marry some nice, Christian guy in another two years and have a bunch of kids. She told him children were a blessing from the Lord and that she wanted a lot of blessings. She had seven brothers and sisters and loved having a big family. The last thing he was thinking about was kids. Still, there was something about her that made him wonder if they would ultimately wind up together.

The clock crept closer to eight and now he had to almost shove her out of bed. Sometimes he thought she wanted to get caught. She was always waiting until the last second to leave. He got up to put on his boxers and his jeans, throw his t-shirt over his head. "You have to get up!" he insisted. "It's 7:45."

She lazily pulled up on one elbow. "I'm so tired," she said. "Lately, I've just been exhausted. I could lie here forever."

"But we don't have forever!" He threw her bra at her -- boring white, no designs or colors or lace on these bras -- somehow Marti's mother seemed to think that boring bras and panties would keep her virginized, or something, she'd said – and then he picked her jeans and sweater off the floor. "You've been telling me you're so tired for a while now. You should go to bed earlier."

"But my boyfriend likes to stay up late, Skyping." She smiled at him, winked, as she pulled on her panties and hooked her bra at the front and then pulled it around the back. He'd always wondered how girls did that -- got their bras to hook in the back -- until he'd seen her get dressed. It was true about the Skyping -- she had to wait until everyone was asleep in the house, usually around midnight, before she would sneak into the basement with her lap top, and they'd Skype for an hour before he fell asleep in the middle. But he never felt tired in the morning and she didn't used to either, not until a couple of weeks ago. Now, every night, she was the one who fell asleep in the middle, who came to school with bags under her eyes, and had even been late a couple of times, missing first period. "It's no big deal if I miss first period," she'd said when he'd asked her about it. "I have a ninety nine in that class." That was true. She was taking AP English and not batting an eye. He didn't know how she managed to skip such an important class now and then and still maintain such a high average. He couldn't help but feel like she would be wasting her brain, becoming a hair dresser. Not that being a hair dresser was a bad thing. It just wasn't...Marti could be anything.

Finally, she got up, finished dressing, and went into his dad's bathroom to look in the mirror while he straightened the sheets and blankets, trying to figure out how they looked before he'd gotten entangled in them. Luckily, his dad never made the bed -- that had always been something his mom had done. "I can't start the day without a made bed!" she'd say, smiling. And then she'd always said,

"There! Doesn't that look better!" when she was done. When he was little, it had been his job to hold the pillows and then to fluff them into place. She'd tousled his hair and praised him every time. "Great job, Ari!" she'd said. He blinked. Where had that memory come from? He hadn't thought about it in a long time.

Marti came back into the room and kissed him lazily. "You're so good at this," she said, and for a moment, she sounded like his mom, praising him as though he was five again, and he grimaced.

"What's wrong?" She tipped her blond curls at him.

"Nothing, we just have to go, that's all." He grabbed her by the elbow and steered her down the stairs, out the back door, just as he heard his father pulling in.

Chapter 7

Hannah

Hannah sat next to Kristin at the lunch table, turning her purity ring around and around on her finger. "You should come Sunday," Kristin said. "It's going to be a blast."

"I can't. My dad will never let me." Every time Kristin asked her to a church event, Hannah had to say no. It was one thing to wear the ring, without her father knowing, of course -- but to go to church? It felt a little creepy, though she was curious, too. She was the rabbi's daughter. She couldn't just take off and go to church.

"But after services we're going to have the Fall Festival! And services are only an hour. We're going to carve pumpkins and bob for apples and there's going to be funnel cake and ice cream and...*everyone's* going to be there but you." Hannah wouldn't mind going to the Fall Festival but because it was held on the church grounds, her dad would forbid it. He knew she was friends with Kristin, though she knew he thought it was more of a school friendship, not a best friendship. He was constantly trying to get her to invite one of the kids from Hebrew School over—but they had nothing in common.

"You could just say you're coming over to my house! Please!" Kristin begged. And then she lowered her voice. "If I bring a friend who's not in the church, I get a ten dollar gift card to Claire's. I'll split it with you." They both grinned. They loved to go to the mall, to go to Claire's and buy hair ribbons and crazy socks. Five bucks went a long way there.

"I'll see what I can do," Hannah promised and then she wondered. How could she go to the most popular event in town without anyone telling her dad?

It wasn't fair. She wasn't even Jewish by birth. She was Buddhist or Christian or atheist or whatever. She didn't know all that much about being Chinese, and she forgot about it, sometimes, until she looked in the mirror and saw the dark, folded in eyelids, the shiny black hair. Then her reflection shocked her. She was not American. But she felt American. She loved the July 4th fireworks and ate burgers and fries and...she didn't give it much thought until she looked at herself in the mirror, and saw the truth.

She'd never felt this way when they'd lived in Manhattan. There, everyone had seemed different. There were loads of foreign-born kids in her class at the Jewish Day School -- kids who had been adopted from Uganda and China and Guatemala. There were kids of mixed race, with an African-American parent and a white, Jewish parent. No one seemed to notice. Or if they did, at least Hannah didn't feel them noticing.

But here, on her very first day at the school, in the middle of fifth grade, some kid said to her, "Where are you from?"

"New York City."

"No," he said, looking her up and down until she felt like she needed to take a shower and wash off her tanned skin. "I mean where do you come *from*?"

"Manhattan," she said, though she knew by then exactly what he meant.

He'd turned on his heel and walked away and by the end of the day, no one else had reached out to her. Except Kristin.

"My mother says we should be nice to everyone," she said as the two girls walked towards the busses. "So just ignore other people. They can be so rude."

"Thanks," Hannah had said gratefully. She'd gotten the impression throughout the day that she was the only normal one, or maybe she was the only weird one, she didn't know, that she was destined not to have any friends here, but this girl seemed pretty nice. At least she talked to her.

Kristin had looked at her sideways. "It's just...there aren't too many Chinese people around here."

"I'm not Chinese," Hannah said. "Not really, anyway. I'm American. And I'm Jewish. My parents adopted me from China when I was like, a baby."

"You're Jewish?" Kristin had asked, tipping her head to one side. "Like, God's chosen people?"

"I guess." She'd heard that phrase in temple of course, at services, or in Jewish History class. She liked the idea that God had chosen her for some grand purpose, though what did that mean, exactly? But since she had been adopted into the religion, was she even allowed to consider herself one of the chosen people? She certainly didn't want to ask her dad that. Still, how did Kristin know about the Chosen People?

"I'm Christian," Kristin said. "Jesus died for our sins, and we promise to live our lives in His name." She sounded like she was quoting from somewhere.

"Oh, okay," Hannah had said. "Maybe you can tell me more about it another time," and she'd changed the subject. She vowed to ask her father more about Christianity when she got home. Then maybe she would have more to say the next time they talked about it, and Kristin would start to like her, and they could become best friends. No one else was talking to her, and she seemed nice. She had beautiful, thick blond hair she wore in a braid down her back, and Hannah could tell that she was popular. On the playground and at lunch, everyone had swarmed around her, and whenever Kristin raised her hand, the teacher called on her. It had been a year until Kristin had begun to show interest in Hannah again, but when she did, Hannah had made sure she did whatever she had to in order to keep Kristin's favor.

Chapter 8

Mark

Mark rushed home to have a quick dinner with the kids before he had to rush back to temple for a meeting. But only Hannah was there, holed up in her room. When Mark told her dinner was ready -- he'd picked up a bag of salad and an already-roasted chicken at the grocery store and topped it with honey mustard dressing, adding a couple of rolls he found in the way back in the freezer -- she said she'd eaten a big snack after school and would skip it. Aaron was out and not answering his cell phone, which seemed to be a problem more and more these days. When Mark had confronted him about it last weekend, Aaron had insisted Mark was always calling him when he was driving, and he didn't want Aaron to answer the phone when he was driving, did he? Mark hadn't known what to say. His wife would have.

So he ate dinner in front of the six o'clock news, by himself, as usual. He had to be back at Temple by seven. Tonight was the first meeting of the new Interfaith Council. The schools had come to them, actually, over the summer, to say they'd noticed more tension over the past year between the faiths. They wanted some of the local religious groups to work together to help all of the kids respect each other's religions.

Mark had been thrilled. This was exactly the kind of thing he thrived on -- planning youth events, helping people understand Judaism better. It still bugged him to no end that the schools didn't give off for Rosh Hashanah and Yom Kippur, even though he'd asked twice -- both years he'd been there. Although only a small population of the kids in the schools was Jewish, there were quite a few Jewish teachers who always had to use personal days for their holidays. He saw the matter as one of equity, while he sensed the members of the school board felt differently.

For tonight's meeting, he'd reached out to the Catholic church and their friendly priest, a middle-aged guy who had sent his youth group over to clean off the side of the building last spring after someone had spray painted Go Home Jews. He found the Episcopal chaplain, a woman bursting with personality, to be enthusiastic about the newly formed council. He'd also invited the non-denominational pastor from the church across town that many of the kids at school attended.

He was especially interested in meeting the pastor. Now that Aaron was dating Marti, and Marti was active in the pastor's church, Mark was curious about the kind of church the pastor ran. Marti was a sweet girl, bright in sort of a no-nonsense way. She seemed to know what she wanted and how she would go about getting it. He hadn't met her parents -- Aaron had made it clear they weren't too happy about Marti dating him. Mark assumed it was because he was Jewish but Aaron had explained that the Jew part was secondary. They hadn't wanted Marti to date anyone until she turned eighteen, and then only for the purpose of finding a husband. They didn't want her parents to criticize her for seeing him too much, so they didn't spend a lot of time around her family.

Mark hadn't liked that part. He'd told Aaron he thought he should come clean, be honest, though the truth was, from the description of Marti's parents, he had a feeling coming clean wasn't going to help at all. He assumed they kept everything close to home, and distrusted anyone who wasn't a Christian. They may not have ever had relationships with Jews before. They didn't want their daughter fraternizing with males at all. When Mark had asked Aaron why Marti had not gone to a private Christian school, he said there was no private Christian school nearby, and it had been too far to commit to driving her every day. Her parents owned their own plumbing company, and didn't have the time.

As Mark set his dishes in the dishwasher, tied a rubber band around the bag of salad, and set the diet soda back in the fridge, he looked even more forward to meeting the pastor tonight. Maybe knowing more about Marti's religion would help him help Aaron. He just wanted the best for his son.

Chapter 9

Aaron

At the same time that Mark was cleaning up after his dinner and Hannah was perusing a site on Aaron's computer about the requirements you needed to become Christian, praying fervently that her dad wouldn't come upstairs and see what she was doing, Aaron was sitting in his car with Marti.

She'd told her parents she had a Student Council meeting after school, but she wasn't on the student council. She just said that so she could see Aaron. Usually they would drive somewhere to make out for hours, talking in between, but today she'd looked deadly serious when she'd gotten in the car, and she hadn't said a word on the drive.

When they'd first started going out, she hadn't told her parents at all. They didn't want her to date until she was ready for marriage, and then only under the strictest of circumstances, the boy coming to their house, spending time with their family, maybe taking a walk around their large property. But dating in high school? No, they hadn't wanted that, and dating a Jew? Not that either.

But after a while, she'd felt guilty sneaking around, she said, so she'd decided to tell her parents. Aaron had been scared that they wouldn't let her see him. Or, that they would hate him because he was Jewish. It turned out neither was true. They were mad, yes, but they asked him over, and he'd sat with her dad for a long time and talked about what they expected of him and how it would work. Her father also told him how Jews were the Chosen People and how he had great respect for them, and that although he wanted Marti to marry within their faith, he respected Aaron's Judaism, which Aaron took to mean he would not try to convert him. And he never had, though they were always inviting him over for their holidays and to their church. Not an exact push to convert, but enough of a suggestion...As far as Marti's parents knew, the two were rarely alone, instead doing "wholesome" things like school events, group activities. Marti's father told her he liked Aaron very much, that he seemed like a good boy, and for Aaron, as long as they allowed them to continue to date, that was all that had mattered. Now, he kept a hand on Marti's leg the entire time he drove, finally steering the car to the empty funeral home lot just a couple of miles away. They'd gone there before -- in the beginning, before they'd started to sleep together last spring, when all they did was hold hands and kiss a little now and then. Marti hadn't wanted to do anything else and he had tried hard to wait until she was ready, but it had been tough. Even just holding hands, his balls felt like they would fall off from desire. Within a couple of months, they'd moved on to heavy petting. She would touch him in a way that could almost make him moan now, thinking about it, even though she was crying right next to him. He willed away the thought and focused.

He pulled into the far part of the lot, by a Dumpster that was never used. It was deserted over here -- the funeral home had moved across town last year to a bigger space. Were more people dying? He didn't know. It just worked out well. They could be alone here. His car was hidden by two big trees. It would get trickier once the leaves came down in November. Then people might be able to see them from the street.

"What is it?" he asked as soon as he shut off the engine. She literally flung herself into his arms, her blond hair smelling of strawberry shampoo and falling into his face as he held her. She buried herself even further into his arms, still crying.

"Look, it can't be that bad." He held her back for a second, a hand on either side of her head. "Just tell me. Whatever it is. I love you." He had a terrible thought then. Had her parents found out? Had they grounded her? Had they threatened her? Had they demanded she stop seeing him? It was both of their worst nightmares.

"It is," she said, barely catching the words. "It is."

"Just tell me. We can get through it -- together." He smiled a little then. Marti could be dramatic. When she'd gotten a C on a Chem test a couple of weeks ago, she'd cried all afternoon. She'd never gotten a C on anything before. He'd been afraid then that her parents had found out. But it had just been a test. And last month, when she'd told him her parents were making her go away on a church retreat the very weekend of Homecoming, so she wouldn't be able to go to the dance, she'd cried then, too. Sure, it wasn't so great that he wouldn't be able to see her for the weekend -- in fact, he'd been very upset, too -- she was like a drug that he needed, and three days without it would feel awful, like withdrawal, but it hadn't been so bad. They'd made it through. He'd gone to the dance with a group of guys and had a pretty good time, and she'd texted him from the retreat every five seconds, telling him how much she loved him and how she couldn't live without him. When they'd reunited Monday night, things were hotter than ever.

He'd asked her, once, how she could really see him, not to mention sleep with him, given her faith. He had been afraid to ask – what if it opened up a can of worms and she realized she could no longer be with him? It was right after they'd had sex, though, so she was especially relaxed and he really wanted to know. It had been on his mind.

"It's hard," she had admitted then. "When I go to church, I always pray to God to forgive me. And sometimes, at night, I do cry..." He suddenly wished he hadn't asked. He didn't want to know that she cried over him, that being with him caused her any pain.

But she continued. "Because I know God doesn't want me to be doing this. But God...He understands. And He knows I love you. And sinners are forgiven. So I put my trust in Him." He hadn't asked any more questions after that.

Now, she said, she didn't want to tell him why she was upset. She just kept crying and crying. "I can make it better," he finally whispered into her ear.

"Are you sure?" she asked.

"Well...I don't know what it is, but of course. You can count on me. You know that." He wiped the tears from her cheeks and patted them gently. "Did your parents find out -- about us?" It was funny how much Marti loved her parents, how she wanted to please them so much, how she looked up to them, but how, at the very same time, they couldn't deal with Marti and Aaron, and how that didn't seem to make Marti mad. She just accepted it. "No! No, they...they don't know."

"Okay, then, as long as we can still see each other, what could be so bad?" He stretched out his legs. Girls could be so dramatic. Hannah was the same way, at least she had been for about the last year. She'd fling herself on the bed and cry. She didn't think anyone could hear, because she blasted her Glee music while she cried. At first he'd been concerned. Maybe it was about their mom. But when he'd asked a few female friends, including Marti, about it, swearing them to secrecy, they'd laughed and said all girls cry -- a lot -- especially when their hormones started changing. He'd been embarrassed then. He didn't want to think of Hannah that way. To him, she was still a little girl they'd rescued from all the way on the other side of the world. She was a little girl holding tight to his mom, who didn't speak until she was over four, who hummed to herself a very strange tune that his mom said was a lullaby from China.

"It's bad," Marti said now, and he ripped himself out of his day dream.

"Okay. Just tell me how I can help."

"You can marry me." She pulled a tiny, white stick from her purse and showed him the two pink lines.

Chapter 10

Hannah

Hannah hated being alone at night. Even if Aaron was here, locked in his room on his laptop, Skyping with Marti, at least someone else would be home. Last summer they had gone for ice cream together at least one night a week. It would start with Aaron coming home from his summer job as a day camp counselor. He would shower, and their dad would be at Temple, working on something, and Aaron would casually come into her room. "Hey," he'd say. "Wanna get some ice cream?" She would never know when it was going to happen, but she always made sure she was still dressed when he got home, that aside from shoving on flip flops, she wouldn't have to do anything else. They'd blast the car radio – he even let her pick the station –and ride downtown to the homemade ice cream place. Whereas her dad always made her get a single scoop, Aaron would say generously, "Order anything you want." She'd get a sundae, usually, mint chip with hot fudge, and they'd sit outside in the humid night, eating slowly.

Her dad was almost never home in the evenings; she was used to that. When her mom was still alive, they would watch t.v. together while her mom knitted, or they would bake cookies. That whole last year, every evening at 7:30, no matter what kind of homework Hannah had or what kind of day, bad or really bad, her mom had had, they'd cuddle together in her parents' bed and watch Wheel of Fortune. Her mom was really good. She always got the puzzle after just a couple of letters, screaming out the answers at the confused contestants. She'd always wanted to be on that show.

Hannah flipped on Wheel of Fortune now, just to have some noise in the room. When would Aaron be home, anyway? Their dad always asked him to be home by seven on the nights that he was out, and Aaron would get pissed. "I'm seventeen!" he would tell their dad. "I'm going to college next year. I'm not going to be here for Hannah anymore." Their dad would wait until Aaron's rant was over. "But you're here now," he would say quietly, and then leave the room. Hannah liked how her father stuck up for her, but she wished he didn't have to. Aaron used to like hanging around her, or maybe he had just pretended to. Tonight, Hannah knew he was out with Marti, though he wouldn't admit it. He would say he was with the guys, shooting baskets. He was at the library, doing homework, working on college essays. A student council thing ran late. Hannah didn't know why he lied so much.

She fingered her purity ring. She knew it meant she was supposed to wait until marriage to have sex. She couldn't imagine ever having sex. It seemed pretty gross to her. When Kristin told her that was part of being Christian, the promise to Jesus that you would remain pure until marriage, Hannah had thought, "Piece of cake." Why would you want anyone touching you that way? She'd happily slipped the ring on her finger.

Being Christian seemed much easier than being Jewish. For one thing, you didn't have to get up in front of an entire congregation of people and chant words you didn't know in a foreign language. You didn't have to spend more than a year preparing for this big day that you wished meant something to you but really didn't, and you didn't have to promise to be grown up before you really thought you were. In fact, Christianity encouraged kids to stay kids, Hannah thought, what with the purity pledge. Why were Jews so interested in getting you grown up before you were really ready?

And when you were Christian, God was your best friend. Hannah loved that idea. You had this best friend with you, all the time. If you misbehaved, don't worry, God was with you. God wanted you to listen to Him, but God knew that people made mistakes, and He forgave you every time. God knew you might stray from your path, but God would be there, waiting until you came back, helping pull you back in, even.

Jews believed in God, if they wanted to at least, in the kind of Jewish Hannah was. They didn't know if God was a male or a female, but that wasn't what was important. God's name was said lots of times during services, but with most of the prayers being read in Hebrew, Hannah didn't even know what she was saying.

Also, the Christians were so sure. Of course there was a God. Of course He loved you. Of course He would take care of you. Of course He would follow you. All you had to do in return was try to be a good person. Try to follow His word. It was all so simple.

The bonus round came on. Soon it would be eight o'clock, and still, no Aaron. Hannah hoped he got home before her father, otherwise her father would kill him. Most of the time, their dad had no idea that Aaron spent a lot of evenings out. He knew about Marti, but Hannah could tell her dad wasn't thrilled by that situation. Marti wasn't Jewish, and their dad had told Aaron more than once that though she was a nice girl, a good girl, a pretty girl, a smart girl, and though he was glad that Aaron had made friends in their town, he shouldn't be dating non-Jewish girls. For one thing, how did it look that the rabbi's son was dating a non-Jew? It looked bad, he told Aaron. Very bad. For another, Aaron himself was planning to go off to college in less than a year, and a break up was hard, Mark had said. Trust me, he had told his son, in front of Hannah. You don't want to go through that, not at this young age. You have plenty of time to become serious.

Hannah wondered if Marti and Aaron were having sex. Probably not, since Marti was a Christian. But once -- okay, more than once -- she had stood outside of Aaron's room, listening to his muffled voice, along with a few of his friends, and she wondered. One day last summer, instead of going to Kristin's, she had stayed home. Aaron and his buddy Ryan were locked in his room. She had snuck up to the doorway and put her ear to the door. She couldn't hear much, and was wondering if the glass-against-the-wall-thing really worked when she heard Aaron say, "Man, her boobs, they are like, perfect." Ryan laughed. "Are you using protection, though?" Aaron had turned on some loud music then, and she hadn't heard the reply. Marti wore the ring, too, but maybe Ryan just didn't know what that meant, and maybe Aaron didn't want to admit he wasn't having sex with his girlfriend. She didn't know.

Marti and Kristin were sisters and she knew how Kristin's parents felt about it. Kristin had told Hannah about the ring ceremonies their father had made for each of the girls when they turned twelve. It sounded so beautiful to Hannah. He had taken each of them out to their favorite restaurant -- he told them they could go anywhere they wanted. Kristin had chosen the most expensive restaurant in the county, with fancy glasses and china and huge steaks, and when their mom had protested to their dad, he had said gently, "It's worth it to make my little girl happy, and if we want her to take her vow to Jesus seriously, we need to do everything we can to ensure she will. It's worth every penny if she'll wait until marriage." Then he'd hired a limo -- Hannah had never been in a limo -- and Kristin had dressed in a fancy dress -- her mom had taken her to a special store for it -- and she and her dad had gone off in the limo and had their fancy dinner, and then they'd gone to their church, where all the other twelve year old girls were waiting with their fathers, dressed in suits, the girls, adorned in their sparkly dresses, and they'd had a party. A huge party that sounded like the party after a Bat Mitzvah service, but just with cake and punch, and no dancing, because apparently people in their church weren't supposed to dance. But they'd had a ceremony, and each father had written a special statement for his daughter about keeping pure and having faith and waiting for the one man God had set out to find her. Then Kristin's father had placed the purity ring -- always made of gold, it looked just like her mother's wedding ring, actually -- on his daughter's ring finger, and kissed her gently on the cheek. It sounded magical to Hannah.

Chapter 11

Mark

When Rabbi Friedlander got back to Temple – and here he definitely felt like Rabbi Friedlander, not Mark, not Hannah and Aaron's dad, not anyone else – the light in the conference room was on, and a young man, maybe around thirty or so, was standing at one of the bookshelves. Mark cringed when he realized that the man seemed so young to him; there was a time, not that long ago, when thirty had seemed so old, and then normal, and now the thirty year olds seemed like babies just out of the nest. With his head cocked to one side, the man was peering at some titles.

Rabbi Friedlander cleared his throat. "Can I help you?" The man definitely wasn't a regular congregant, though he could have passed for the father of a younger student whose company didn't force suits on their employees. He had sandy brown hair and limp brown eyes, and he wore an earnest expression on his face.

"Oh, yes. Rabbi Friedlander. I'm Jim Jameson." He strode toward the rabbi even though they were only steps apart. Ah, the pastor from down the road. The Rabbi had heard he was young, and he'd gone on the church's web site, but all of the pictures of Pastor Jameson had been unclear or blurry or taken from a distance.

"Great to meet you, Jim. So glad you could come." He shook the man's outstretched hand and motioned for him to sit down. "Everyone else should be here in a few minutes. Can I get you some coffee?"

"Coffee'd be great. Long day."

"How do you take it?" Rabbi Friedlander was relieved. Getting Jim coffee was something to do, instead of creating small talk. He hated small talk, yet so much of it was required as a rabbi, with your congregants, your board, everyone you came in contact with. The weather, local politics, an accident at the same intersection the police had been promising to put in a light at for the last year...what was the point of it all? He liked talking about real issues, real problems, real solutions. Even during rabbinical school, his mentors had told him that if he didn't learn to small talk, he'd have a hard time with a congregation. They'd suggested he consider other areas of the rabbinate, but he liked the idea of counseling people he could get to know from the time they were born until the time they died. He liked the idea of multigenerational families and presiding over their Brises and their Bar Mitzvahs and their weddings, and then doing the same for their kids. He had started that in Manhattan, and it had been okay that he wasn't so great at small talk – everyone in Manhattan was too busy for it anyway – but here - here small talk was everything. The only person he'd liked small talking with had been his wife.

He headed towards the small kitchen in the back of the synagogue, hoping that the Catholic and Episcopalian priests would be in the conference room by the time he got back. He fixed his own coffee – black, strong, he knew he would be up until midnight working on his Rosh Hashanah sermon, not to mention gathering something to speak about at Saturday services this week and a short speech about the Bar Mitzvah boy for his service. He didn't know what to do about that one. How do you say something positive about a kid who spends all of Hebrew School class blowing spit balls at his classmates and speaking rudely to every teacher? Maybe he could use the word energetic to describe him. . .

The pastor had requested black coffee. Good. Easier that way. He couldn't mess up the amount of milk or sugar or wonder if he wanted Sweet and Low or Equal. And since he liked his coffee black, too, it was something for them to talk about, he thought, and that made him feel better. He headed back to the conference room, noticing the carpet needed a good vacuum, wishing the synagogue could afford more than once a week cleaning. Between the old paint and dirty carpet, the temple was looking dingy and old these days.

By the time he got back, the pastor had been joined by Erica, the Episcopalian priest, and Michael, the fifty-something, gray-haired, kindly priest from St. Joe's. They were all sitting at the table now, engaged in conversation. "I can get the two of you coffee, if you'd like," Mark said, sliding one of the cups over to Jim. "I'm fine," Erica said, just as Michael tugged at his backwards collar and said, "No need." So he took the empty seat near the doorway and shut the door.

"I'm glad all of you could come tonight," he said, clearing his throat, hoping he didn't sound too lame. Then he almost laughed at himself. His son would be the one using the word lame, not Mark. "I wanted to address the, uh, tensions I've heard have been arising, especially at the middle and high schools, among some of our students."

"I was glad you brought this up, Mark," Erica said, her short, dark bob nodding with her. "I've had several students come to me, very upset, about what they perceive as a challenge to their faith." She glanced at Jim.

"I haven't had any problems," said Michael. "But I know they can exist. This town is growing more diverse. What have you been seeing?"

"I have a gay teenager," Erica said now, quietly. "And he feels, well, that some of the kids are giving him a hard time."

Mark sighed. "Such a difficult age. And sexuality...Does he have support at home?"

"His parents have been pretty good, surprised, when he told them, but working on being supportive. The school is trying. It's just..."

Jim Jameson cleared his throat. "Who is counseling this young man?" Jim was tall, but thin, and sitting down he looked almost child-like, even though he tried to make his voice sound big.

"Counseling, well, not sure what you mean. He's not seeing a professional. Do you think that could help?" Erica scratched her head. Mark knew an adolescent psychotherapist he could recommend; he'd sent several teenagers to her and had heard only good things. He started to say so but Jim continued.

"I mean, counseling him to get the help he needs. To see that being gay is against God's way. It's best to get this early. I'm sure I could have some of the teens from my youth group counsel him, help him see, and support him as he transitions back to healthy sexuality."

Mark sputtered, and had to control the swig of coffee in his mouth from spewing all over the table. "What are you saying, Jim?" Maybe it wasn't what he thought.

"Just what I meant. These are young minds. We're helping form them. It's our job to get as many good influences to these kids as possible, and I have some great influences in my youth group. Kids who will show this young man that heterosexuality is the only way, the right way, God's way. . ."

"What would these kids from your youth group do?" Mark wanted to control the angry blush he felt creeping up his neck. "I'm just not sure what you mean."

Erica nodded. The priest, who had been silent, nodded too.

"Educate the young man, of course. We can show him the Bible passages where it clearly says that being gay is a sin. We can introduce him to nice, quality young ladies, and we can help him with his temptations. I'm happy to do it." He leaned back in his chair, a smile on his face.

"But that's not what he wants," Erica said. "He just wants to feel accepted."

"Of course he can be accepted. Accepted for being unsure about his path in life, as most of us are, at one time or another. But we have to teach him the right ways, and I'm sure we're all happy to do that here."

The priest held up a hand. "I see where this is going, and that's into dangerous territory. The Church says homosexuality is a sin, too, but I've seen too many in my time to think we can change them. So even though we teach against it, I counsel those in my parish who are struggling to pray about it, think about it, and then, well, I don't advertise this, but it does seem to be biological." He sighed.

Mark nodded. "We don't teach against homosexuality here. We embrace it. I have a gay couple in this congregation and I hope they feel welcomed and accepted."

Erica added, "We embrace. We listen. These are teenagers. They need our support."

Jim looked around at his colleagues incredulously. "You tell people that it's okay to have relations with someone of the same gender?"

Mark almost laughed out loud. This guy couldn't be more than 30, 32 tops. Who said "have relations with" at that age? Or, at all, for that matter? "I don't tell them to have sex, of course, but I don't tell my heterosexual teens to have sex either. I just offer them a place to talk and to be who they are."

"But being who they are, if they're with people of the same sex – that's not natural." Now Jim looked confused.

"For some people, being who they are is being gay. Now," the priest said. "Can we get back to the subject at hand? I like to be in bed by ten. It's getting late." He tapped at his watch and looked at the others expectantly. "Unless you forgot, we were talking about ways to forge a brotherhood," and here he winked at Erica, "or a sisterhood, as the case may be, that would support all of our young people, and help them respect the religious affiliations of the other students at school."

Mark supposed that was enough about homosexuality for now. He wasn't going to get very far with this Jim Jameson. He was glad he didn't run into this attitude more often – so many people still held prejudice against gays, especially in some religious communities. It would take years to stop the prejudice, and he couldn't do it all himself. To him, it was about helping the teens develop healthy attitudes towards it, so when they became adults, the prejudice would be gone, or at least, greatly diminished.

Mark suggested, "Maybe we could start an interfaith campaign that we use in our individual houses of worship. We'll design it together -- and with input of some of our kids, I have a few I know would love to work on this – and present it to our youth groups. We can teach the kids about the other faiths they will encounter in town, just so they have a more basic understanding, and can be tolerant and respectful, and know what they're talking about, of course." Everyone chuckled. "We can probably do most of this via phone and email. I'm happy to serve as an advisor on the Jewish faith to anyone who needs it."

Erica and Michael nodded.

"I can't go along with this," Jim cut in, still sitting. "My job isn't to tell my students how other religions work. It's to teach them to embrace their own faith."

"But isn't part of our job," and Mark looked around the small table, "to teach all of our congregants tolerance and acceptance of other groups?"

"Actually, no, at least not mine. My job is to teach those in my congregation how to embrace their own faith, and to help others see our faith as a viable choice, to accept Jesus as one's savior, and to work hard to get into Heaven," Jim said. And then he continued. "Look, I came because I wanted to meet all of you, glad to get to know you, all of that. But the truth is, it's my job to recruit my flock, to teach people Christ's ways. There is only one way to live. And that's by Christ's law. And we can't go muddying that up with but maybe this faith is okay and maybe that faith is okay and maybe," and here he swallowed, "the sin of homosexuality is okay. So thank you," and now he stood, stuck out his hand as he tugged at the collar of his tightly buttoned starched white shirt, "for the meeting. But I'm not going to do this. I won't. And I can't." He strode out of the room, leaving his colleagues behind.

Chapter 12

Aaron

Aaron never prayed. But now, as he sat in his room at two a.m., wide awake, he prayed fervently. "Please let it be wrong. Please let it be negative. Please let it be not real. Please. I'll do anything." He even pinched himself. The house was quiet, his father and Hannah long ago sound asleep.

After he'd dropped Marti off, a block from her house like usual, at nine, he'd driven around for hours. His dad had texted him at 10. Where R U, as though he were seventeen, like Aaron.

Home by eleven, he'd texted back shakily. Hopefully his dad wouldn't give him a hard time. Likely he would just go to bed and talk to him about the late hours he was keeping tomorrow. Aaron wished that was all they would be talking about.

He hadn't known what to say to Marti. He felt like the biggest idiot on earth. He'd been taught about birth control since seventh grade health and yet...he'd ignored it. He'd trusted his girlfriend. He never thought this would happen.

But it wasn't her fault. She had learned this way. She said it would work. It had worked. For a long time. But not now. Shit.

He didn't promise to marry her. He said they would work through this together. It was the best he could do. Shit! He thought again. He told her they should consider all of their options but then her eyes got big. She knew exactly what he was talking about. "You know I can't," she said. "I won't. It's a life. It's part of us." Then she'd put his hand on her stomach and he'd gotten really creeped out. He didn't want to feel anything. Could you even feel it now? He doubted it, if he couldn't even tell she was pregnant when he looked at her.

"How far along?" he'd asked as she'd cried into his shoulder.

"Nine weeks. I think."

"Nine? How long have you known?" Couldn't you find out pretty quickly these days? He saw those whatever-you-called them-EPT test commercials on t.v., and you could find out at like, nine days. Or something like that.

"Well," she said, gulping. "I missed one period but I just thought it was a fluke. So I waited and didn't get my next one, either. And then my boobs started getting big and I was tired all the time. I guess I was just, you know, in denial." She cried even more loudly then, and flung herself against him all over again. And he wanted to make her feel better, he did, but even touching her now felt so…wrong.

"A fluke? Have you ever missed one before, like that?" He could hear his voice raising.

"Once or twice. And then I always got the next one. So I didn't really think anything of it. Until, maybe, last week?"

"Why didn't you say anything?"

"I didn't…I just did…"

You didn't what?" Steady, he told himself. Calm down.

She'd broken down crying, and he couldn't get her to stop, so he had driven her home, awkwardly patting her knee the entire time. "We'll figure it out," he'd said mechanically, more than once. Exactly how would they figure it out? He had no idea.

And now, in his room, at two a.m., he tried to get himself to calm down. She was only what? Eight or nine weeks along? Plenty early enough to try to convince her to have an abortion. He knew her religion was big on no abortion; she had, more than once, spent hours protesting in front of the abortion clinic down on Route 7, holding a sign with a picture of a baby, red paint smeared over its face, chanting Don't Kill Your Baby at women coming into the clinic. But, still, now, she had to be practical, right? They couldn't have a baby! He was going away to college next year; she knew that. She wouldn't want to be a single mom, would she? Wasn't that stigma, for her religion, just as bad? Or even worse, he thought hopefully, and then felt ashamed of the thought but still kept it in his mind anyway, because no one needed to know about the abortion. They could skip school one day, do it first thing in the morning, come back to his house. They could stay here all day, and he's take great care of her. He pictured himself bringing her soup and wet washcloths and holding her hand.

He stripped down to his shorts and buried himself under the covers. Tomorrow was his first big AP Physics test and he wasn't prepared. He had been planning to study tonight, after he'd gotten home. And he hadn't even cracked open a book. He definitely needed some sleep but he didn't know how he could get any with the thoughts pressing on his mind. He wished his mother were there. She'd know what to do. She always did.

Chapter 13

Hannah

Hannah had been looking forward to Saturday all week long. She and Kristin were going to spend the whole afternoon together; lunch and shopping at the mall, maybe a movie at her house afterwards. Her dad had promised she could go after she went to services Saturday morning; she would just have to get through that. Her new strategy was to bring a paperback that fit inside the prayer book, so no one could tell she was reading. They just thought she was the good, devoted daughter.

She was trying to decide what to wear Saturday morning when her phone rang. It was Kristin.

"My dad said he can drop me around 12:30," Hannah said breathlessly, not even bothering with a hello. "I know that's a little late, but services won't end until 12. I'll be there as soon as I can."

"I can't go," Kristin said miserably.

"What? Can't go? Why?"

"Our pastor is holding an emergency meeting for anyone in middle or high school. My parents said I have to go. They don't even know what it's about! It's just…the pastor says it, so it must be important." If Kristin were in front of Hannah right now, Hannah was sure her friend would be rolling her eyes.

Hannah threw the shirt she had been considering on her bed. It wasn't fair. "Maybe the meeting won't go that long?" she asked hopefully. "We could just go later, have dinner at the mall instead of lunch." That would be good. All the cool kids came to the mall later anyway, and hung out there until after dinner.

"My parents won't let me. They said they have no idea how long the meeting will go, and then there's going to be a potluck afterwards. My mother's making something in the crock pot for it now," Kristin said, sounding just as annoyed as Hannah felt. That was something anyway. Kristin didn't want to go to the meeting; she'd rather hang out with Hannah.

When Hannah got downstairs, her Saturday services skirt and blouse on, now wishing she'd never gotten up, her dad was waiting for her in his suit and bright tie, car keys in hand. "You don't have time for breakfast now," he admonished, looking at his watch. "Grab a granola bar or a toaster pastry and meet me in the car in two minutes." He hurried into the garage to back the car out and start it. Hannah's mother would have shuddered at her breakfast choices. When she was alive, Saturday morning breakfast was always challah French toast, the bread left over from Shabbat dinner the night before, or chocolate chip pancakes with warmed syrup; Hannah had never even tasted a toaster pastry until after her mother had died.

"What's wrong?" her dad asked as he drove them the ten minutes to temple. Hannah munched half-heartedly at her pastry. It was brown sugar cinnamon, her favorite, but it tasted like cardboard.

"Kristin can't get together. Now I don't have anything to do this afternoon." A long, boring Saturday afternoon. Nothing to do.

"Maybe you could call another friend," her dad suggested. What was wrong with him? Did he not know that Kristin was her only friend? That the other kids only put up with her because Kristin was so popular, that they acted like her slanted eyes and yellow-brown skin were contagious? Or that being Jewish was weird? That she just didn't fit in? Or when they did talk to her, it was because they wanted math "help" as in, Let me see what answer you got for problem number three.

But she didn't want to go into all of that now. They were only minutes from temple. "I don't think so," she said. Even her new book, which she'd been looking forward to reading during services and was tucked into her bag, didn't make her feel any better. It was going to be a long weekend of nothingness.

The service was two and a half hours long. Hannah envied the Catholic kids, who went to an hour long service once a week and an hour of CCD and that was it. They didn't even have to go to their service first thing in the morning; sometimes they went instead at five on Saturday evenings and then out to dinner, almost as though the service was a warm up to a fun evening out. Their services didn't drone on and on; they could sleep in on Saturdays, and they at least heard their prayers in English. In fact, Hannah noted as she glanced at the watch of a woman sitting next to her, she bet most of the kids from school were still asleep, or zoned out in front of Saturday morning television or lying in bed with their computers right now. She heard her father ask everyone to stand, and she knew the service was just about over. He intoned the names of the newly dead. She wondered what had it been like for him, at their old temple, to intone his own wife's name for the first month after her mother had died. And all of the weekly readings of her name during the list of prayers for the sick prior to that. Her mother had been sick for two years. Had he gotten used to it, like you get used to taking a terrible tasting antibiotic every day to get rid of an ear infection? Still, you only had to take the medicine for ten days or so. Two years was hard to imagine now, even though Hannah had lived it.

Or maybe, Hannah wondered, did you pretend you were reading the name of someone who wasn't yours? Like Hannah pretended that she didn't care she was adopted; like her brother pretended – but Hannah knew otherwise – that if he didn't get into Columbia he would be perfectly happy just to go somewhere else. She cocked her head at her father as he continued down the list. A lot of people sure had died in the past few weeks. Hannah always thought people should die in the middle of winter, January or February, when it was so cold and depressing out anyway. But her mother had died in May, on a warm spring day that the weatherman had called one of the top ten on the news that morning. It hadn't seemed right.

Her father finished the last prayer and all around her, people were wishing each other a good Shabbos. It was so fake. They'd only come to the service for the Bar Mitzvah. Soon they'd drive over to the hotel on the other side of town for the party – the real reason they were there. There were only maybe fifty or sixty people at the service, maybe ten or fifteen kids. She bet at least a hundred people were going to the party; they just didn't go to the service. Too boring. Her dad came off the podium, chatted with a few of the regulars – older people who came to everything. He caught Hannah's eye and winked and Hannah felt almost – something. Maybe her dad wasn't so bad. Maybe he really did love her. Maybe she really...did love him. She came over to stand next to him. "Why don't you go down to my office," he told her. "I'll meet you there in a few minutes."

Maybe she could convince him to go to lunch and a movie or something. Sure, she'd much rather be with Kristin at the mall, but at least it would kill the day. They could go to the diner. Her dad liked it there, and there wasn't much else in town, except McDonalds. She hadn't been to the movies in forever. They might be able to pick something out they could both agree on. She felt almost hopeful – maybe the day wouldn't be so bad --as she hurried down the hall to her father's office. She could check the movie listings on his computer if she could remember his passcode. Her stomach was rumbling. She couldn't wait for lunch.

Chapter 14

Mark

After Mark had dropped Hannah in the sanctuary that morning before services, he had hurried to the cantor's office. He had gotten an idea because of Hannah's broken play date – though Hannah had expressly told him to stop referring to her get-togethers as play dates. Those were for babies, she reminded him, and she and her friends were just hanging out. Apparently there was a big difference. Now was the perfect opportunity for her to do something that had been on his mind for a while, something he had come up with that would help Hannah and help him.

He'd liked the cantor from the minute he'd met her. Though she was much younger than he was, she had a wise, calm manner that often reminded him of a much older soul. This was her first job out of cantorial school, and she bubbled over with enthusiasm for her work.

Despite that it was her job to sing at all the services, her voice actually was not amazing, though certainly it was better than decent. He'd known that from the second they had practiced for their first service together. It was slightly flat and lacked the robust quality he had been used to from the cantor he had worked with in Manhattan. He wondered how she had decided to be a cantor when she clearly didn't have the greatest voice. It wasn't bad; it just wasn't what he had expected, quality-wise, from a professional singer.

But what she didn't have in voice quality she had in bright happiness. She was excellent with the kids. Last week he had overheard her working with Nathan, a kid who appeared to be completely tone deaf. "I'm never going to get it," he'd wailed, and the rabbi had heard a kick of the chair.

"Let me have your hand," the cantor had said. And soon he could hear her tapping Nathan's smaller hand against the desk. "Okay," she said, "start up again." He sang a line, and it was right on the beat. "You got it!" she said, and he could hear the pleasure in her voice. And she loved services. She loved belting out the familiar tunes to prayers and songs and then mixing them up and presenting new ones, trying to get the congregants to join in. A few months after he'd first gotten here, he suggested they try to stick to the standards, just for one service, instead of changing them up and she'd looked at him in mock horror. "Everyone should try to learn at least one new thing a week," she'd said. "I bet almost everyone at services today hasn't learned one new thing this week yet." The next week, he'd taken her advice and decided to start learning a few words of French. He'd taken Spanish in high school and always regretted not taking French instead, such a beautiful language. It was because of the cantor that he found a simple online lesson and was building his vocabulary.

It was because she was so good with the kids that he was going to her now. They only had ten minutes before the Bar Mitzvah boy and his family would bustle into his office, looking frantic and overwhelmed. He already knew the mother would have perfectly coiffed hair she'd convinced her hair dresser to do at seven this morning in exchange for double or triple what she usually paid. The father would be sweating bullets, not about the Bar Mitzvah boy's speech, but over the bar bill that was sure to come and the tips he was supposed to divvy out to the wait staff and DJ and dancers when the party was over. There would also be a proud grandparent in the room who was scheduled to read a prayer but didn't know how, and the poor Bar Mitzvah boy in an already-too-short suit his mother had purchased for him three weeks ago.

So with all of that in mind, he practically ran down the worn carpet towards the cantor's office. Her light was on and he could hear her warming up, running up and down a scale as though she were taking a walk down the street on a spring day.

He knocked on the door even though it was open. Her back was towards the doorway and he didn't want to scare her.

"Hey!" she called brightly when she turned around to see who was there. She was wearing dress pants and a blouse. He was going to have to talk to her about that again. The Board expected her to be in dresses or skirts at all services and events, and they had told him twice to make sure she was. He didn't know how this was his responsibility. Technically, he was her boss, he supposed, as the head of the temple, but she had been there longer than he had, and the board oversaw both of them, as well as the other employees. He hated that they expected him to talk to her about this, but he had tried. He did it in a round-about way, telling her how "formal" his Manhattan synagogue had been, how everyone had worn dresses and skirts and suits to every service, and how his wife had hated the expense of the suits he'd had to buy. He'd even told her that his wife said she had hated that she had to wear dresses to everything, and longed to wear pants, just like the cantor, but it had been expected, and so she had done it. It had taken him four days to come up with that story, and he thought it was pretty good.

The cantor had just laughed and said she much preferred pants, especially in winter, and that she had ugly knees she liked to avoid showing people. That had seemed perfectly reasonable to him, but he hadn't known if he should relay that back to the Board. In the end, he'd ignored the problem, hoping it would go away.

"Ready for today?" he asked her now, sliding into the seat on the visitor side of her desk. He reached into the glass jar on her desk and fished out a Tootsie roll, unwrapped it, and started to chew. Thank goodness it was fresh.

"Yeah. The kid knows his stuff."

"So, um, I was thinking..." He didn't quite know how to ask, but for Hannah, he had to. And for him, too, he supposed.

"What's up?" She pulled heels out of a brown shopping bag and began to slip them on her feet. He hadn't even noticed she had been barefoot.

"Hannah, it's, she's...well, she's twelve and a half now. Of course you know that. . .And, well, I..." He cleared his throat.

"Yes?" She pulled breath spray out of the purse sitting on her desk and squirted it into her mouth a few times.

"Well, Hannah needs, what I mean is..." He took a deep breath and admonished himself. *Oh just say it*, he thought. "Hannah needs a...woman...for...woman things." He smiled weakly and hoped she would know what he meant without saying the actual words. "And I know you're probably busy but I thought, since, anyway, maybe you could take her shopping for...you know, things?"

"What kind of things?" she asked and he swore he saw a little twitch in her lip.

He sighed. He was going to have to say the words. "Bras. And." He gulped. "Feminine protection." One of the things his wife had worried about was Hannah going into puberty, and she had thought ahead. First, she had gone out and bought some training bras and told him to give them to Hannah when she needed them, and to tell her she could use them whenever she wanted. He'd only halfway done what she said. He'd slipped the bras into her underwear drawer when she was at school, still in their package, and had never said a word. She hadn't commented, but when she had turned eleven, he could see the faint outline of their straps underneath her t-shirts.

He hadn't dealt with the period issue at all, and it was only sheer luck that she hadn't gotten it by now. He knew they did a unit in school, during health, and he hoped she would ask her female teacher anything she needed to know. He hadn't had the guts to give her pads and tampons, wouldn't have the faintest idea of how to help her with them. And though his wife had lamented that she wouldn't be here for the milestone, and Hannah would have to go through that difficult time alone, they hadn't discussed what he should do. Or not do. So he had done nothing. Which was obviously the wrong move. Hannah was still wearing the training bras though he was sure by now she needed bigger ones, and he was afraid that at any moment, the period would come, and she would have to ask him for supplies which would embarrass both of them. He'd thought about asking his mother to help, but she lived in a retirement community in San Diego so she couldn't be there, plus, what could be worse than a grown man asking his mother about periods? He shuddered at the thought. But he could no longer put off the inevitable.

"Sure, I'd be happy to," she said, now standing at her desk. "I'm free this afternoon, actually. Do you think she would like to go to lunch and shopping then?" Thank goodness the temple standard was not to invite the clergy to the Bar Mitzvah parties, or they would never get a free Saturday afternoon.

He couldn't believe his luck. "Yes, that would be great!" he said, a little too enthusiastically. "Let me give you some money, and I'll tell Hannah. I know she'll be happy." Actually, he didn't know that, and he suspected she would be mad. She got mad easily these days, a sign of things to come, he knew, a sign of hormones raging and a period that would show up, and soon.

"Lunch is my treat. Just leave me a little for our supplies" – he liked how she said that, generically and no-nonsense – "and I'll drop her back at your house afterwards." She'd been there once before, when he'd hosted a coffee for all of the temple board members and employees, something his wife should have been doing but he had known he had to, as the rabbi, when he had first started.

He stood up, too, and stretched. Should he shake her hand, kiss her cheek? He decided on an earnest thank you. They marched out of the room together to go meet the Bar Mitzvah boy and his family.

Chapter 15

Aaron

Aaron opened one eye on Saturday morning and let out a groan. He'd barely slept for the last four nights, ever since Marti had told him the news. That's how he thought of it – as *the news*. He couldn't think of it any other way.

He'd already started his campaign to persuade her to have an abortion but it wasn't going well. Mostly she cried and told him she couldn't kill their child, that she would go to hell if she did, that it was murder, that at nine or ten weeks – she wasn't even sure, exactly – it already had a heart beat and arms and legs and was moving around inside her, even though she couldn't feel it.

He'd hoped to convince her it was just a bundle of cells. At first, that's what he had thought. He thought she was just, well, he admitted to himself, touchy, because of her religion, who knew what they taught her – it wasn't a baby yet, it was a….thing…that *could* become a baby, but that didn't turn out to be true. In fact, he saw as he consulted the Internet, the baby was forming every day, getting more and more developed, and soon it would have everything it needed. It already had ear buds, for crying out loud. And Marti had been right – it was moving around and testing out its arms and legs. No matter that it was less than an inch, or something. It was a baby, or at least more of a baby than he had originally thought.

But it still wasn't practical for her to have the baby. No way. And it was up to him to convince her. He rolled over on his side, his eyes still closed. His eyelids felt stuck to his face, as though he couldn't open them even if he wanted to. Which he didn't.

So far neither of them had told anyone, but he was afraid Marti was going to break soon. If she told her parents, it was over. If she told a friend, it was over. All of her friends were very religious Christians from her church. Now that he thought about it, he was her only non-Christian friend. They would all try to ram the "Your baby is a real person already, a soul that God has given you to protect" idea down her throat.

But it wasn't. It might have arm and leg buds, ear buds and a place for eyes, but it didn't have thoughts or feelings or ideas. It wasn't a real person. He was sure of that. He was supposed to go over to Marti's today so they could talk some more. If he could get her out of there, maybe go for a drive, they could talk reasonably. He could show her all the advantages of having an abortion. He just had to. His stomach clenched and then he felt the rest of his body tense up, too.

He got up, got into the shower. He was supposed to be there by twelve. Meanwhile, his dad was pressuring him to work on his college applications. He still hadn't confirmed his teacher recommendations. He wanted to ask his AP Physics teacher, Mr. Renales, but he was afraid to. He'd been an A student last year in AP Chem, now he was barely passing Physics with a C. This week had been disastrous in that class. He'd failed the chapter test and bombed the lab. He hadn't been able to concentrate. Mr. Renales had even asked him if he was okay, if he needed to speak to the guidance counselor. He'd been so embarrassed. What was he supposed to say? That his girlfriend was pregnant and about to ruin his life? And that he had no one to blame but himself, he couldn't help but feel angry at her? And then angry at himself for feeling angry with her?

The shower water felt good on his face and helped him wake up. It wasn't Marti's fault. He should have insisted on using the damn condoms, even when she said she didn't want to, because he knew that was right thing. He had always been responsible, that's what his mother had said, anyway. Yet he'd done one of the most irresponsible things he could ever do.

He toweled off, grabbed the same pair of jeans he'd worn yesterday, searched his dresser for a clean shirt. He should have done laundry last night. His dad had stopped doing his laundry last year, said that if he was going off to college soon, he should know how to do it. His mother never would have done that. He found a shirt, sniffed it to make sure it smelled clean enough. It smelled like his mother's laundry detergent. He closed his eyes, tried to blink back the tears. If only she were here right now to talk him through it. She was the one person he could go to about stuff like this.

He didn't bother to eat breakfast; just grabbed his car keys and headed out the door. It was nearly twelve now and he didn't want to be late. Marti hadn't wanted him to leave her side all week. If he was late, she would freak out that he wasn't coming at all. He had been ten minutes late the other night because his father had made him pick Hannah up from temple and drop her home first. Normally, Marti wouldn't think anything of it. That time, she had started texting him when he was one minute late. He wasn't allowed to text while he was driving. She knew that, yet by the time he got to her house, ten minutes later, she'd sent eight messages. Where R U, When will U B here, Y R U late? As he had driven down the long back roads toward her house, his stomach flip flopped and he desperately wanted to close his eyes, if only for a few minutes. What could he say differently today than he had all this week? She needed to have an abortion. He needed her to have one. It was the best thing. Really.

He pulled into the long asphalt drive that led to her front door. How many times had he driven up to the driveway, his heart beating with anticipation that soon he would be kissing her? That he would bury his face in her hair and smell that smell he'd gotten so addicted to? That she would let him touch her like no other girl had? But now all he felt was dread, like he had a case of the stomach flu. The last thing he wanted was to ring her doorbell, to say a calm hello to her mother, to shake her father's hand, to make small talk. Yes, he was working on his college applications, no, he hadn't heard that the town drug store was going out of business and they would all be forced to use the impersonal chain store down on Route 9. He didn't want to look into Marti's glassy, red rimmed eyes and pretend he didn't see her complete fright. He didn't want to wait until her parents went into the next room so he could make his case, a case he didn't even know how to make. He didn't want to suggest they go for a walk and hold hands while her whole neighborhood watched and reported back to her father. He just wanted to be a normal seventeen year old kid again. But he knew, no matter what, he never would be.

Chapter 16

Hannah

Hannah kept her eyes down, staring at the floor as though the most fascinating t.v. show was playing on the soft carpet. She was at Nordstrom's with the cantor, in the bra fitting department. Her dad had told her right after services that she would spend the afternoon with Cantor Strauss, and that they would have lunch and "girl time." She had looked at him as though he had two heads. Girl time? She hadn't known what it would mean. And the cantor? Sure, she was nice, but the most they'd ever talked about was prayers. And singing them. Okay, once the cantor had asked her if she watched American Idol. The cantor did, and loved it, even though they kept changing the judges from year to year. Hannah didn't watch it though; she preferred The Voice, and that had been the end of that conversation.

As soon as they got into the cantor's car, which Hannah had been surprised to see was a bright yellow convertible, not the kind of car she would imagine a cantor driving, the cantor had turned to her and said, "Out of Temple, you can call me Robyn, okay?" Hannah had nodded. She'd never before called any adult by her first name. Her mom had told her it was rude and inappropriate. Plus, this was the cantor. Even the adults called her *Cantor*. She didn't think she knew even what her first name was before. Robyn was a pretty name, Hannah thought. And the cantor even looked a bit like a robin, her size anyway. She was tiny and thin, as though you could push her over with one hand and she would go tumbling to the ground.

They'd gone to lunch first, at Cheesecake Factory. Hannah had never been there before – her father was always too busy to make the thirty minute drive to the nice mall several towns over – but she'd heard kids at school talking about it, how big the menu was, pages and pages, and how many different kinds of cheesecakes there were for dessert. She'd felt odd at first, sitting across from the cantor – Robyn – studying her menu. But Robyn had been fun, way more fun than she was when they practiced for her Bat Mitzvah, and she told Hannah stories of growing up as the only Jew in a small Massachusetts town an hour from Boston. Hannah could relate, kind of.

"When I was fourteen, do you know what I did, Hannah?" the cantor – Robyn -- asked as Hannah buttered a piece of wheat bread. Who knew wheat bread could taste this good?

"What?"

"I hung a Christmas stocking out of my bedroom window. I hated that we were the only house on the block without Christmas decorations."

"You did that?" Hannah couldn't believe it. This was the cantor. Wasn't she supposed to be, like, a Super Jew, or something?

"Yup, sure did. I bought it at the five and dime, which is sort of like a Target, I guess, only a lot smaller, and I came home from school, lifted my window sill, and hung it there. My dad came home from work and pulled up and saw it and he went ballistic! He was screaming and yelling. I could hear him even though all the windows were closed. He came running up the stairs and into my room and opened my window. He grabbed it and flung it into my garbage can!" The cantor laughed. "I was grounded for a week."

"Weren't you mad?" Hannah asked. She would be furious if her father did something like that.

"At the time, yes. I was. I didn't speak to him for two days. But now, we joke about it. He was right. Sometimes there's no point in trying to fit in. You just have to accept who you are."

And now they were here, in the trying-on area of the department store, and an old lady – she had to be in her fifties at least – was gathering a tape measure around Hannah's chest and squinting at the numbers. She snapped it back and said, "Okay, then. You're a 32 B." She was mortified, but thankfully, the cantor had said, just as the lady was taking the tape measure from around her neck, "I'll wait out there," and left the room before the old lady had started. "I'll go get you some things to try on," the fitter said, and she looked kind. "Do you have any color preference?"

Her cheeks burned. "No," she said, even though she had some seen some cool-looking hot pink bras on the way in. Maybe the bra fitter would just know to get them.

She did know. She brought back the hot pink Hannah had admired and some green striped ones, and also some tan and some white ones, which would be good for under light colored shirts, she had explained to Hannah. "I'll just go wait by your—"

"—friend," Hannah said. What else could she call Robyn?

"Friend," the woman replied, smiling, as though the whole thing were normal. "Just call me if you need anything."

She finally decided on four, but they were expensive. She didn't know how much money the cantor had. Had her father given it to her? She supposed so. Her face burned again, just thinking about her dad knowing she needed bras. Even though, she reminded herself, her dad had left the old bras in her underwear drawer a couple of years ago. At least she thought it had been her dad. Who else would it have been? Sometimes she missed her mom so much, she could cry. She felt tears forming in her eyes and tried to think about something else.

They paid for the bras and then headed back to the car. "It's such a beautiful fall day!" Robyn exclaimed, turning up the music on the radio and putting the top down. It was very warm, and the trees were just starting to turn, and it all made Hannah feel hopeful.

"Are we going home now?"

"One more stop." Twenty minutes later, they pulled into the CVS parking lot just a mile from her house. "I can wait in here," Hannah told the -- Robyn. She wanted to text Kristin, if her meeting was done, maybe they could hang out tonight.

"Oh no, you need to come in with me."

She trudged out of the car. They walked down the long aisle of the CVS, Hannah nodding at a few kids she knew from school, hoping none of them would wonder who Robyn was. They all knew her mother had died.

"Here we are!" Robyn trilled, as they stopped in front of a long display. Hannah looked up. "What?" she asked, confused.

"Hannah, you're almost thirteen," Robyn said gently, her voice quieter than Hannah had ever heard it before. "And I'm sure you know a lot about periods and what they are and how they happen, but I was wondering if you needed any supplies?"

Hannah had not admitted to anyone that she had gotten her first period a few months ago, over the summer, during sleep away camp. She'd had to tell her counselor, who had taken her to the infirmary. There, they had handed her a bunch of pads and asked if she wanted to call home. "No!" she had shouted. She did not want her father to know. So the nurse had said fine, given her a talk on how often to change the pads and about the cramps she could expect, the acne that might come, the difference between pads and tampons, and sent her on her way. It all sounded quite awful. She had gone back before she left camp and asked for more supplies, hoping they would last her a long time. But they had only lasted through September, and she was due to get it again pretty soon. She hadn't known what she was going to do – maybe go to the nurse at school? – but without telling her father, which she was not – NOT going to do – she wouldn't have enough for more than a day or two and the first time she had needed them for five.

She nodded to Robyn now, so together they selected an overnight pad, a regular pad, light pads for the first and last days, Robyn told her, and a small box of tampons, which Robyn had said she could practice using and were a lot more comfortable than pads, but Hannah had no intention of ever doing that. Hannah prayed fervently that no one from school would come over to this aisle and see her, and not only that, but they could get back down the aisle, packages in hand, without anyone noticing.

When they pulled into her driveway just fifteen minutes later, it was a relief to get home, even though, strangely, Hannah had really liked hanging out with Robyn.

Robyn turned to her. "I had so much fun," she said, smiling at Hannah, as though she could read Hannah's mind.

"Me, too!" Hannah said, caught up in the moment. "Even though…you know, bra shopping isn't that fun." Her ears burned and she felt like Robyn definitely had to know it was embarrassing to say that.

"Yeah, bra shopping isn't too much fun, but Cheesecake Factory sure is. We'll have to do that part again soon." Robyn smiled.

"Yeah…Well…thanks." Hannah unlocked the door and jumped out of the car. As Robyn pulled away, Hannah ran into the house. Next time she was going to get the key lime cheesecake. And maybe they could shop for actual clothes. There were some good stores in that mall. She ran up to her room to hide her supplies and bras in her underwear drawer. Her father would never look there; her brother would never look there. She slammed the drawer shut just as she heard her brother coming home.

Chapter 17

Mark

Mark was in his office Tuesday afternoon, making good progress on his New Year's sermon, when Anna Nachman came to his doorway. "Knock, knock," she called, barging in. "Am I coming at a bad time?" Every time you come is a bad time, he wanted to say, but instead he plastered a smile on his face and said, "Of course not!" and jumped out of his seat to give her the perfunctory kiss on the cheek. The woman smelled of heavy perfume and he nearly gagged, stopping himself before she noticed.

"As you know, Mark, the Board met last night," she said. "And we've been thinking. About the issue of Outreach. We have a new idea."

"Great, I'm open," he said. He'd been thinking about outreach, too. It was part of his job as the rabbi to bring new families in, preferably young families who would be at the synagogue for many years, educating their children, and most importantly to the board, paying dues. He hadn't come up with any ideas, though, and he'd planned on bringing the subject up at a regional rabbinical conference he was scheduled to attend next month. It was an age-old problem, bringing in new members, and all rabbis struggled with it.

"We thought, since the holidays are coming up, that you could put together a costume – we'd be happy to give you a modest budget for it – and go the bookstore where there will be a lot of young children, and talk about our customs, read a story. Maybe hand out some apples and honey as part of the New Year."

"Costume?" He scratched his head.

"We thought it might garner some attention – maybe even some local news or Patch attention – if you were in a get-up."

"I'm not sure what you mean, get-up."

"We'd like you to dress as an apple, to symbolize the New Year. Or the Torah. Or just about anything that would draw attention."

"You want me to dress up like an apple?" He pictured himself in a bright red felt suit, rounded about him, his arms laying uncomfortably outwards, a felt green core stuck to the top of his head. His stomach turned over.

"Yes, exactly," she said proudly. "Maybe on Saturday afternoon, after services, and then again on Sunday afternoon after Hebrew School. You can find anything on the Internet these days. I'm sure you could find an apple get-up. We'll reimburse you for that, and for the apples and honey, too. Just put them on a platter, offer them to the kids, talk to their parents."

"An apple," Mark said again. "That is, I mean to say..."

"Brilliant, right? I came up with it myself, and the board members are fully behind me. Take care of it, and make sure you save your receipts!" she said, and jauntily left the room.

He made a beeline for the cantor's office down the hall, ignoring his secretary, a Hebrew School teacher, and two children who called out "Hi Rabbi Friedlander!" Robyn was sitting at the small table she used for Bar Mitzvah lessons, her eyes closed, ear buds firmly in her ears.

He waved an arm frantically but it still took an uncomfortable amount of time for her to notice him. "Oh, Hi Mark," she said. She pulled out her ear buds. "I'm listening to a new song that maybe we can try Friday night. It's an easy tune to learn; I can teach it to you in a few minutes."

He slumped down in the chair next to her. She smelled of fresh spring air. "You're not going to believe this."

"What am I not going to believe?"

He relayed the story and she burst into laughter. "An apple? That's a new one. That Anna." She chuckled softly again.

"You're not outraged?" he asked. "I'm supposed to be the dignified face of this temple. I can't dress up like an apple!"

She thought for a moment. "I suppose you're right. But...I could."

"You could? Why would you want to do that?"

"Oh it'll be fun. I don't mind; I'll go into the book store. I'll find a short Rosh Hashanah story to read, or something. I'll tell you what. I'll dress up as the apple if you carry the platter of apples and honey and offer them. We'll be in this together. How's that?"

"You really want to do this?"

"It'll be fun. Come on, what do you say?"

He didn't even want to be seen with someone dressed as an apple. And he didn't want the cantor to embarrass herself. Maybe, because she was so young, she didn't realize how it would look. "I don't think you should," he said finally. "I think you'll embarrass yourself, frankly."

"Embarrass myself? Come on, it's just an hour dressed up like an apple. We really should do more to connect in this town. Do you know how often I see that Jim Jameson around, talking to kids? He's always in town, offering candy and music gift cards to get kids to come to his church."

"He does?" Mark supposed that he didn't go into town much. He worked too much for casual strolls or lunch out. "That seems an awful lot like bribery, though."

She shrugged. "He's just making himself seem like a fun guy. Like the party is at his church. And he's trying to get teenagers. He's got the right idea. If we want to go after young families, we need to be in town, talking directly to them."

"We're not supposed to be proselytizing," he reminded her. "It's against our basic core values."

"We're not proselytizing. We're educating. We want people to know we're fun, that their kids will like coming here. I don't see what's wrong with that. It's called outreach, though; make sure you use the right word." She winked.

"Why? So it won't feel as wrong?"

She didn't answer, just leaned back in her seat. "So, are you with me? Two o'clock Saturday. You can still wear your suit, if you'd like." She winked again.

He pulled his collar away from his neck and swallowed. "Okay."

It wasn't until after he had left that he realized it was the first time she'd called him Mark, not Rabbi Friedlander.

Chapter 18

Aaron

Aaron fidgeted all the way through AP Calculus. He looked at the clock incessantly and drummed his pencil against his desk. He looked anywhere but at his teacher.

"Are you okay?" she asked him after she'd caught him three times.

"Yeah, uh, sure," he said, burying his face back in his book. He'd managed to put the appropriate look of concentration on his face and go back to the problem at hand for five minutes, until he began looking at the clock again.

He sprinted out of his seat the moment the bell rang. Normally he liked to hang around after school, talk to his teacher, Ms. Barnes, who was the best math teacher he'd ever had. They'd talk about differential equations first, and then his college choices and how he was considering engineering as a major. He'd had Ms. Barnes for Pre-Calc last year, too, and on the last day, she had told him that he had been one of her best students ever. He'd finished with a 98 average.

But today he didn't have time for Ms. Barnes, even though he knew he needed to ask her for a college recommendation. She would be perfect. He didn't have much time left to ask; some teachers would only do so many. He had no idea if Ms. Barnes had that kind of policy. He thought about writing her an email, but his guidance counselor had told him that wasn't appropriate: he needed to ask face to face, and soon. And when you asked, you were supposed to hand the teacher the already-stamped-and-addressed envelopes so they could slip the recommendation into the mail. Emailed recommendations would not be accepted.

He hadn't even gotten around to writing out the envelopes yet. In fact, he had been supposed to spend all of yesterday on his essay and applications, But instead, he'd been on Skype with Marti from the time she'd gotten home from church until after midnight. She'd made an appointment with a clinic he'd found outside of town after school today. He was going to take her, and they were going to discuss "their options." He was afraid, though, that her idea of options was keeping the baby and possibly adoption, and to him, the only option was abortion. He'd promised to keep an open mind if she would. But he also knew he wasn't keeping an open mind, and frankly, neither was she.

"You could still go to college if we got married," she'd whispered on Skype after they'd already been debating for two hours. "You could go to Community College and then Ramapo," she'd suggested. Ramapo? That's where people went when they couldn't get in anywhere else. Or when kids couldn't afford to go away and stayed in town instead, schlepping out there for classes, coming home at night to work in the town diner or at McDonalds. He wasn't going to Ramapo. *God*, he admonished himself. *You sound like such a snob*.

"It's not that far," she said, as if she could read his mind. "It's only forty minutes or so. And you can major in math or science there. And I know my parents would let us live here." Marti's place was certainly bigger than his, even with all of the kids they had. They had an enormous, finished basement with two bedrooms, a bathroom, a mini kitchen, and a living area.

"Marti," he'd said, hoping to sound gentle and loving, "I love you." He did, didn't he? Sometimes, with everything going on, now he wondered, because if he loved her, wouldn't he want to marry her? Wouldn't he feel that was a good option? "And I want to do the right thing. But...I'm not sure marriage is a good idea right now. We're only seventeen. It's not even legal!" He tried to laugh, like he knew it was ridiculous, and she should, too.

"You'll be eighteen in March; I'll be eighteen in April. Besides, my parents would sign consent, wouldn't your dad? We can't let this baby be a bastard." Did people really still consider children of single mothers bastards, he'd wondered. The only time he said bastard was when he was kidding around with his friends. And no, he didn't want to tell her, but he doubted his father would consent for him to get married at seventeen.

Today they would find out a lot more. He rushed to his car and threw his back pack in the back seat. Marti would meet him in a minute. Their appointment was at three, and it would take them at least twenty minutes to get there. He'd already programmed the address into his GPS. He started the car and fiddled with his ipod. What kind of music would be good for the ride over?

Soon she appeared, appearing as pale as she had on Skype yesterday. He looked her up and down. She was still beautiful, and her jeans clung perfectly to her body. She didn't look any heavier. You couldn't even tell she was pregnant, although she complained about her bras getting too small already.

"Hey," she said, weary, and pecked him on the cheek. "I have to be home by five."

"Why?"

"I have to take my sister somewhere. I hope the place is on time. Maybe we should reschedule?" She whipped out her phone, ready to make the call.

"No!"

"We can do it tomorrow, or the next day…or…sometime later this week. It doesn't have to be today." She scrolled through her phone, looking for the number.

He tried to grab the phone from her, a little roughly. "No, we need to go. We need to get more information." He was so afraid she would delay and delay and then it would be too late to get the abortion. He didn't even know what week you could get them until, but he knew earlier was better. Plus, once the – thing – looked like a baby, seemed like a baby – forget it, she would never do it. But now, when she wasn't showing and no one else knew, he thought he had half a chance of her agreeing to it.

"Stop it, Aar," she said. "You don't have to grab my phone away." She held it from him and he put the car in drive.

The clinic was two towns over, in a medical arts building right off the highway. The door was locked, but they rang a bell to the side. A female voice came over a crackly intercom. "Name?"

"Marti. Appointment at 3:00."

The voice didn't answer, but they heard a buzz and the doorknob clicked in Aaron's hand. "I don't like this place," Marti whispered into the back of his jacket. "How did you find it?"

He'd found it online under abortion, but it also took care of pregnant women and would help people who wanted to place their babies for adoption. He'd made sure of that. And it took cash and first names and you didn't have to be eighteen to go there. He'd made sure of that, too.

"It's fine," he whispered back, reaching a hand back to hers as he walked in front of her, and squeezing. God, he was such a prick. He needed to be more sensitive. She was going through a lot. And it was his baby, too; that thought surprised him and he felt a whir in his chest, like a startled newborn bird. He'd been working so hard to think of it as nothing. It certainly didn't seem real. But here they were.

The entry way was small, and it smelled like Lysol and something not so good underneath that. Inside the waiting area was a square box, plastic chairs running each side, a cheap, worn-looking children's play area in the middle. Several women were waiting already, a few clearly pregnant, others clearly looking like they wished they were anywhere but here. A toddler was trying to grab at some of the toys on the floor. Aaron couldn't figure out which woman was his mother. None of the women seemed that interested in him.

But while he signed Marti in, and took the paperwork to fill out, a huge sheaf of papers on a brown clipboard, she had gone right over to the little boy. "Hey there," she said softly. "Can I play with you?" He nodded strongly, as though he'd never had anyone ask before, and he reached down with one hand holding him steadily against the table, and handed her a truck.

"Mart, we have to fill these out," Aaron said. "There's a lot of paperwork."

"In a minute," she said, making vroom vroom noises and running the truck around the little boy's feet. Her face was soft for the first time in weeks, a genuine smile instead of a pained expression, and her shoulders were relaxed.

"I guess I'll start then," he sighed, and began with her name, home address, and cell phone number. He put his cell number down as a contact as well. That was okay, right? Because even though she was the patient, he was in this with her.

After he got done checking off that they had no income – he had made $1500 last summer when he was a camp counselor, but his father had made him put all but $200 of it in his college savings account, did he have to say that was income? He decided he didn't. That was past income, and he didn't even get to keep it – he got to the next line, which read LMP.

What the hell was LMP? It had spaces for a date. "Mart?" he asked again. "I don't know the answer to this question."

"Let me look." She scrambled off the floor, wiping the dust from her butt. He pointed to the letters. "LMP? I have no idea," she said, shaking her head. "Excuse me," she asked a very pregnant woman sitting next to Aaron and pointed to the letters. "Do you know what this is?"

"Last menstrual period," she said loudly. Aaron's ears burned.

Marti looked up at the ceiling, tapping the pencil on her chin. "What if you don't know it exactly?"

"That's okay; you can estimate."

"Thank you," she said, scribbling down July 15. July 15? That had been three months ago! How could she have not gotten her period all that time and not thought anything of it? Aaron knew she thought she had missed two; when he'd gone online, that put her at about eight weeks along, maybe nine. But twelve weeks? Maybe thirteen? He started to sweat.

Marti quickly filled out the rest of the forms and handed the clipboard back to the receptionist at the front of the room, a sliding glass partition between them. The receptionist said something to Marti, and she came scurrying back. "It's ten dollars for today. I don't have it, do you?"

Aaron reached into his back pocket for his wallet. He'd actually stolen a couple of twenties from his father last night, when he was in the shower, and he felt horribly guilty about it. His dad had always given him money whenever he asked. Going to the movies? Here's $20. Out with Marti for pizza? Here's $25. He'd never had to sneak money before. He would have to go into his college fund if – when, he told himself firmly now – she had the abortion. He had no idea how much that would cost. He hoped not too much. But whatever it was, it would be worth it.

When Marti's name was called, he squeezed her hand and said, "Good luck," but she said, "You have to come, too." Did he even want to? What kinds of things were they going to do to her? It would be bad, he was sure, bad and uncomfortable and he wouldn't know where to look or what to do. "I should stay out here," he said, "to give you some privacy."

"I don't want privacy!" she said, probably louder than she should have. She grabbed his hand and pulled him up. "We're in this together." And so he went, dragging his feet, with her, towards the nurse waiting for them.

Chapter 19

Hannah

Hannah got off the bus with Kristin, who had invited her to a youth group meeting at church right after school. Hannah's dad would be at temple until late and who knew where Aaron was – probably making out with Marti somewhere. That's all he ever seemed to do.

She hadn't hesitated when Kristin had texted her during third period. Hannah had been in English, normally her favorite class. They were reading *The Book Thief* and she was loving it. Still, when her phone went off, she checked it, hoping her teacher wouldn't notice.

Hannah knew she wasn't supposed to go with Kristin to any church events. Her dad had made that clear. She wondered what her punishment would be if she got caught. Not that she would get caught. She was very good at covering her tracks. Plus, she said to herself, what was she supposed to do? Sit at home the rest of her life, while all the other kids went to the movies and the mall together? If she went to Kristin's church thing, maybe they would do something non church-y next time.

Also, she had to admit, she was curious. She had been to church in Manhattan – her dad had been big on interfaith services at Thanksgiving, and once a year they did a huge food drive with a church down the street. The people had been nice but it hadn't felt much different than temple. There were prayers – though in English, not Hebrew – and there were lots of older people in dresses and suits. She wanted to feel a difference; otherwise, what was the point of having various religions? She had a feeling that at Kristin's church she would.

The girls ran into Kristin's house and headed straight into the kitchen. Her mom was on the phone; she put up a hand to them to signal quiet and continued talking. Kristin's mom's hair was the same kind of wavy that Kristin's was, and they had the same blue eyes, too. Hannah was always jealous that Kristin and her mom looked so much alike. "We can do tomorrow at 1:30," she said. Kristin rolled her eyes. Her mom was constantly getting work calls for appointments or complaints; their business number hooked into their home phone. Kristin said they rarely had an uninterrupted conversation. Hannah bet that with eight kids it was hard, too. As Kristin's mom was typing information into a laptop on the kitchen island, Kristin's baby brother, Clayton, clung to his mother's knee and whined. Hannah wondered how Kristin ever got any peace. On the other hand, her house was too quiet, and for that, she envied Kristin. There was always someone to talk at Kristin's house, even if her mom was busy.

"Hello, girls!" her mom said, getting off the phone. "Who's hungry?" She went over to the pantry, took out a bag of Oreos, then to the refrigerator, where she pulled out a gallon of milk, and finally to the cupboard, and reached for two glasses. How she could carry all of that stuff without dropping it, Hannah had no idea, and Clayton was still attached to her knee.

Her mom sat down with them at the table, reached for one of the Oreos, and sighed. "How was school?" The phone rang again and Kristin shrugged. Hannah reached for an Oreo, pulling it apart to expose the crème filling. Was it her, or were they skimping on the vanilla center lately? But she couldn't ask Kristin what she thought because her mom was holding up her hand again.

"Meet me out in the car," her mom mouthed as she looked at an appointment calendar, holding up a hand and motioning to the door that led from the kitchen to the garage. Kristin just shrugged again and signaled for Hannah to follow her.

Hannah started getting nervous on the way over to the church. She really, really, really hoped her dad wouldn't find out. "We're so glad you could join us," Kristin's mom said. "You'll love Pastor Jim. He's very dynamic."

"What is this meeting about, anyway?" Hannah wanted to clap her hand over her mouth as soon as she said it; she knew she sounded rude. But she wanted to be prepared, so she could think of things to say and how to say them.

"Oh, just about how important it is to follow the Bible, and its teachings, and to help those who don't do that to find their way." Kristin's younger sisters and brothers were so loud in the minivan, whining and crying and calling out Mommy. But it was like Kristin didn't hear them, and her mother seemed to tune them out pretty well, too.

They were at the church in just minutes. It was large and it didn't have a steeple as so many other churches Hannah had seen. It looked more like an auditorium, and when she got inside, she could see that's just what it was, a large auditorium, with a few smaller rooms off a long hallway. There were about twenty kids waiting—

most looked to be somewhere between thirteen and sixteen. She recognized a few from school or from around town. None was as old as her brother. She was glad. If any of them knew Aaron and she were siblings, they could report back to Aaron who would tell her father. But she didn't think anyone in this crowd knew him. She relaxed a little.

"Let's get a seat up front," Kristin said, leading the way.

"Up front?" She would be more noticed that way. She didn't want anyone to remember her, but hers was the only nonwhite face in the crowd.

A man with sandy brown hair, jeans, and a plaid shirt came striding up the aisle and stood right in front of them. He was so close to her that she could reach out and touch his sleeve if she wanted to. "Good afternoon!" he yelled. It sounded fake.

But all of the teens yelled back, "Good afternoon, Pastor Jim!" They didn't sound fake. She twirled her purity ring on her finger.

"I called this meeting because we have God's work to do. I want to follow up on our emergency meeting from a couple of weeks back. When God calls, we can't wait until the next youth group meeting to discuss what He wants. Am I right?"

"You're right!" the crowd yelled, sounding more like a hundred people than maybe twenty or twenty five. Hannah set about counting them, but it was hard, because she was in the front row, and everyone was behind her. She tried to turn around to look, but Kristin grabbed her hand and held it.

"There are some wayward souls in our midst. God has sent me a message; and that message is that we must help those souls find their way back to Him. And God has let me know that we are called to help them. It's our duty."

It was silent for a moment, and then a car without a muffler roared past, jolting Hannah a bit.

"Last time I asked each of you to think about how we can help others. This time I want to give you some specific ideas. So what we're going to do," said Pastor Jim. "Is spread our message. We're going to spread the message that God loves everyone, that it is not too late to change, to behave as God commands us to, in the Bible. Does everyone understand?"

Hannah did not understand. Who were they helping? How were they supposed to know they were helping the right people? And what were they helping them with? But no one was asking questions. No one was trying to get more information. They all just nodded.

Hannah tried to whisper to Kristin. “Who?” But Pastor Jim looked right at her. “Ah,” he said. “We have a newcomer in our midst. How wonderful! Good job, Kristin!” Kristin blushed and Hannah wondered if this was the point at which the Pastor would hand over a $10 gift card to Claire’s. With her part, Hannah was going to get a new necklace. “Who are you, young lady?”

She hadn’t expected to be pointed out like this. Kristin hadn’t told her that part. Was she supposed to say her name? Could she just say she was Jewish and he would pass over her? She felt her hands grow sweaty.

“Hannah,” she said as quietly as she could.

“Hannah; wonderful. And what brings you to us?”

“Well, her,” she said pointing at her friend. “She did.”

“Yes, but why did you decide to join us today?” He paced in front of her and her palms grew even sweatier.

“Just, it’s, well, Kristin said it’s so much fun here so I wanted to try it out,” she said meekly, and swallowed hard.

“Very good. It *is* fun,” he emphasized, nodding. “But we also do important work. We help people come to Jesus Christ and follow his ways.”

Hannah nodded.

The man put his hands up to the audience, many of whom were getting twitchy and restless. “So, welcome Hannah.” He cleared his throat and the room grew pin-drop quiet again. “If you see someone in need, if he is not living according to what our Bible tells us, it is important to try to talk to that person.”

“What would we say?” came a voice from the back.

“You could ask him if he’s okay. If he would like to pray with you, go to church with you. If he knows how he’s hurting himself or his family. You can come to me, and I can talk to him. The important thing is that we’re dedicating ourselves to God and that we want others to dedicate themselves to God.”

A girl right behind Hannah raised her hand. “Pastor? I’m not sure what we should be looking for. Like, how do we know if we’re helping the people you want us to help?” Finally, someone was asking the question that Hannah had wanted to ask.

“You’re all of an age now where you can hear certain things and wonder is that right? What does that mean? Things you didn’t think about a year or two ago, even. And maybe some of you have older brothers and sisters in high school, and they tell you certain things...about...sexuality." He waited a moment, and again, not a peep.

"It's come to my attention that there are some children in our town, children as young as you..." Hannah looked around. She didn't consider herself a child. She was almost thirteen, practically a teenager, about to leave childhood behind. Maybe she'd already left it behind. It certainly felt like that a lot of days. "And they are misguided. They...they believe they are homosexuals. And we know that God created everyone in his image, and that image specifically is a heterosexual one. And so we want to help guide these children back to the Lord, so that they may grow up and marry properly and have more children to give to the Lord. And live Godly lives."

Hannah was pretty sure her father would be having a fit if he knew what she was listening to right now. Who cared if someone was gay? Hannah knew a bunch of same-sex couples back in New York. In fact, she'd had two friends who were kids of same-sex couples. One was a Korean adopted girl. She had two moms and it was no big deal. The other couple was two men, and right when Hannah and her family had left to come to New Jersey, they were about to have a baby boy born through a surrogate. Hannah hadn't thought about them in a long time.

And what about Kristin and her parents? Did they believe this? They seemed so nice and normal...she wondered if Kristin's parents even knew the pastor was saying this stuff. Being Christian was about loving everyone and forgiveness. Kristin had told her that a bunch of times. That was one reason she wanted to be Christian. Finding courage, she raised her hand. "Um, Pastor?"

"Yes, Hannah."

"Um, what if these people are happy just as they are? I mean, why would we want to change that?"

Pastor Jim knelt down in front of her, on one knee, and she could smell his breath, a combination of eggs and a breath mint he'd obviously tried to mask the smell with. He took her hand, and she was embarrassed by her sweaty palms. She wondered if he was embarrassed about his breath.

"Hannah, these are not happy people. There are confused, conflicted people. And they spend their lives trying to work this out. If we help them, they can be at peace."

"But..."

"When it comes to God's words, there is no but. There is just God. Just Jesus Christ. We want to live Christ-driven lives. We want everyone else to live Christ-driven lives, too."

But not Jews, Hannah wanted to say. We don't live our lives by Christ. Did the Pastor want Jews to live Christ-driven lives even though it said right in the Torah that they were God's chosen people? Wasn't that higher than anything else? She wasn't sure how Christ fit into Judaism, though she knew that Jews didn't believe he was God's son. That whole thing, in her opinion, made no sense. God was not a person, so God couldn't have a child, could he? And Mary, Christ's mother. How could anyone believe her when she said Christ was God's son? Mary was just a pregnant teenager. Some poor teenage boy was Christ's father and he didn't even know. How Mary had managed to fool all of those people was beyond Hannah.

"So, now, does anyone have any questions?"

"No, Pastor," the kids said in unison.

"All right then; go forward. Help those among us who can't help themselves. Bring them to the church, tell them they can speak to me at any time, day or night. Tell your parents to call me if they have any questions. We must take this charge of duty very seriously."

And they were dismissed.

Chapter 20

Mark

It seemed to Mark that he had not spent any time with Aaron in days, maybe weeks. They were always on different paths, Aaron at school and with his girlfriend and at his myriad club activities and Student Council, Mark at late night temple meetings and Bar Mitzvahs and marrying couples some Sundays. The weddings were the hardest, watching two earnest young people promise to love each other in sickness and health, when he was fully aware of what the sickness part really meant. They had no idea. They didn't know it meant watching the person you loved wasting away to nonexistence. They didn't know it meant that you might be left someday to raise two children when you felt completely inadequate to do so. He had stopped in Aaron's room late last night, after he'd gotten home from Friday night services, a headache already forming on the back of his skull. He couldn't wait to take some ibuprofen and head to bed; he groaned when he remembered he had to set his alarm for seven. Normally he liked getting up early, or at least didn't mind it. He did his best thinking in the mornings. But the headache was a doozy, and he knew that more than anything, he needed a solid night's sleep to get rid of it. But first he needed to check in with his son.

He found Aaron lying on his bed, his computer on his lap, typing furiously. "Hey Ari," he said, coming in without knocking, which he'd promised Aaron he would never do. But the door had been open a crack, and Mark hoped that meant Aaron might be receptive to a late night chat. He only wanted about five minutes, which was all he thought he could manage before the headache overtook him and he would need to go to bed. He could hear his late wife chiding him. "You're not spending enough time with him," he knew she would be saying if she could. "It's his senior year; it's a big deal, you need to reach out."

"Dad!" Aaron quickly shut his lap top. "Um, hey."

"Hey," Mark smiled. He wondered what Aaron had been looking at. The look on his face said something he didn't want Mark to know about. "So," he said, making room for himself on the edge of the bed, which was cluttered with dirty socks, text books, and a box of tissues. "What's up?"

"Nothing."

"Nothing? You shut down that screen pretty fast."

"Just, you know, stuff."

"Talking to Marti, huh?" Mark had been concerned about the relationship. Aaron and Marti had been dating over a year now, at least, maybe longer. He tried to remember how long it had actually been. In any case, it seemed as serious as ever. He'd wanted Aaron to play the field a bit more, see different girls, and at first, he had nagged Aaron about it, until Aaron had explained that he only wanted to date Marti. Mark had tried to go into a discussion about condoms and protection, his face turning red. What would his wife have said about that? They'd talked a lot about what she would miss, the milestones the kids would go through that she wouldn't be there for, that Mark would have to deal with, but they'd talked mainly about Hannah, bras and puberty and periods and first crushes and hormones. Perhaps his wife had thought he would do better with a boy, know what to say with Aaron. But he hadn't.

"Um, yeah," Aaron said sheepishly. Aaron's eyes darted around the room, and Mark wondered if he was telling the truth.

Mark had come to accept that Aaron would likely finish out his senior year with Marti, and then, he hoped, find a nice, Jewish girl in college. Marti was sweet enough, she seemed bright and well meaning, but they were too young to get serious, and she wasn't Jewish. When he'd tried to bring that point up, Aaron had bristled. "God, Dad," he'd said. "It's not like we're getting married or anything. We're just going out." And to the condom talk? Aaron had brushed that off, too. "She's a *Christian,* Dad. Are you kidding me? They won't do anything before marriage. I can barely hold her hand." Well, Mark had certainly been relieved about that, at least.

"So how are college apps going?" Aaron hadn't come to him with any questions, not even to ask for the application fees.

"Fine," Aaron said absently.

"Do you need the app fees yet? I can give you the credit card."

"No, not yet. Soon, though." The air between them felt thick.

"And school? Any problems?" There were never any. Aaron was a straight A student. When he'd gotten an A – in AP History last year, he'd nearly had a fit and couldn't sleep for days. Mark had done his best to reassure his son that it wouldn't affect his applications, but Aaron wouldn't calm down until he made an appointment with his guidance counselor, who'd reassured him as well.

"No," Aaron mumbled. "No problems."

"Great! That's good. I mean...But you should really get going on those applications."

"Yeah, yeah."

"And maybe," Mark said, hesitating. "We could get together, you know, a men's night out, one of these days."

"Yeah, that would be, uh, great."

"Dinner? You can choose the restaurant." Likely Aaron would pick the diner in town. If it were Hannah, she'd want to go to Cheesecake Factory. She hadn't stopped talking about it since the cantor – "She told me to call her Robyn outside of temple," Hannah had said, grinning – had taken her there, and the huge menu, the dozens of cheesecake options at the end. But Aaron wouldn't care about something like that.

"Sounds good, Dad," Aaron said huskily, and Mark thought he caught a look of – sadness? Disdain? Pity? – run across his son's face. He wasn't sure what it was, but it wasn't good.

"Son, you okay?" he reached out to touch the boy and Aaron jerked back as though he were on fire. Mark dropped his hand and felt his entire body deflate. He could no longer touch either of his children without them acting like he was going to give them the Bubonic plague.

"Yeah, yeah, fine. Just you know, tired."

So Mark got up, walked to the door, pushed the dirty clothes away from it so he could get on the other side, where it was safe, he thought, and cringed. As if to make up for the disturbing thought he said, "Let's definitely plan that dinner. Next week. Look at your calendar, okay?" Aaron nodded, already pushing his laptop cover open and typing his password onto his keyboard. Mark suspected Marti was sitting on the other side, Skyped in, waiting for him.

Chapter 21

Aaron

Aaron quickly turned his computer back on the second he heard his father pad into his own bedroom. He hadn't been Skpying Marti, but they had been messaging, and he hoped she hadn't left.

"R U there?" he typed.

"Yes," she typed back.

"Sorry. Dad came in...I no its hard," he typed, "but we have to."

"We don't have to. We can have this baby. I M going to."

They had been going round and round in circles since Tuesday, when they had been at the clinic. It was all bad news there, bad news that Aaron hadn't been able to get off his mind.

She was fourteen weeks pregnant.

It wasn't too late to have an abortion, the doctor had reassured them, if that's what she wanted. Well, the doctor had said "they," but Aaron knew that the doctor meant "she." Aaron couldn't force her to do anything. He was still in shock about how far along she was. He had wanted to scream, "But you only missed two periods!" Not that it would matter. It already was what it was.

After the doctor had examined her internally, which Aaron considered the most embarrassing moment of his life --he'd looked up at the ceiling the whole time as Marti had squeezed his hand -- the doctor said they could do an ultrasound, if they wanted. "I can do it abdominally," he said to Marti. "I think you're far enough along. Though if you're thinking about an abortion, you might not want to." But Marti had nodded.

The doctor had spread this gel on Marti's stomach then, and for the first time, Aaron had noticed it did look a little bigger. Not that he would ever tell Marti that, or anything. Girls hated to think they looked fat. And then the doctor had turned off the lights and turned the screen towards himself. He'd moved the wand over Marti's stomach and typed some things into the computer part of the machine. That's when he told them. "Okay," he said. "You're fourteen weeks." He jotted that down in Marti's newly-made chart.

"Can I see?" Marti had said, craning her neck.

"Yes, you can; if you're sure?" Marti nodded and Aaron thought about going outside. He didn't want to see. To know. It was just a – ball of cells. A thing. But if he didn't stay to watch, Marti would never forgive him. So he stayed planted on the stool above Marti's head and he nodded, too.

The doctor had turned the screen back to them. On it was the clear outline of a baby, small, yes, but it looked like it had everything. "So according to your ultrasound, you're actually due on April 21."

Marti's eighteenth birthday.

And now they were here, late on a Friday night, messaging about what to do. Aaron had managed to get through the rest of the week, barely, but whenever he closed his eyes to sleep, all he saw was that tiny image. It had even been moving. He didn't know babies could move that early. He knew nothing at all.

He hadn't wanted to admit how the screen shot had affected him. He'd nodded at the screen and then looked away, the image burnt on his mind, trying not to react, while Marti had stared at the screen, transfixed. The doctor hadn't said anything else right then, just turned the screen back away from them and made some more notes and then the room had been silent. "You can still have an abortion," he'd told them. "It's legal until the twenty-fourth week in New Jersey."

Marti had gasped. "Twenty-four?"

"Yes, but after week fourteen, you have to have it done in a hospital, so we'd schedule it for over there whenever you want. "

"Would she be…awake?" Aaron had asked.

"No, we can put her into twilight sleep." He looked at Marti. "You'd be comfortable, and not aware. The procedure only takes a few minutes; you'd be home in a very short time, resting. And then the next day you'd go back to most of your regular activities. . .You still have time; not a lot; I'd say. If you're going to have it done, it should be done sooner rather than later. But you can think about it; call us next week, or before, if you have any questions." He'd patted Marti on the shoulder and disappeared.

Aaron typed now, "I don't want to do it either, but we have 2."

"Why? If we don't want 2?"

How could he explain that his life would be ruined if he didn't? That he would be stuck in this God-awful town in the middle of God-awful nowhere for the rest of his life, pumping gas or something while he provided for this baby he didn't want and certainly had no idea how to take care of. And how could he also explain, at the same time, that he couldn't stop thinking about the baby, whether it was a boy or a girl, and that it held his DNA, his mother's DNA. That before the ultrasound he'd really thought it was a clump of cells, and it had felt okay to...have the procedure when that's all it was, just a clump of cells trying to divide... but now...it felt different. And he didn't want to admit that. Not to himself, certainly not to anyone else. But still, he wanted her to have an abortion. Yes, he needed to convince her.

"I no u don't want to, but no other choice," he typed back.

"I can have it. Give it up for adoption." He'd thought about that, too. He'd imagined watching the baby being born and then giving it to some nice couple at the hospital, some people who couldn't have a baby but really wanted one. That could be a middle-of- the-road option. Could he live with that?

But he had rejected it. For one thing, then everyone would know. His father would know. And he would always have this kid out there, which would be weird. And they'd have to get through the next six months and then Marti would have to live with it forever, too. Truth be told, he wasn't sure that she would give the baby up, when it came down to it. And he couldn't take that risk.

He said that now. "U wouldn't be able to give it up."

"I would!"

"No U wouldn't. I NO U. We R 2 young to have a baby." And ruin our lives, he wanted to add, but he wasn't sure that was entirely true, either.

"Ill be 18. U 2."

"Still 2 young. College."

They went round and round for at least another hour, and then Marti had said she was exhausted and needed to go to bed. Aaron wondered if, like him, she tossed and turned all night, going over the choices, wondering what would happen next.

Chapter 22

Hannah

Hannah's Saturday afternoon was turning out to be boring. Kristin couldn't hang out, her dad had to be at something downtown, and Aaron was with Marti again. She wandered from room to room, turned on the television and turned it off, tried to read the new Megan McCafferty novel. Nothing was working to take away the itchiness she felt. She wanted to *do* something.

She could play on the computer, she supposed, check Facebook to see what was going on. When sixth grade started, she realized most of the girls had one. Kristin had one. So one night she hopped on her Dad's computer to make herself one. Her dad had come into his office. "Whatcha doin', Honey?" he'd asked.

"Making a Facebook account. But they ask here for your birthday and it says you have to be thirteen..." She twisted her tongue in her mouth. "I'll just change the year, then." She began to type it in, but her dad said, "No."

"What do you mean, no?" He was standing over her at the desk now, and he grabbed the mouse from her.

"I mean, if it says thirteen, then you need to be thirteen. You're only eleven. You'll have plenty of time for this stuff later."

"Da-ad," she'd said back, drawing out the syllable so he would know how stupid he sounded. "It's no big deal. All of the kids at school have them, and they're all only eleven and twelve."

"All of them but you," he'd replied, and exited out of Facebook. "On the day you turn thirteen, you can have one, but not the day before." He'd smiled then, as though he thought he was being such a great dad. But he wasn't. She'd rolled her eyes at him and slammed out of the room, not daring to look back, to give him any chance of thinking she would get over this.

So she'd made one on her brother's computer. For a smart guy, he wasn't very smart about keeping his password secret. His password was his birthday. Duh. Please. So easy. It had taken her only three guesses to get it right. She used her account to spy on the kids at school, and to see if she was missing anything. Some of the girls were so cruel to each other; she couldn't get over it. Her mother used to say that if you couldn't say anything nice, don't say anything at all, and Hannah thought that was an excellent rule.

She went into her brother's room and dug his laptop out from under his bed. It smelled pretty bad under there. She bet he was eating in his room again and not throwing out his garbage, even though their dad had told him a million times not to. They'd had to get the whole upstairs sprayed for ants last spring because of his eating. It had been disgusting. But Aaron wouldn't get in trouble or anything for disobeying. It was like her father had different rules for each of them, and she didn't know why. She pulled open the top and was surprised to see Aaron's computer was still on. Normally her brother was a fanatic about turning it off at the end of the night. The screen lit up. His Facebook was still on, too, and instead of logging out of it so she could get onto her own page, she quickly scrolled through some of the posts to see what the high school kids were talking about. Nothing interesting. College applications. Homecoming. Boring.

And then she saw at the bottom of the screen, a conversation between him and Marti. It was minimized, but there. She always wondered what they talked about.

Should she look? This was trespassing. It was wrong. Her heart galloped. She would kill her brother if he trespassed in her room, although she had nothing interesting or private in there, unless she counted her new bras, which fit so much better than her old ones, and the pads she was hiding in her underwear drawer. She'd gotten her period again this week, and it was such a relief to have those pads for it. In a couple of more periods, she would need more, and she was already worried about how she would get them. She couldn't ask her father. She just couldn't.

Curiosity won out over right and wrong. She clicked on the messaging box.

The conversation was long. She scrolled to the beginning so she could read it all. Why was her brother asking Marti how she felt? Had she been sick? And why did he keep saying, "You have to do it." What did she have to do? And she kept saying she couldn't? Was he trying to force her to have sex with him? Eew, how gross, also, that was so rude of her brother.

14 wks. Already baby.

What?

She read further. She scrolled quickly, hoping her brother wouldn't walk in, her heart pounding. "Oh my God," she said over and over out loud. "Oh my God. Marti's pregnant."

Chapter 23

Mark

Mark couldn't believe it when he honked his horn at Robyn's condo and she actually came out dressed as an apple. Where had she found the get up? She wore red tights on her legs and a big red apple suit-like thing. On top of her head was a green stem. He burst out laughing as she gingerly made her way into the car, pushing the stem down so it wouldn't get caught on the roof.

"Isn't this great?" she asked enthusiastically. "I found it online and had it shipped overnight."

"Good luck getting the temple to reimburse you for overnight charges," he said as he put the car in Drive and headed downtown.

"Oh, I don't care. I think this is so much fun. Did you get the apples?"

He pointed to the back seat. He'd had the grocery store make up a platter with a ramekin of honey for dipping right in the middle, and then he'd swapped out the store's cheap plastic tray for one of his wife's old serving trays that he had found still packed in a box in the basement. He'd forgotten all about how she'd loved to entertain – they'd had lots of parties in their Manhattan apartment, but only in the warm months, because they needed the extra space out on their terrace for guests. She'd be excited all day before the event, cooking and chopping and arranging hors d'oeuvres platters and cleaning the kids' toys out from under the couch. He'd been in charge of drinks; always wine and soda, sometimes some hard drinks, too, depending on the occasion. They hadn't really been big drinkers.

"Do you know Jim Jameson?" Mark asked Robyn now. He'd been thinking about Jameson all week. He wasn't sure what the man was up to, but he hated the idea of innocent teenagers struggling with their sexuality running into him.

"Who doesn't?" Robyn asked. "Why?"

"I knew his name, of course, but I never met him before this week. He was, uh, quite a character."

"If you mean that he's loud and obnoxious, you're right." Robyn grinned.

"I guess that's one way of putting it," Mark said. He was so used to watching every word with everyone outside of his wife. You never knew who was repeating what to whom within the congregation, even other staff members, and certainly congregants. He'd seen what happened to loose-lipped rabbis and none of it was good.

Mark maneuvered the car into a parking space just steps from the book store. "So what about him?" Robyn asked, opening the car door.

"Here, let me help you." Mark ran around to the other side of the car and opened the door. He let Robyn grab his hand in order to stabilize herself. Her nails were perfectly manicured, clear polish on them, her hand warm. "Oops," she said, as she tried to balance herself. "Is my stem straight?" and she laughed.

Mark smiled and adjusted it. "So anyway," he said, grabbing the apple platter and honey from the back seat. They began walking. It was a crisp October day, the leaves turning, the air fresh. He breathed in the scent.

"Right, Jim Jameson." He made sure to talk softly, even though he saw no one around them. You really could never be too careful. "Yeah, we had an interfaith pastoral meeting last week. To talk about bullying and religion and what we could do about it. He got very, I guess you would say, overzealous."

"About gays."

"How did you know?"

"That's the guy's MO. I've heard it around town."

Where had Mark been? How could this be going on and he had no idea? "I'm worried about how this might affect the teenagers. He pretty much said he's going to try to stop them from being gay."

"Like that'll work," Robyn said, rolling her eyes. They reached the bookstore and Mark opened the door. "After you," he said, ushering Robyn inside. But she grabbed the door from him. "You have the apples," she said. "So after you." He stepped forward. He was so relieved not to be the one dressed as an apple. But as young children began surrounding Robyn, touching her costume and hugging her red legs, and as she returned their hugs and slapped their little hands with high fives, he almost wished for the affection.

Chapter 24

Aaron

Aaron and Marti were walking down the road away from her house. He was nearly in a panic. "I can barely snap my jeans," she said, showing him the strain around her waist. She was fifteen weeks now, and they were no closer to a resolution. The other night, she'd asked him, "What if it hurt?"

"Having a baby? It *would* hurt."

"No, I mean the other thing."

"Abortion?"

"Don't say the word," she'd said and covered her ears as though she was four years old and afraid of a playmate talking about the bogey man.

"I don't think it hurts. I'm sure they give you something for it. . . Is that what you're worried about? It hurting?"

She'd hesitated. "No...not really, I don't think. I guess more...it's going to hurt me, inside." She touched her chest, by her heart.

"I know," he'd said and put his arm around her. "But it would be the right thing to do. We can't love this...we can't love *it* the way we need to." He couldn't say the word baby any more than she could say the word abortion. They were still pretending it wasn't real. But it was.

"I could love it, I already do. But....I know if I go through with having it, everything, you, me, our families...it would all be a mess."

They hadn't said anything more about it that night, though he sensed from her words that maybe she was really thinking abortion, maybe considering it, for real.

Then, yesterday, as he had grabbed her hand and squeezed it on the way into school, she had pulled away. "I'm not doing it," she had said, and floated in the direction of her first class, leaving him with his mouth open, wondering if he had imagined their conversation the night before. He had slept well the night before for the first time in weeks, and he'd planned on asking his teachers for their recommendations today. He even felt confident about his Calc test. But it had all fallen apart when she said those words.

Now she said, "I want to tell my parents."

He stopped, faced her, and he felt the adrenalin rush through his body. "Are you crazy? They'll disown you!"

"I don't think they will," she said thoughtfully, forming a slight pout with her lips. She crinkled her eyebrows. "Will they be mad? Yes. Will they scream and yell? Probably. But Jesus tells us to hate the sin and love the sinner, so I think that's how it'll pan out."

He looked at her again. She was nuts. "Marti, they could throw you out of the house!" What would he do then? She couldn't...live at their house, could she? His father would never allow it. Plus, did he really want her to live with him?

But he knew why she was doing this. Her convictions and faith were strong, and if he admitted it to himself, though he didn't understand or want to be part of her religion, he loved how strong she was in her beliefs. He loved that she really did believe God was there for her and that if she only followed Him, things would be okay. It was a simplistic view of life, he thought, but there was something...sweet about it. Something that was so uncomplicated, unlike Reform Judaism, a religion that practically begged you to question, that wanted you to wonder and dissect and not be able to reach any conclusions. A religion that thought it was okay to question God, to wonder if God even existed. In her faith, with her beliefs, Marti simply did believe. Simply did not question.

Still, he didn't know if her parents would be so forgiving, even if that's what Jesus would do.

"I have to tell them sometime. I'm starting to show," she said calmly, as calm as she had been in weeks. "And I want them to know. I want to start making plans. I think I should go back, now, to the house. They're both there. You leave; I want to tell them alone."

She wanted him to leave while she told them? That was so...not right. Shouldn't he be there? Still, he had not pictured this ever getting that far, and his stomach sank. "I don't know," he said. "Shouldn't I be there, with you?" He had no idea how to do this, but it seemed to him that at least he should be there.

"I think it will be better if I tell them myself. You can come back another time. I just – I can't hide behind you. I'm going to be a mother, and I have to advocate for my child. And you need to tell your dad, too. We should tell them separately, at the same time." They stopped walking, and she turned to face him. "You're going to be a father, that's all there is to it. I can't kill this baby. It's a person, growing inside me, waiting to come out to the world and do good things and be loved and give love. It's got a brain and a heart and all of its organs. It's expecting us, as its parents, to protect it." She waited a moment and then, "And all you keep thinking about is yourself," she spat.

"I'm just trying to think of you…" But that wasn't completely true, and he knew it. "And…me. Our futures. And the," he swallowed hard. "Baby. Because wouldn't we only want a baby we could give the best possible life to?" Marti was practical, if nothing else.

"Who are we to determine what kind of life it will have? He or she will have, I mean? We can be great parents."

"Would you consider adoption?" She definitely wasn't going to abort this baby, and he should have known that right away, from the beginning. At least with adoption, there would be an ending to this nightmare. He was going to be a father. But what if she adopted it out instead? It wasn't the perfect solution, but neither was abortion. At least with adoption, they could both still have lives after high school, as much as he knew how selfish that sounded. And the baby could go to some nice, rich family who would raise it Christian – he knew Marti would insist on that – a family who really wanted a baby, who was dying for one. So then the baby could have the wonderful life Marti wanted for it. It didn't sound so bad, now, against his only other option.

"I'm not sure I could give it up," she said, which he knew would be a problem and scared the crap out of him. "But even if I did, we would still have to tell my mom and dad. And your dad, too."

The thought of telling his dad was almost as bad as telling her parents in some ways. He wondered what his mom would have said. Oh, she would have been furious. But somehow she would have understood, he thought. She would have paved the way to tell his dad, who would be most concerned about his congregants, about his job with the temple. But his mom would have been there for him – after she got over the shock, of course. She would have walked him through the different scenarios and even talked to Marti. God, she would have been great with Marti. She could convince anyone to do anything. She'd been a lawyer before she'd had him and she'd been great at debating. She would have rationally explained to Marti why she couldn't keep the baby and she would have been really supportive during her pregnancy and helped her find a good home. She wouldn't have been happy about the baby being raised in a Christian family instead of a Jewish one, but she would have known that there was nothing she could do about that. Aaron felt the weight pressing down on his shoulders, the wish once again that his mother were alive to help him. And the reality that wishing it would not make it so.

Chapter 25

Hannah

Hannah shut the computer with a slam and then ran from the room, as though the computer had a virus that would contaminate her if she stayed there. She paced the hallway and then went downstairs and closed her eyes. Could this be true? Maybe she'd misunderstood it. Maybe it wasn't what she thought. Pregnant? So she ran back upstairs, heart pounding, and opened the computer. She read the words again, tried to find another meaning. She might be only twelve, but she wasn't stupid. Marti was pregnant. Aaron was going to be a father.

She went to her room and tried to calm down, doing the yoga breathing her mother had taught her. It wasn't her problem, she kept reminding herself. This was Aaron's problem, his mess. It did explain how weird he'd been acting the last couple of weeks, even weird for him. When she had come into his room for help with a math problem last week, he'd screamed at her. "Get out, Hann," he's roared, in a voice she had only heard when he was mad at other people, not her.

"But you said I could always come to you for math help." She hadn't meant to, but she knew she sounded whiny.

"I'm in the middle of something. Can't you see that, Stupid?"

The word hurt. She'd hurried out the door then, feeling like she'd been punched in the gut. And then the next day, when she got marked off for not completing her math homework, she'd felt her stomach hurt all over again. Did her father know? He couldn't know, because he'd been acting totally normal. She doubted he would be if he knew. How would Aaron tell him? Would he sit his father down and tell him right here, in the house, or would he take their dad somewhere else to do it? Would they have to move or would they stay here? Would Marti and Aaron get married? And then would they live with them? Hannah could babysit the baby. She loved babies, was a natural with them. She loved their long eyelashes, their sweet smell. She didn't think she would even mind changing diapers, not for her niece or nephew. She was going to be aunt! Or would she? Would they give it away, like she had been given away? Oh that would be awful. She felt the pit in her stomach grow, until it felt like it reached up to her throat and down to her feet. Could they really do that? She would have to tell Aaron, it wasn't like he imagined it would be. Give the baby away to a better life and then snap, just like that, the baby would grow up happy and content. The baby would wonder what had happened to its parents, like she did, and it would look different than its family and it wouldn't like that, either.

On the other hand, she thought, she loved her family and her mom had always told her that if she'd stayed in China, she'd be living in an orphanage somewhere, without a real family to call her own. And she did have a pretty good life, she knew, except she missed her mom so much and she felt so awkward around the kids at school who thought she was an alien, or something.

So maybe Aaron and Marti would give their baby away. Maybe she could still visit it, though, because it wouldn't go halfway around the world, it would be somewhere else in America, wouldn't it? Even if it was in, like, California, it would still be closer than China. It was weird imagining that she'd been on a plane for nearly a whole twenty four hours to come here, when she couldn't remember it. She'd never been on a plane otherwise, and when other kids asked her if she'd ever flown, she always said no, because really, how did she know, except that her parents had told her and there were pictures of her as a baby, her mother cradling her as they walked off the plane together. There were balloons that said "It's a girl!" and her mother's mother, her grandmother, who she had not really known because she'd died a year later, in a wheelchair, her mother bending over the chair to show her. In the picture, her mother was wearing strange, out of date clothes, and she didn't look even a tiny bit sick, just regular. It had gotten to the point, Hannah realized, that she almost couldn't remember her mother as anything but sick and frail, a bandana on her head so no one would see her bald, (though she had shown Hannah) so she was relieved when she remembered that she could just pull out those pictures and see her mother as she had really been. The mom Hannah wanted to remember. And then, she also couldn't remember the last time her father had looked happy. It had been too long.

She could distract herself with a snack. She decided to fix herself half of a pb&j. While waiting for the bread to toast, she grabbed the peanut butter from the cabinet and a jar of strawberry jam from the fridge. There wasn't much jam left, so she wrote a note on the pad on the refrigerator; her dad would not remember to get it if she didn't. Her dad was a terrible grocery shopper. He forgot to go until they were out of milk and down to the last slice of bread, the heel of the loaf, which she hated. And then he got the wrong brands or forgot half the things and had to go back, sighing as he slammed back out of the house. She might need to take over the grocery shopping if they had this baby and decided to keep it, though she didn't think her father would ever agree to something like that. She would be good at the grocery shopping, though. She didn't think it was too hard; she couldn't figure out why her father had so much trouble with it.

The bread popped out of the toaster and she smoothed the peanut butter over it until it reached the very edges, just the way she liked it. Then she plopped a little bit of jam in the center and ran the knife over it to make it even with the peanut butter. She folded the bread over and cut it, went back to the frig for some chocolate milk. As she sat at the table, she felt a little better. Things would be okay. Her dad would figure out what to do about all of this.

Just as she was finishing the sandwich, her dad walked in. He had a smile on his face so he couldn't know what she knew. It was the first time she had seen that kind of smile in a very long time.

Chapter 26

Mark

As Mark drove towards home, he felt a sense of happiness in his chest that he hadn't felt since, well, forever, it seemed. He was a little embarrassed that he'd ever scoffed at the apples and honey idea. The kids loved the apples and honey, so he'd had a rapt audience who munched on apples while he read the simple book he'd chosen about Rosh Hashanah. Afterwards, parents had milled around, asking questions about the temple, telling him how much they had enjoyed his presentation. Sure, many had not been Jews, but he liked that they'd stayed anyway, that they'd asked questions, that they'd seemed interested. How better to build his synagogue than through word of mouth. Maybe some of those non-Jewish parents would tell their Jewish friends about him, about how much fun their children had had at the bookstore, and they would come check it out. Two of the mothers had said they'd been thinking about looking at the temple, and had asked specific questions about the Hebrew School and becoming members.

He suspected that it hadn't been just his reading that had prompted the positive reaction. Robyn really had a way with kids. She got down on their level and talked to them. They'd wanted to feel her stem, and she let them, even when one particularly aggressive boy had tried to pull it off her head. She'd just laughed and patted him. She had even led the group in a couple of easy to learn holiday songs, and they'd enthusiastically sung along. On the ride back to her house, she said, "Wasn't that great?"

"It really was," he'd agreed.

"We should do it for Chanukah."

He laughed. "I wonder if you could even find a potato latke costume."

"I could make one."

He laughed again.

"No, I'm serious. I'm kind of handy with a sewing machine. My mother taught me."

"If you make one, I will definitely come with you," he'd said, and he realized he really hoped she *would* make one, so they could do this again. When they'd arrived at her condo, he'd run around the car again, helping her out. "No man my age ever opens the door for me," she'd laughed, and he wondered again how old she was. Definitely no more than thirty, he decided. As young as the crazy pastor, but not at all the same. He walked her up to her doorway. "No need to walk me up," she'd protested. "I'm a big girl."

"My mother taught me always to walk the lady to the door," he'd joked back, realizing how old he must sound.

She smiled. "Your mother taught you well. How sweet." She blushed.

"So I'll see you tomorrow for Hebrew school?" he asked, as she looked for her key in her purse.

"Nine a.m., sharp. God, I wish I could sleep late on weekends," she said. "Like a regular person."

"Me, too," he'd said back, though he hadn't really cared. He was often up by six anyway. "But we do what we have to do." She'd nodded then, and tipped her head, and then finally produced her key. She held it up. "Better go in. I'm going to have a nice, long bubble bath and a glass of wine."

"Maybe I'll take the kids out for dinner." When was the last time the three of them had been out together? He couldn't even remember. Aaron was always with Marti or off doing something and Hannah...he took her out, now and again, but just for a quick meal. Tonight maybe they could do that and rent a movie. There must be one movie they could all agree on.

He'd left Robyn's apartment feeling buoyed. And he was still feeling that way when he came into his own house, and found Hannah, and a counter messy with peanut butter and jelly stains, and a look on her face that said something was very, very wrong.

Chapter 27

Aaron

Aaron drove home from Marti's as slowly as possible. Normally he would gun the engine through yellow lights, even if he knew they really were about to turn red, and he'd squeak around corners a little too tightly, even though he knew he shouldn't, because it felt good, and powerful. But tonight he drove as though he were a sixty five year old grandmother, letting other cars pass him on the main drag, using his signal, and stopping even if a light had barely tuned yellow.

Right now, at this very moment, Marti was telling her parents. He needed to do exactly the same, at the same moment, like Marti had said. He'd gotten her into this mess, and he should be a man about it. He should have gone with her. No, it wouldn't have been easy, but he should be with her. He had been relieved though, when she insisted she go it alone, as cowardly, as ashamed he was with the relief he felt. His entire body tingled.

Marti's parents couldn't know and his dad not know. Plus, it would be all over town in about ten minutes. He cringed.

Once Marti told her parents, he knew the abortion option, as minute as it had been, would cease to exist. It had probably never been there in the first place, he knew now. Sure, Marti had said she would consider it, but she never really had. Her religion wouldn't let her. It pissed him off, but he also respected the way she felt, and the way her parents would feel. And the idea of abortion had been bothering him, a little, too, he admitted. He couldn't get the image on the ultrasound screen out of his mind. When he tried to go to sleep, when he was studying – or not studying but trying to, was the way it felt these days – when he was in the shower, or driving somewhere, he saw the little limbs moving, the heart beating, and he thought, something I made is alive. We can't kill it.

Still, he would have gone for the abortion. It would have been the easiest choice, overall, of the three. He would have felt guilty for a long time, he supposed, and he knew Marti wouldn't have forgiven herself, but it would have been complication-free for the rest of his life. Now they had *keep the baby* or *give the baby up for adoption*. Marti wanted to keep the baby and raise it. She wanted to get married, for Pete's sake. He was seventeen years old. He would not marry her. And he didn't think his dad would let him anyway.

Give the baby up for adoption was the next alternative. He didn't like the idea -- that a piece of him, a piece of his mother, would be out there somewhere, him not knowing how it was doing, or being able to see it grow. Marti had said that maybe they would find a couple who would let them stay involved, but then how was that true adoption? His parents had deliberately gone to another country to adopt Hannah so they wouldn't have anyone else in the picture, his mother had said. They wanted to be the baby's parents and not worry the birth family would come back and try to get the baby, or be too involved in the baby's life.

Aaron had been five when Hannah was adopted. He remembered the drive to the airport well. He'd loved looking at the planes flying in and out, and his father had bought him ice cream from a stand while they waited. He couldn't wait to see his mother again. She had been gone a long time, it felt like forever but maybe it had been two weeks or so, and he'd missed her. He and his father had held a sign that said Welcome Home, Hannah Joy, her middle name for all the happiness she would bring them, his mother had said as she'd said goodbye to him what felt like so long ago, as she had gripped his hand tightly, so tight it almost hurt.

He suddenly realized that he had no idea why his parents had adopted his sister. Had they been unable to have another baby? Did they just want to do some good in the world? His mother had been very into doing good in the world. He should ask his father sometime why the adoption had happened. But not now. Maybe not for a long time.

Despite his slow pace, he got to the house in record time. His father's car was there. He started to sweat. He needed to do it, he told himself; he just couldn't wait any longer. Marti was telling her parents right this second. So it was good that his father was home.

He walked into the house, dropped his keys on the end table and took his jacket off. He could hear his father and sister talking softly in the kitchen. He made his way through the dark living room – they never used it, it didn't even have any furniture in it and they'd never installed lighting -- towards the back of the house. He entered the kitchen to find his sister crying in her father's lap, his dad rubbing her back. When they heard him come in, they both looked up, and he saw that somehow, some way, they already knew.

Chapter 28

Hannah

When her dad had come into the house, Hannah had felt the tears start up immediately. She had wanted to tell him so badly, but she knew she shouldn't. She abandoned her pb&j and ran into his arms, and he had held her for a long time, stroking her hair and whispering he loved her and to tell him what was wrong.

"Are you hurt?" he'd asked over and over and she had shaken her head each time. But she couldn't speak, either, and the words she wanted to say, longed to say, were stuck in her throat along with the salty, pungent taste of the peanut butter. The sandwich churned in her stomach. She was sorry she had eaten it.

When she had finally taken a breath, he had pulled her away from him and said, "Tell me," and for that moment, she felt like her father really cared, like a dad should.

"I can't," she had said, and thrown herself back into his arms. She knew that it was for Aaron to tell, still, the secret lodged itself in her, and she wanted to say it. But it all seemed too crazy, that Marti was pregnant, that Aaron would be a father, that her father – and she'd looked at him for a split second when she realized it – would be a grandfather. It wasn't real, yet it was.

"You have to," her father had said. "If you're this upset, something is very wrong, and we need to deal with it."

She'd calmed down a bit by then, and rubbed her red eyes. Her father gently put her back upright in her seat and had gone into the guest bathroom briefly. He returned with a roll of toilet paper and gave her some. "Blow your nose," he'd said. After she had, he had said again. "You have to tell me. Whatever it is, we can deal with it."

She just shook her head slowly, and her father had again held her for what seemed like a long time. He rubbed circles on her back. "Is it Kristin?" he asked. "Did you two have a fight?" She shook her head. "Did someone say something mean to you at school?" Again, she'd shaken her head. "Did you get in trouble?" he asked, and he sounded so horrified that she had almost laughed. Her father knew she was a goody two shoes with straight A report cards and perfect comments about her behavior. If anything, her teachers had told him, she was too quiet.

"So then what?" he asked, stroking her hair.

She blurted out, "Marti."

"Marti? Aaron's girlfriend?"

"Yes," she whispered, and then she was mad at herself. Why had she even said the name?

"What about Marti? Is she hurt? Did she and Aaron have a fight?"

"No."

"Is Aaron with her now?"

"I don't know," she said miserably, though she suspected he was.

"Then what?"

"I can't say it," she said, hoping that would satisfy her father, for now, that Aaron could come home and either tell him or push him away, and they could deal with it. She'd already said too much, gone too far.

"You can," he father said. "You can and you will." He sounded stern, like he did when the Bar Mitzvah kids came in for practice and hadn't done their homework, or they acted out or the boys said crude things that her father hated. Everyone listened when her father was stern, which wasn't too often.

"I'm not sure I can. We need to wait for Aaron."

"Why do we need to wait for Aaron?"

"It's just...it's...we just do."

That seemed to satisfy her father, at least for a short while, and he continued to stroke her hair, neither of them saying a word. Ten minutes later she heard Aaron's car pull up, the opening of the front door. "There he is," her father murmured. "We're going to get to the bottom of this." And as Aaron came through to the kitchen, they both looked up. Aaron's face was pale white, and his forehead was slick with sweat. *Oh*, Hannah thought, *he was going to tell us anyway*.

Chapter 29

Mark

The second he had seen his daughter's face, Mark had known something was terribly, awfully wrong. She looked like an animal separated from its mother, and the last time he'd seen that wide-eyed look, his wife had just died, and Hannah was getting ready to go to the funeral, putting on the dark dress that his wife's friend had brought over. She was easing Hannah into it, but Hannah had looked just the same as she did now. Like she wanted to be anywhere but here. Like she needed comfort yet no one would be able to provide it.

He had tried to coax it out of her, but he could see she was dead set against telling him. When she said *Marti*, though, he knew. What else could it be? And now he had just waited, holding a shaken Hannah in his arms, for his son to come and tell him. A million thoughts swirled through his mind, though he tried to temper them on the off chance he was wrong. And also to try to give his son the benefit of the doubt, which was very hard when you saw his entire future being flushed down the toilet.

He tried to be calm for Hannah. It was hard, but there was something soothing about running his fingers through her jet black hair, over and over. It was knotted at the base and he wondered, in the midst of his mind jumping from thought to thought, when was the last time Hannah had gotten a haircut. A long time, he realized sadly. He had been that neglectful of her basic needs. And this thing with Aaron – if it was what he thought it was – that was neglect, too. He just wasn't a good father. He was trying, he had told himself more than once, but now he wondered, was he? He hadn't been there for his kids, and they were all going to pay the price.

He heard the front door open and shut, the rattle of Aaron's keys onto the end table, and his footsteps coming closer to the kitchen. He tried to raise Hannah out of his lap so he could confront his son, eye to eye, man to man, but she was like the dead weight of wet sand.

He looked up and Aaron was in the kitchen.

"Dad," he said, and he took a step further in.

"Hannah, why don't you go into your room? Aaron and I need to talk, and then we'll all talk as a family." He smiled weakly.

"I don't want to," she said, and clung to him. This was not a conversation he wanted to have with his daughter present. She was still a little girl, and she shouldn't hear the complicated discussion they were about to have, the words that might pass between him and his son.

"You must," he said, trying to sound both fatherly and commanding. But she clung to him some more, and he sighed.

Aaron tried, too. "Hanny Bananny," he said, using the nickname that he hadn't heard in years. "I think you should go upstairs, okay?" Surprisingly, then, Hannah slid off of her father's lap, squeezing against Mark one last time, and slunk past her brother. Once she was safely upstairs, Mark nodded to Aaron. "Take a seat, son." Aaron complied.

He sat in Hannah's chair but said nothing. His hair had grown too long, looking more like the way he wore it as a preteen sixth grader, still innocent, when his most pressing problem had been whether he would ever grow as tall as the other boys. He had. He was six one now, with broad shoulders and his mother's eyes. Mark cleared his throat. "Is there something you wanted to talk about?" He was determined not to make it easy for his son, and in fact, had to control the simmering anger he felt.

You know."

"I don't know anything."

"You know. Come on, Dad," he whined, and Mark thought he sounded like a seven year old being told he had to go to bed before midnight on New Year's Eve.

"I don't. I know something's terribly wrong, otherwise why would your sister fling herself into my arms the minute I got home, looking as though the world has ended?" He stopped for a second, hoping to get his son to say the words.

But Aaron just blinked, and Mark realized he would have to go further.

"And when I questioned her, the only word I could really get from her was 'Marti.'"

Aaron looked down at the floor. "Yeah." But he didn't say anything else.

"What's this about, Aaron?" Mark put his hand on Aaron's shoulder now and felt, mixed with his anger, sorry for his son.

"I came home to tell you. Tonight. I was going to tell you tonight. I swear."

"Tell me what?" He looked into Aaron's steely gray eyes—his wife's steely gray eyes, the eyes she used when she was looking for a jury decision in the courtroom, or the time she had used those eyes on him to get him to agree to adopt a baby from China.

"Marti," he whispered.

"Marti. Okay. Say it."

Aaron took a deep breath and whimpered. He looked down at the floor and mumbled. "She's pregnant."

He had hoped against hope that wasn't it but the moment he said those words, and it was actually true, not just a scared thought in the back of Mark's mind, everything shifted.

Chapter 30

Aaron

Aaron moved the chair he was sitting in further away from his father, so they couldn't touch. He couldn't bear the thought of his dad touching him right now, or he might break in two. He felt as nervous as he had when he was at college interviews this past summer, except instead of bragging about himself, talking about his accomplishments in school, he was about to face an inquisition. An inquisition he deserved, he reminded himself.

His father didn't say anything. He just looked at Aaron, his arms crossed. Aaron looked back at his father, too, unable to know where to start. Should he start with the condoms, and how he insisted on using them until Marti had insisted, just as strongly, that they weren't necessary because she was watching her cycle, had it down to a science? Did he start with how he had thought he loved Marti, but had begun to realize over the last two weeks that what he felt might not really be love, and how that was scary? Or about how he had begged his girlfriend to get an abortion, knowing how she felt about it even when he knew it would be the easiest thing and how selfish that felt? So many openings to choose from, and none seemed a good starting place.

So he opened his mouth and then closed it again, the words not forming the way he wanted them to. He needed his dad so badly, needed him in a way he never had, even when his mother had died right before his eyes, but he didn't know how to reach him. How to make him understand. How to get him on his side.

"Aaron," his dad said, and he did sound gentle. "You need to say the words."

So Aaron closed his eyes for a second and he was so tired that he could imagine falling asleep in the chair, if he was not so revved up, if his heart was not pounding so hard in his throat. "Marti's pregnant." He kept his eyes closed. "And it's mine."

"I see," said Mark. There was another long pause, and Aaron realized his dad wasn't going to ask questions, he was just going to expect Aaron to talk. And talk. And Aaron, for everything he was good at, good grades and student council and all of that, was lousy at talking about feelings, talking about hard choices. He could bullshit everyone with his smooth talk about some stupid subject but he never talked about the real stuff. And now he was going to have to.

So he laid it all out for his dad – everything. And when he finished, he waited for his dad to say something, but he didn't. He just sat there, his arms slightly less firmly folded than fifteen minutes before, when he had started talking.

"And now you know everything," Aaron concluded, embarrassed. Because it was embarrassing to admit to his dad everything that had happened, to say the words sex and condoms and birth control and abortion out loud, talking about himself and his stupid choices that had landed him in his incredibly big mess.

"I'm glad I know everything now," his dad said.

"But you already knew. I could tell when I came in."

"I didn't know, not for sure, but Hannah was upset, and she said Marti's name, and I just put two and two together. Of course, I'd hoped it wasn't true. You've gotten yourself into a big mess, son."

"She'd better not have gone through my stuff!" Aaron would kill her if she had.

"Hannah going through your stuff – if that's what happened – is the least of your problems right now."

Aaron supposed his father was right, and he wanted to be really mad at Hannah, but there was so much else.

"Marti's not having an abortion, Dad. That I know."

"She's Christian, son, it's considered a sin; a big one. And they learn from very early on never to have abortions. It's not like the Jews, where we accept that they are necessary sometimes."

"They learn from very early on not to have sex before marriage, either, but she did that!" Aaron knew he sounded ridiculous, like a stubborn little boy who thought he got gypped out of a Little League trophy. "Anyway, it was weird. Seeing the baby," he gulped. "On the ultrasound screen. It felt so – real. And I didn't know after that, could we do it? I mean, I knew we should do it, it's the right thing to do, our lives wouldn't be – ruined. But now, I have to accept that she's going to have a baby. I'm going to be a father."

"I should talk to her parents," Mark said. "Do you have their phone number?"

"Dad, no! She's just telling them tonight. We have to give them some time. They're going to be furious."

"I wouldn't call them tonight. I would wait until tomorrow, or Monday, even, of course. But if I wait too long, they're going to think you're abdicating your responsibility, and we don't want to give them that impression. Because whatever happens, you need to be in this, you need to own it, Son, and you need to do what needs to be done. Even if that means some of your dreams and your plans get put on hold."

"I know," Aaron replied. "And I'll do whatever I need to do to make this right. Dad, I don't want to marry her, and I'm so afraid that's what they'll make me do. But I love her. And that's confusing, because shouldn't I want to marry her if I love her?

"Love doesn't work that way. You can love someone with all of your heart and still know logically that marriage isn't a good idea. No one can make you get married. So if you don't want to do that, if you don't love her enough to do that, then you won't. Plus eighteen's pretty young to get married, don't you think?" Aaron thought he saw his dad almost smile.

"Yeah, yeah. I told Marti that, but she wants to do the whole marriage thing. Dad, I want to go to college, and I don't..." He felt ashamed now, of having sex with Marti (even though he knew she had wanted to, too, that she had encouraged it, that it hadn't been a one way decision), of not thinking more clearly, of letting his stupid hormones get the best of him.

"So this is what we'll do," his dad said. "We'll hang out here tonight, just the three of us. I'll go out and get pizza, or something, and then I'll call Marti's parents very soon, and we'll arrange for a meeting. Until then, no Internet. Don't go online. Don't tell anyone, though I suspect by Monday the entire town will know." Aaron bet people already did know.

Aaron nodded.

"Tonight we'll think about how to do this, what the best way is to act. And we'll get through this, Son. We'll get through this together. But next time, please don't wait this long to come to me. I'm your father. I want to help you. That's what here I'm for."

It was the first time since Aaron's mother had died that he felt his father was there for him. Really meant what he said. And despite the circumstances, maybe it would be okay.

Chapter 31

Hannah

Hannah's father still made her go to Hebrew School Sunday morning, despite the "crisis." That's how her dad had been referring to it since last night. "The crisis," as in, "Don't bother your brother during this crisis. Your brother needs special care and consideration during this crisis. I don't want you on the Internet during this crisis."

They had spent Saturday night trying to eat pizza. Aaron looked awful. His eyes were red from crying. (And Hannah had not seen him cry ever, not even at their mom's funeral, not even when they read the Kaddish and slowly lowered the coffin into the ground, when everyone else was crying. Aaron had just stood there, his hands in his pockets, not even really looking at it.)

They hadn't succeeded in eating much. They were too upset. And then her dad had tried to find a movie On Demand they would all like. Hannah wanted to watch The Vow but Aaron had said it was too girly and too romantic and they almost got into a shouting match over it, but then her dad had said No way, it was too adult for her, even though everyone at school had already seen it. Aaron had suggested some chainsaw massacre movie, and of course her dad had nixed that idea. He kept suggesting Disney movies, and both of them were too old for those. Finally they had given up and gone to their rooms at nine, which was a ridiculously early hour, Hannah thought, especially for Aaron, but they had trudged upstairs anyway, her dad calling after them, "No Internet!"

This morning it had been cold out, the first chilly day of autumn, and Hannah's dad had to pull her from her bed. When she realized that Aaron was going to skip his volunteer job as an assistant teacher with the kindergarteners, she'd protested. "Why do I have to go and he doesn't?" she'd whined. Though of course she knew the answer. And even though she actually agreed that Aaron should stay home, she found herself arguing against it. Her father had just sighed and stood over her while she brushed her teeth and put in her contact lenses. "Are you going to watch me go to the bathroom too?" she'd snarled, and then he finally left. She wanted to slam the door after him, but Aaron was still asleep, and her father had already emphasized how much he needed his rest.

She was already feeling weary as she climbed the stairs to her second floor classroom. Next week was Rosh Hashanah, and she dreaded the long services, hours of sitting in a hard seat, trying not to look too bored, right in front where everyone could see her, the Rabbi's daughter. She wondered if Aaron was going to get out of Rosh Hashanah, too.

She entered her classroom. Two of the bitchy girls, Jillian and Claire, were whispering in the corner, but they stopped as soon as she came inside. "Um, hey," she said, taking off her too-small windbreaker. She needed a new one, but who knew when she would get one, now. They stared at her like she had a disease or something, and as she was going to look down to see if there was toothpaste on her shirt or God forbid, she hadn't zipped her fly, Jillian said, "I hear you're going to be an aunt." And then Claire laughed this horsey laugh and Hannah fled.

She ran downstairs and out the side door of the temple and away from the parking lot, where she could hear other kids slamming doors and saying goodbye to their parents. She ran around to the side of the building, which was bordered by trees. Maybe she could go there and hide. Hide until Hebrew School was over and everyone had gone home. Or maybe even, like forever. But then she heard some footsteps behind her, trying to catch up, and she kept running. She didn't want to look back, to see who it was, so she headed for the forest of trees and wondered what was beyond that. She would run and run forever if she had to.

But the steps grew closer, even as she kept running, and then an arm reached out and grabbed her and a voice said, "Hannah, wait."

Chapter 32

Mark

Mark tossed and turned all night, had finally given up on sleep at six a.m., taken a hot shower to ease the knotted muscles in his back. After Hannah had fallen asleep, he and Aaron had trudged back down to the kitchen, Mark's hands folded in front of him, as they talked about their options.

He knew Marti would never go along with abortion, nor would her parents. They were devout Christians, some of the highest up in their church—Jim Jameson's church, he reminded himself, and they were strong in their faith. He hadn't thought about Jim more than in passing in a couple of days, but strangely, now, as he walked slowly into synagogue, feeling far older than his forty seven years, he thought about Jim again, and wondered if he would insert himself into the issue.

Reform Judaism allowed them to accept abortion, mostly in the first twelve weeks. Mark had counseled struggling couples before, and had let them know they were not doing anything against their religion if that's what they chose. After the first twelve weeks, it got dicey, but still, if the mother's health or life were at stake, and indeed he included the mental health of the mother in that, he told them they should go ahead and do it if that's what they wanted and felt what was best. But he know Marti's family would not agree; in their faith, they could never accept abortion, not under any circumstances.

He was going to be a grandfather. At forty-seven. The reality hadn't set in yet. He hurried down the hall to his office, determined to make as normal a morning for himself as he could, despite the swirling thoughts in his head. His wife would have been a grandmother at forty-four, far too young, but she would have known what to say and do, and found some way to make the situation work. He would have to call Marti's parents soon; today, maybe even, and go over there and try to figure out a way to make all of this better, or at least, he thought grimly, tolerable. He would have to promise all kinds of things, and figure out a way to get Aaron to college and figure out a way to convince them that no, Aaron would not be marrying their daughter, not at seventeen or eighteen.

He unlocked his study door and went to his desk. He turned on his computer and shrugged out of his trench coat. And then Robyn came flying through the door.

"I just heard," she said. "I'm so sorry."

"Heard what?" he asked, puzzled.

"Oh, I mean, well, about Aaron."

He knew his feet were still on the ground but he couldn't feel them. "You heard? Already? How?"

"It doesn't matter how…you didn't think anyone would find out? This is a small town. A gossipy town. You know that." She sat down in the visitor's chair opposite him and crossed her legs. They were smooth and muscled, like she worked out, or maybe, being so young, they were naturally like that.

"I just…Naively, I was hoping no one would find out so quickly. Aaron only told me last night. It's all still new to me." He slumped into his chair. Every bone in his body ached, he realized now. Not enough sleep, or stress, or something.

"Just last night? I assumed you'd known for a while."

"Literally, last night, after our day in town." He smiled just a second, and she did, too, both remembering the fun they'd had. He quickly resumed a solemn pose. "I don't know what the hell I'm going to do. Damn it!" He tried not to curse, a promise he'd made to himself as he'd entered his first day of rabbinical school. Curses were ugly words, and there were better words to express frustration. But since his wife had died, the words had come out too often. "Everyone knows?"

"I think so. It's all anyone was talking about at the diner this morning when I stopped to get coffee. And everyone here, well, I'm sorry. But yes, I think most everyone knows."

"I have no idea what we're going to do. I wish my wife…"

He had never actively talked about his wife before, not to Robyn and not to anyone else here. Another promise he had made himself, when they'd moved here a year and a half ago. In Manhattan, in their neighborhood, in their synagogue, at the children's schools and in their building, they'd been known as the family-who-had-lost-their-wife-and-mother and he'd hated it. Oh, not in the beginning. In the beginning he had been too shocked, even though after two years of a downhill battle against cancer, he knew it was coming, and their friends and congregants had helpfully left complete dinners at their doorstep, so he hadn't had to think about meal preparation the first couple of months. And the women had also taken care of the kids and they'd helped him organize a calendar to keep track of their activities.

But after a few months, it was too hard to be the young widower. And he didn't want to talk about Julie everywhere he went. He didn't want to feel her in the sadness of everyone's faces and have to constantly hear the invocation of her name at synagogue events. He was touched when the congregation decided to honor her memory with a new plaque in the sanctuary, but he couldn't bear to look at it every time he delivered a sermon. So when he moved to New Jersey, he realized now, as much as it had been for the kids, to give them a fresh start, like he'd always said, it had been for him, too. To not have to think about Julie all the time. But lately, he'd been thinking about her a lot. And now, with Aaron, how could he not?

"I'm sorry your wife isn't here to help you," Robyn said quietly. "What do you think she would say?"

He thought as Robyn sat silently, and he appreciated that she wasn't trying to fill the silence with words. He could hear the hallways filling up with kids coming to Hebrew School, parents making their way to the media center, where they could enjoy a cup of fresh coffee and a bagel and some visiting time while their kids learned. Sunday mornings were usually his favorite time of the week. People were in good spirits, rested from a morning without hearing the blare of an alarm, a whole day of relaxation stretched out in front of them. But today would be horrendous.

"I think my wife would tell me not to worry about what people are saying, and to focus on Aaron and Hannah and get in touch immediately with Marti's parents. I was going to do that soon anyway, but maybe soon isn't soon enough. I'll do that today." Aaron had given him their home phone number last night, and he had thought about waiting until later this week, after they'd had time to think, but mostly, he admitted now to himself, because he had no idea what he was going to say. "And my wife would probably not have sent Hannah to Hebrew School this morning, knowing that it would already be leaked. I've got to go get her..." he stood up just as a girl from Hannah's class came running in. "Rabbi Friedlander," she said breathlessly. "Hannah's run away!"

"Let me go," Robyn said, touching his arm as he jumped up. "I'll find her."

Chapter 33

Aaron

Aaron didn't sleep all night and as morning came, his eyelids felt plastered to his face. He had felt a momentary relief when he'd told his dad, when his dad finally knew everything. It always felt better to confess, and he remembered back to when he was just a little kid and told a lie. It would build and build and build in him until he confessed, always to his mother, at night, when she was sitting on his bed and reading him a story. In the end, she'd always absolved him, but of course those had been small lies. I didn't brush my teeth when you told me to, I didn't do my homework, I lied to my friend about how good I am at baseball. No one was going to absolve him now.

But in the end, all telling his father did was make the situation feel more real. This was really happening, he would be a father in a few months, a father when he'd only had his driver's license a year and couldn't vote in an election yet and couldn't decide what to write about for his college essay. Fathers were supposed to be strong and confident and know...things. He didn't know anything. If he could somehow convince Marti to adopt the baby out, things would be a little better, but he'd always have this kid out there and always wonder, and always hope the kid didn't resent him for being adopted. Maybe he could talk to Hannah about what it felt like to be adopted. Get that, he thought, Hannah helping him, instead of the other way around, like it had always been before. Everything just went around and around in his head until the early morning hours, when he wrestled with himself not to go online and then finally decided to do it anyway.

He'd almost signed on several times overnight but he had been afraid. Afraid to see Marti and wonder what she would say about what her parents said, afraid that she hadn't told them but now his dad knew, afraid that Marti had told her friends so everyone now knew, and then afraid she wouldn't be online so that then he would be imagining the worst.

Finally, at five a.m., he typed in his password and held his breath. Maybe it wouldn't be that bad. Maybe people would understand. They weren't the only teenagers to ever get caught having sex or having a baby. It must have happened in Marti's church before, even. And some of his friends already knew they had been having sex; surely some of hers knew, too. Things couldn't be that bad, right? And he couldn't hide from this forever.

He had three hundred and fifty three Facebook direct private messages. There weren't even three hundred and fifty three people in his senior class! Did he even know that many people? Marti wasn't online. Had her parents kicked her out, as she'd told him they'd implied they ever would if they ever found out she was having sex? Would she come knocking on his door any minute with a suitcase?

He started going through the PMs. None were from Marti. Ninety per cent of them, he calculated quickly, were hostile, antagonizing, or downright threatening. "You'd better marry her," one of Marti's friends who he'd never liked wrote. "Couldn't keep your fly zipped huh?" another guy wrote. "Way to score!" a stupid creepy AP Physics, a kid who'd probably never even kissed a girl, quipped.

He reread the nice ones. "How are you holding up?" one of his best friends asked. Another girl had written, "U will be a great dad," but he didn't recognize her name. Had someone made a fake account? He wished Marti would sign on, if only to know she was okay. Even though he wouldn't have any idea what to say.

He wondered how it had gotten started. Maybe Kristin had overheard Marti and her parents fighting and had told one person, who'd told another, and another...maybe Marti had told a friend? He'd suspected for a while that her best friend, Molly, might know, and that she might blab.

He shut the computer off and tried to go to sleep. He laid there silently as he heard his dad start to move around at about seven, popping up the heat and starting a pot of coffee, and then quietly waking Hannah and urging her in a loud whisper to get dressed and hurry. He waited until he heard them leave the house, and then he peeked outside his window to make sure that he saw his dad's car drive off in the direction of the synagogue. Then he turned his computer back on and read some more messages. He went to Columbia's web site and clicked on the application form. Flipped over to Dartmouth and did the same. Clicked on Northwestern and read through their list of majors; looked up Tufts statistics one more time. Then he shut the computer down and lay back on the bed. He closed his eyes and finally fell asleep before he could text Marti to ask her how she was.

Chapter 34

Hannah

Hannah felt the hand on her arm and heard the voice and turned around. "Cantor!" she said, surprised. "It's Robyn when we're not in temple, remember? We're not technically inside temple right now." Robyn smiled but she was panting hard, bent over. "You can run fast! Maybe you should join the track team!" She smiled at Hannah and Hannah tried to smile back, but instead, she burst into tears.

Robyn let Hannah cry for a few minutes, and she was grateful. When she collected herself as best she could, Robyn signaled to her. "Let's walk," she said, pointing in the distance. "It's a beautiful morning." They walked in silence for a while; the sound of the first fallen leaves crunching pleasantly under Hannah's feet. It had been cloudy when they had left the house, but now the sun was breaking through, and she could tell it would be a nice day.

"So why did you leave Hebrew School?" Robyn asked.

"They said...they said..." Hannah could feel the words getting hitched in her throat and the tears threatening to come out again.

Robyn put her hand back on Hannah's shoulder. "Who's *they*? And what did *they* say?"

"Two girls. In my class. They knew about Aaron. And they said...Wait, you don't know about Aaron."

"I do know."

"I guess everyone does."

Robyn didn't confirm that, but didn't deny it either, so Hannah knew she was right.

"Aaron's going to need a lot of support in the coming weeks and months," Robyn said.

"My dad told me that, too. And I know. It's just...it's not going to be easy."

"Let's head back, okay?" Robyn said. They walked slowly. "When I was young, people weren't nearly as tolerant as they are today," she said, keeping a firm arm around Hannah's shoulder, as though if she let her go, she might run again. Robyn's arm felt good, so she didn't mind. "Kids were teased a lot more about things they couldn't help."

"Like what?"

"The usual, of course, braces and glasses and things like that, but also...bigger things. Things about their families."

Hannah didn't get it.

"My brother," Robyn said.

"Your brother had a baby when he was a teenager, too?" Hannah's eyes got big and she thought *What a coincidence.*

"No. Not a baby. But he is....was...my brother's mentally challenged. He went to the same school as I did, so everyone knew who he was, but he was in a special class. He didn't talk. Or walk very well. He drooled all the time, so he had to wear a bib. His eyes crossed so he was kind of scary to look at, if you weren't used to it, and he didn't really know proper boundaries, and he was friendly, so he hugged everyone, all the time, even people he didn't know or who didn't want to be hugged. So I got teased. A lot."

"But it wasn't your fault!" Hannah cried.

"No, of course not. It wasn't anyone's fault. It just sort of happened. My parents didn't plan on having a baby with a disability, but they did. So they did the very best they could for him. Sometimes I would come in after school, crying, and tell my mother what had happened, the mean things the kids said, and she would look at me so sadly, and tell me she was sorry, that people shouldn't say things like that."

"They shouldn't." *How awful for Robyn*, Hannah thought. At her school, there was a special ed. class and everyone was extra nice to them.

"They shouldn't, but they do."

They were almost at the temple now, and Hannah stopped walking. "I don't want to go back in there."

"I know. And I didn't want to go to school the next day when I got teased, either. But I did. And the day after, and the day after. And I got through it, and I know you're going to get through it, too."

"But this is different," Hannah protested.

"It's not so different. And in the end, you're going to have to live with it. Something happened, something that's not good for you, and that might cause you embarrassment. Same as me. But I found the good in it – eventually – my brother was sweet, the sweetest boy, and he taught me tolerance. That was the good that came of it."

"Where does he live now?"

Robyn closed her eyes. "He died. Ten years ago. When he was eighteen. He had a heart attack one day, just out of the blue."

"Oh. That's so sad." Hannah wanted to reach out and touch the cantor, but she didn't think she could.

"Yes, it is. But the point is…hold your head up, Hannah. You didn't do anything, and this baby, whatever happens to this baby, didn't do anything either. You have to remember that."

They'd reached the stairs leading up to the door of the synagogue. Robyn opened the door and ushered Hannah in.

Chapter 35

Mark

By Wednesday night, Mark was completely wiped out. Aaron hadn't been to school all week, and though Mark had tried to persuade him to go, he hadn't persuaded too hard, and Hannah was barely saying two words to him. Rosh Hashanah was in a few days, and he was desperate to get his speech done. Anna Nachman had come to see him on Monday, demanding to know how he was going to handle "the scandal" as she'd called it. Mark had tried to reassure her that everything would be fine, and that he could do his job in the middle of this ongoing personal crisis. He was worried, though, because he wouldn't put it past Anna to use it as an excuse to get rid of him at the end of his contract in June. He desperately needed a renewal, now, with a baby on the way and no idea what was going to happen, he needed at least the stability of his job. He couldn't handle a job search on top of everything else. And he didn't have any money to tide him over should there be a period of unemployment. Just thinking the word unemployment scared him. He was still paying the hospital two years after his wife had died. And though she'd had a little life insurance, it had gone to pay for her funeral and for a sitter for the kids after school and on weekends while they were still living in New York. Plus, college was coming up. His stomach knotted. He had very little for Aaron for college and had been counting on scholarship money. When he looked on the Parent Portal, he saw Aaron's grades sliding down. Who knew if he would even be able to go away to college with all of this.

He called to Aaron to come downstairs and grabbed his keys off the kitchen counter. Tonight they were going over to Marti's house, to meet with her and her parents, Joan and Ken. Mark had called them on Sunday night and asked for the meeting. Ken had been cold on the phone, but he had agreed. He supposed that was a start. Mark couldn't get a handle on what they were like. Strict, Aaron had said, of course, but also, he had told Mark, Marti loved and respected them so much. Yes, she didn't always listen to them, but she admired them. She wanted a life like theirs.

They drove over to Marti's house in silence. Mark tried to start a conversation, get Aaron to talk, but Aaron had not said more than three words in the last three days, after his big confession

Saturday night. "The important thing," Mark said, as they walked up to the house, Aaron's hands in his pockets, "is to remain calm. To listen to their side, to be open to their ideas, but to get across how you feel, too."

"I know, Dad!" he finally said, breaking his silence. "You already told me thirty times, or something." Ah, so his son had been listening to him. Well, there was that, anyway.

Joan came to the door and ushered them inside. She looked straight at Aaron in a sad, disappointed way, but Aaron kept his eyes trained on the tile floor. "I'm Mark Friedlander," he said, shaking her hand. "It's nice to finally meet you, even under these difficult circumstances."

"Rabbi," she said, and pulled her hand back. She smiled wanly. "Yes, I wish the circumstances were different, too."

"Please, call me Mark." They followed down the hallway to the back of the house into a large family room covered in shag carpet. A burly man stood up, reached his hand out to Mark. "Rabbi," he said. Marti's father. Mark could see why Aaron would feel intimidated. Ken had a thick neck and was well built for a man of his age, and although Aaron was six one, this man was at least six four.

"He prefers to be called Mark," Joan said to her husband. "Please, sit down."

"Where's Marti?" Mark asked.

"We believe its best that she isn't in this conversation," Ken said. "She's just a girl in a bad situation."

Mark groaned inwardly. Were they back in the fifties? What was going to happen next? Were they going to send their daughter to a home for unwed mothers?

He tried again. "I brought Aaron and I thought Marti would be joining us as well, so we could see where they are, with their thoughts on the matter."

"Marti is agreeable to whatever we think is best," Ken said. "She's already told us that. And perhaps if she had listened to us about this months ago," and here Ken glared at Aaron. "We wouldn't even be having this conversation."

"Certainly the kids should have talked to us; believe me when I say I'm sorry Aaron didn't talk to me either. And disappointed. But now they have a big decision to make," and then he added hastily, when he saw the looks in Ken and Joan's eyes, "with our help of course, but still, I'm really interested in what they both have to say."

Ken shook his head strongly, and Mark wondered if it made him dizzy. “No. Marti is too young. I can tell you one thing, she will not be killing her baby. She told me that’s what you wanted.” He looked again at Aaron, who looked like he wanted to melt into the floor. “She said you took her to an abortion clinic to kill your child.”

Aaron started to speak, but no words came out of his mouth.

Mark took over for him. “From what I understand, they went to a prenatal clinic to explore all of their options. I think that was very responsible of them, don’t you?”

“Responsible? Are you kidding me? I don’t know what kind of religion you practice, Sir, but we don’t kill our children, no matter how convenient it might seem at the time. That was an abortion clinic. They lie about the counseling. It’s just a place to kill innocent children that the Lord wants on this earth.”

This wasn’t going anywhere. They needed to get back on track. “I understand. And I’m sorry if Aaron upset Marti. What we need to do now is consider the available options. I understand abortion is out of the question.” Originally he had thought maybe he could convince them, but Aaron had been adamant. They would not agree to one. And now Mark could see that his son had been right on target. This baby would be born, no matter what. What happened to it – and to Aaron’s future – beyond that was anyone’s guess.

“Good, then we agree on that.”

“Adoption is a good solution, I think,” Mark said, and he realized he didn’t sound strong enough in his conviction.

“We think it would be best for this young man to marry Marti. He can join our church, so we can pray for his soul properly, forgive me Rabbi, and he’s going to need it. . .” Mark tried to speak but Ken held up his hand to cut him off. “This child is Christian. I know the Jews believe it’s whatever the mother is, and the mother is Christian.” Mark groaned inwardly again. Ken was right on that point. Jews believed that the child was the religion of the biological mother. “They can marry right away; we can hold a service at church by Thanksgiving, and he can move in here with us. We have plenty of room and then Joan,” and he nodded at his wife, “can help with the baby. I have a spot on my plumbing team. I can train him. He’ll start off at the bottom, just like my own sons will, but eventually, he’ll make good money and the two of them can get their own place, maybe in a couple of years.”

Aaron sat up then, as though he were finally listening. “But...”

"No buts, sir," Ken said, "You got yourself into this mess, you and my daughter. You're going to get her out of it."

Mark touched his son's knee. A signal to calm down and let him do the talking, like he'd told him he would do, if necessary.

"I'm afraid I don't agree," he said. "They're too young to get married."

"I married my wife at nineteen," Ken said, his chest puffing up, "And not because she was in trouble, I'll tell you that. We waited, like the Good Lord instructs us to do. And we've been married now twenty five years."

"Things were...different then. And Aaron has plans to go on to college."

Ken leaned forward in his seat and pressed his beefy arms against his legs. His pot belly hung over his thighs. "Marti had plans, too. She wanted to go to beauty school. And now that's going to be on hold. Being a parent comes first; you should remember that, Aaron." He glared at Mark's son and Mark wanted to kick him in the face. He surprised himself. He could not remember ever having the urge to hurt someone physically since the third grade, when Lyle Hochmann had told him that if he didn't believe Jesus was God's son then he would kick his ass. Mark hadn't even known what an ass was, but he surmised, and he'd run all the way home, before bursting through the door to tell his mother. The next day, Lyle had been absent from recess.

Aaron said now, quietly, so quietly that Mark wondered if Marti's parents could hear. "I love Marti. And I'm sorry this happened. It was a stupid, stupid thing. We should have been more careful, but..." Aaron said. "Even so. I'm not ready to get married. And I would much prefer we find a good home for this baby. There must be a lot of families out there who really want a baby, who can take care of one properly." Aaron sat up then, and Mark was incredibly proud of his son. It would not be easy to stand up to this man. Ken obviously loved and wanted what was best for his daughter, but was that what was truly best for Aaron? Or for any of them?

Ken sat back in his seat. "That's true. There are couples who want a baby; couples in my own church who've been looking, in fact. But with the rate of abortion in this country, these couples can't find a baby."

Mark held his breath. Were they going to agree? The next six months would still be hard, but it would be a way out. He hated the idea that he wouldn't get to know his grandchild, and that the child was likely never going to be Jewish, but it was for the best, for everyone, his son, Marti, even the baby.

Joan nodded. "It's such a blessing to give the infertile the opportunity to be parents."

"Still and all," Ken said. "It's not like these young people would have it bad. My wife is going to be right here, helping them raise it. And giving away your own flesh and blood? When you have the means to take care of them? Doesn't make sense to me."

Mark cringed. They were not going to budge. Not easily.

Chapter 36

Aaron

Aaron was desperate to talk to Marti. It had been a week since everyone had found out, since Aaron's world had gone from bad to worse, spinning out of control like a car going ninety-five miles an hour in a loop. He hadn't figured out a way, though. Hannah had talked to Kristin, and Kristin had told her that Marti was being kept in the house. Aaron couldn't believe it. She said she thought Marti would be stuck inside until she gave birth. Could her parents really do that? Aaron didn't know, but her dad had been scary when they'd talked in his family room. At the same time, he did respect Marti's dad, Ken, and he thought Ken liked it when Aaron had spoken up on his own behalf, even if he didn't agree. Aaron had to admire that Marti's dad just wanted what he thought was best for her, even though it's not what Aaron wanted for himself.

He had taken to staying up all night on Skype, in case Marti had figured out how to sneak on to talk to him. He would doze between three and five, but that was it. He didn't want to miss her. They needed to talk.

He had been going to school, and it was worse every day. Someone had spray painted Daddy on his locker the other day, and someone else yesterday had stuffed it with messy diapers. Of course they weren't actually filled with shit, as he emptied the locker he thought he caught the smell of chocolate pudding, still, it was disgusting. The pudding had gotten all over his Physics book, and his teacher had informed him he would need to buy a new one. They were a hundred dollars apiece, and his father had sighed as he wrote out the check.

His guidance counselor had called him down the other day. She was very cool, with black bouncy curls and hip glasses, and everyone wanted her for their guidance counselor because she would try to get you the best teachers even though she was supposed to let the computer pick. She had told him she'd heard, and how sorry she was, and how she was there if he needed anything. What he could need from her, though, he couldn't see.

"Still," she had said, "You need to focus. You have one of the best shots of getting into an Ivy of anyone this school has ever had.

You can still go, make something of yourself. This is an opportunity you can't afford not to take."

"I might not be going anywhere," he'd said miserably. He had been feeling particularly low that day. Marti's father had emailed him the night before, laying out his plans for marriage. Aaron knew that when Marti's father wanted something done a certain way, it was impossible for him to see another. Last year, Marti had wanted to get a job at the diner in town, just hostessing a couple of afternoons or evenings a week, but her father wouldn't let her. She had replayed the scene for Aaron. "Your work is to help your mother take care of the children," her father had said, when she told him she wanted to apply.

"But, Dad, Mom is fine with them. And Kristin's getting older, so she can help more, and I want to earn a little money, so I don't have to keep asking you for money." She'd hoped to get him on that angle. He grumbled whenever she needed a ten or a twenty.

Marti's father had answered angrily. "Your priorities are God, your family, and school. In that order. I don't want you working where a lot of strange men can harass you, when I can't protect you, during hours you could be helping your mother." Marti gave up after that. She knew not to question.

Aaron hadn't even told his father about Marti's parents' expectation that he would absolutely marry their daughter. What could his father do about it, anyway? He was beginning to think he should just do it. He loved her. She loved him. People got married all the time when they didn't even love each other, so weren't they ahead of the game? He wouldn't become a plumber though. He bet his dad would pay for state college, and then he could still get his degree. They could move somewhere for graduate school or medical school, whatever he decided. And eventually he'd make good money, be able to take care of Marti and the baby. But this idea depressed the hell out of him. Marti was a great girl but they were so...opposite. He couldn't see how they could last. He was furious with himself for not thinking this out earlier. Like when Marti had told him not to bother with the condoms. How could he have been so stupid?

The guidance counselor had waved a hand in his face. "Are you still there?"

"Um, yes," he said.

"So you need to get your applications done. You need to get those recommendations in here, pronto, and you need to write your essay so we can go over it and edit it together."

He felt too exhausted to think about any of it.

"I don't even know what I would write for an essay," he said listlessly. As though this was the biggest problem anyone had. Well, for most seniors, he guessed it was. For him, just a month ago, and it was hard to believe it that only a month ago, finding the right essay topic *had* been his biggest problem.

"Why don't you write about this," the guidance counselor said, spreading her hands wide.

"Your desk?" he asked, confused. His mind was muddled without sleep.

"No," she laughed. "What's going on in your life. Becoming a teen father."

He couldn't believe she would have the nerve to suggest such a topic at first, but as he headed upstairs to AP US History and then as he had driven home and logged onto Skype and toasted a bagel with cheese – the first thing he had been hungry for in two weeks, he had already lost ten pounds – and tackled his Calc homework – he had a test tomorrow and he really needed an A on it – he felt, for the first time in forever, like he could concentrate, hell, he could breathe, without it being painful.

He had written his college essay last night at two in the morning, when he was waiting for Marti. And he had emailed two teachers at three to ask them to write his recommendations. He was supposed to ask in person, he knew, but email was easier for him right now. Marti had never shown up on Skype, but at least he had gotten stuff done. Still, though, he wanted to talk to his girlfriend.

Her best friend, Shannon, had been giving him occasional updates. "Marti says hi," she'd said one morning at his locker, looking over her shoulder as if she didn't know who would be looking or reporting back to Marti's father.

"Tell her I said hi, too, and I'm thinking about her," he'd whispered back, and then flipped around so he was facing the shelf, pulling out his history book.

Two days later, Shannon had left him a note between the cracks of the locker door. It had gotten jammed between two books, and he'd almost missed it. "Marti wants to talk. The morning sickness is gone, and she's feeling better." That's when he'd started leaving

Skype on all night. But that plan hadn't been working. He was no closer to talking to her than he had been before.

Chapter 37

Hannah

Life at home was so beyond weird these days that Hannah spent a lot of time downtown, walking from store to store, and even though it was only October, grabbing a hot chocolate from the coffee shop. As bad as things were, she couldn't stop thinking about the baby in all of this. It would be cute and cuddly and she could babysit it after school, whenever Marti wanted. She hoped it would be a girl and that they use a J name, as is Jewish custom, after her mother, Julie. There were lots of pretty girl J names like Julia and Jennifer and Julianna and Josephine, which wasn't so pretty but very hip and fresh and sounded, well, smart. And if it was a boy – God forbid – there was Josh and Jack and Justin and Jason. Decent names.

She was coming out of the coffee shop with her hot chocolate on a not particularly cold day – she just loved hot chocolate, the cold whipped cream light on her tongue, the underlying warmth of the hot chocolate, smooth – when Jim Jameson held the door for her.

"Hi, you're Hannah, right?" he asked, as she nodded to him for holding the door.

"Yeah," she said, and started walking back towards her neighborhood. Not quickly, but definitely quicker than her stroll down here earlier today. Jim Jameson had a longer stride, though, and kept up with her easily.

"I'm Jim." He stuck out his hand at her and she reluctantly shook it. It was clammy and she wondered if he was nervous, though what would he have to be nervous about?

He didn't say anything else for a moment and she kept walking, sipped her hot chocolate, even though now her stomach felt like a rock was holding it down.

"So, remember what we were talking about? At the meeting?" The meeting she had attended with Kristin seemed like so long ago, but it had only been a few weeks.

"Yeah."

"We'd love to have you join us more often. You know, everyone needs to make things right with Christ, and we could help you." He nodded at her finger. "I see you wear the purity ring. Did your dad give it to you?"

Could he not know who her father was? She certainly hoped not. And how did he know it was a purity ring? It could be something else. He was just assuming.

But she said, "Yeah. Yeah, he did." It was a lie, but a necessary one, she thought. Her mother had told her there were times you lied to protect yourself or others, and that she would know when those times were. This was one of them, she was sure of it.

"So he wants you to be a member of our church, then. Do you attend church anywhere else right now?"

She thought about what to say. "No." In one way, it was the complete truth.

He stopped, turned to her, and she thought she had no choice but to turn towards him, too. "Hannah," he said. "It's important that we honor the teachings of Christ. We must – we must – follow what he says. It's our way to glory. You want to go to Heaven, don't you?"

Her mother was in Heaven, that she knew. She pictured her mother there. It was sunny and warm all the time, and there was no cancer. You could do whatever you wanted all day, and she bet the girls didn't get periods.

"Yes," she said. "I definitely want to go to Heaven."

"Then if you do what I say, if you follow me and the church, you'll get there. Don't worry." And he sounded so sure, and kind, and his smile was nice, so she thought, *He isn't that bad*. In fact, maybe she had misjudged him completely.

Chapter 38

Mark

Mark was at his desk Wednesday morning, Rosh Hashanah behind him, a big Yom Kippur sermon still to write for next week. They congregation had seemed to like his Rosh Hashanah sermon, at least many people had come up to him afterwards and told him how much they'd enjoyed it. He hoped the board members had paid attention to the compliments he had received.

Robyn knocked on his door, even though it was open. "Knock, knock," she said.

He waved her in and smiled. She sat down across from him.

"Thanks again for your help with Hannah," he said. Robyn had gone after her in the woods, and brought her back inside, and spoken to the Hebrew School girls about kindness and they'd left Hannah alone after that, at least he thought so. Hannah wasn't talking much these days. He hoped school was going okay for her. He made a mental note to check on her tonight, wishing he had checked in with her last night, or the night before. Why was he constantly forgetting to do this? Maybe because it seemed simple but was, in fact, rather difficult.

"Oh, you're more than welcome...listen, Mark, Jim Jameson, he's...I hear he's trying to convert some of the kids over to his church."

"What kids?"

"I don't know. I just heard around town, he talks to the kids, scares them, and gets them to convert. And then he uses those kids to report kids who aren't living the "Godly" way...I heard he has a list in his office, and other kids write down, anonymously apparently, who they think is a problem."

"Why would he do that?"

"I don't know...but it's dangerous."

"I haven't heard any of the same stories. Are you sure?"

"I've heard it from very reliable sources. I'm worried."

"It just seems preposterous that he would do something like that." Of course, Mark hadn't believed it when Jim Jameson himself had said that he was going to try to stop gays from being gay...and he hadn't heard anybody complain that he had, so the guy was probably all talk, no action. He would have heard from some of the other clergy in town if Jim was up to something. And he hadn't. In fact, he realized, they hadn't met since the meeting about interfaith initiatives which led to the conversation about trying to take the pressure off of the gay kids. He made another mental note to call the priest and the Episcopalian minister again, just to see if they'd heard anything. Though wouldn't they have called them if they had? Jim was small potatoes. A small time, big ego pastor with old-fashioned ideas. He couldn't hurt a fly. *But did that matter,* Mark mused*, if the pastor himself thought he could?*

"I'll check in with the other clergy and ask around town," Mark said. "Don't worry." And then he asked a question he'd been wanting to ask Robyn for weeks.

"So, Robyn, are you uh, are you...?"

"Am I what?" she asked gently, twirling her hair between two fingers. She was young, Mark thought, not for the first time. For sure she was. And they were colleagues. He had not so much as kissed a woman since his wife had died, not even looked at them for anything but help for his kids. At one time he couldn't imagine being with anyone else, ever, and thought he would die alone.

But Robyn had changed that. She was smart, and funny, easy to talk to and...sexy, he had to admit. He'd woken up last night from a dream about her, and though he couldn't quite remember it, he knew it had been good.

Just say it, he told himself, feeling like a teenaged boy instead of a fully grown man with two children, and he remembered then after forgetting for a few minutes, about to be a grandfather. He shook his head to will the thought away. "Um, are you free Saturday evening?"

"Free?" she asked, like she didn't really know what he was asking.

"You know, for a...date." He hid his hands under the desk so she couldn't see them tremor.

"Yes, yes I am, in fact. What did you have in mind?" She cocked her head to one side, and Mark wondered if she was serious, that she liked him enough to go on a date with him, or whether she was just...pitying him, or thinking they were friends.

"Dinner," he said quickly.

"Sounds lovely," she said. "Time?"

"I'll pick you up, say 7? What kind of food do you like?"

"Anything. I will eat anything." She stood up and turned towards the door, and then turned back to him. "I'm looking forward to it," she said, and scurried out the door. It was the first time Mark had ever seen her even a little flustered.

He waved at her and then went back to his sermon. He completely forgot about Jim Jameson and calling the other pastors.

Chapter 39

Aaron

Wednesday night, Aaron finally caught Marti on Skype. It was one a.m., and he'd finished editing his college essay and his transcripts were ready to go. Two teachers had agreed to write letters of recommendation for him, and his guidance counselor said everything would go out in a couple of weeks. Finally, he was moving forward, feeling like he was accomplishing something.

He was shocked to see Marti pop on his screen, looking like she always had. She had not been to school in three weeks, and he had begun to wonder if he had imagined her, and the pregnancy, dreamt that horrible scene with her parents. But there she was.

"Hey," she said quietly. "I've missed you."

"I've missed you, too," he said, and he had, but not in the way he was supposed to, in the way she assumed he meant. He still loved her, cared about her, but, he realized, his life had been blinded by her for the last year. Blinded by having sex with her. His grades had gone down. He wasn't hanging out with his buddies any more. He hadn't consistently been going to fall track for the first time in eight years since he'd fallen in love with the sport in sixth grade.

"How are you?" he asked.

"I'm okay. Sixteen weeks." She stood up in front of the camera and he could see a slight bulge in her sweat pants. "My mother is going to buy me some maternity stuff," she said. "My regular jeans don't fit anymore. And she took me to her doctor yesterday. Everything is looking good...with the baby."

"That's...that's great," he said weakly. It was. He wanted the baby to be healthy. And somewhere inside him, he didn't want to admit it, he thought it was cool that he would have a child in the world, someone he had made and could, like, become the President or an NFL pro.

"Look, I need to know," she said now. "I need to know...are we going to get married?"

How could he look her in the eye, even on Skype, even with its grainy stop-and-go, freeze-and-release picture? How could he say to her that no, he still didn't want to marry her, that he wanted the baby to be put up for adoption, that he would be there every step of the way, but next September he was going to be on a college campus somewhere and their baby was going to be in someone else's house and Marti was going to have to find her way.

"Is that what you want?" he asked.

"I love you," she said, like she was going to cry, and even with the bad picture, he could make out tears forming in her big blue eyes. His eyes were his mother's gray. He wondered what color the baby's would be. He hoped it had Marti's. They were gorgeous.

"I love you, too," he said back, and he felt it, meant it.

"So then why can't we get married? I don't get this. If you love me, if you love our baby," and he could see her reach down, he supposed, to rub the bump in her sweat pants, "you would want us to be a family."

He could do it now. Just lay it all on the line. It was the perfect opportunity, and she would be hurt, but she would get over it, and the maybe, finally she would agree to adoption.

But instead of saying no, instead of getting it over with, he looked into those big blue eyes and he knew he couldn't disappoint her. He knew, even, that he had a responsibility to her, and certainly to their child, and even though he didn't want to, he needed to, so he said, "Yes. All right, let's get married." And once the words were out, he couldn't stuff them back in.

Chapter 40

Hannah

Hannah imagined that if she had not met Jim Jameson that day last week, she would be as lonely as ever, maybe even worse. Aaron was home a lot but he never spoke to her. She had tried to apologize to him for looking on his computer, but he had barely grunted when she spoke to him. He was in his room most of the time now, bouncing a ball off of his wall over and over, or peeled to his Skype, waiting for Marti to come on. Which, as far as Hannah knew, she never did.

And her dad was so busy at temple. He had told her that they were trying to get new members and of course, it had just been Rosh Hashanah and Yom Kippur and now it would be some other holidays she didn't care about but had to pretend to.

One of the nice things about being Christian, she noticed, was they only celebrated two big holidays, Christmas and Easter, and she bet they were both a whole lot more fun than sitting in temple for hours and hours listening to Hebrew she didn't understand or care about. And being Christian was about loving people and wanting the best for them, and showing them God's light. She liked the idea of God's light, that He was watching over her and protecting her and was always with her. Jim Jameson had said that if she had ever needed God, she only think his name and pray to him, and he would answer her. Maybe he wouldn't answer her in the way she hoped, but always with great love and care, and in a way that would help her. It all seemed so cool that she had no idea why everyone wasn't Christian. And now she could understand why Christians wanted everyone else to be Christian, too.

The best thing was that Kristin was still speaking to her. She had been worried about that. She didn't know if Kristin would be mad since Aaron had gotten Marti pregnant, but actually, Kristin was excited to become an aunt, just like Hannah was. Kristin had invited her over today after school, and since Hannah had nobody waiting for her at home, no one who cared where she was or what she was doing, she had said yes without even checking with her dad. He wouldn't even notice she was gone.

The girls walked home towards Kristin's. It was a late October day, and there was finally a definite nip in the air. Hannah used to love this time of year; her mom would begin preparing the Thanksgiving menu, cutting out recipes from magazines and printing them off the Internet, and Hannah would sit by her side, giving her opinions. Her mom liked trying new things each year, and Hannah got to be her taste tester all of November, as her mom tried one thing after the other. Hannah cringed a little, remembering her mother's last Thanksgiving. She had insisted on doing it, even though by then she was pretty sick from the chemo and had no hair and spent a lot of days in bed. Her friend, Betsy, had come over to actually make the recipes while Hannah and her mom supervised. They'd had great fun that day, but it was hard to remember it now.

"Does your mom know I'm coming over?" Hannah asked Kristin nervously, as they rounded the corner and approached the house. She had not thought before now about how Kristin's mom might feel about her, even though it wasn't her fault Aaron had gotten Marti pregnant and there was this whole mess to deal with from it.

"Yeah, I texted her before, and she said it was fine." The girls reached the front door. "I'm home," Kristin shouted when they got inside. It felt warm and inviting, the heat washing over Hannah, her hands immediately starting to warm up.

Kristin's mom shouted back, "I'm in the kitchen!" The girls wound their way back past the staircase and down the hall filled with pictures of all of Kristin's siblings. There were the two older boys who were away in the army, Marti, Kristin, and then four younger siblings, and Hannah often wondered how Kristin's mom managed to keep up with all of them all the time. But she always came off as smooth and calm, organized in a busy-but-I'm-managing-it way. And she was always smiling. She'd asked Kristin once why she had so many brothers and sisters. "It's what God wants," she had said, "For us to have as many blessings as possible. Children are blessings from God." Hannah still couldn't imagine having eight children. She wanted one or two at most.

Kristin's mom was sitting at her lap top, frantically typing. Marti was standing at the island, and Hannah thought she looked different. Was her top a little tighter across her middle? Could you see a little bulge? She wasn't sure. Marti certainly didn't seem as miserable as Kristin had described her...not eating and not showering and walking around in a fog. In fact, she was smiling and munching on popcorn, like any normal day.

"Hello, girls!" her mother chirped. "So nice to see you, Hannah!"

"It's nice to see you, too, Mrs. Engel." She made a questioning glance at Kristin, who shrugged and grabbed a cookie off a plate of homemade chocolate chip. She handed the plate to Hannah, and she grabbed one, too.

Kristin threw her back pack down on the floor and plopped next to her mother at the table. The table only had six chairs and Hannah wondered what happened when the whole family was together for dinner. With two of Kristin's brothers overseas, and the youngest still in a high chair, she supposed that's how they did it.

"What are you doing, Mom?" Kristin asked.

"I have exciting news!" her mother screeched, a huge smile on her face, her eyes lit up. "Actually, Marti does." Marti took a cookie and shoved it in her mouth. "Eating for two!" she chirped and then smiled. A secret smile. Something was definitely up.

"What?" Kristin asked. Her mom smiled and then Marti smiled again. "Don't you know, Hannah? Oh, maybe you don't yet."

"Know what?"

"Aaron and I are getting married!"

Chapter 41

Mark

Mark was in no mood for anything resembling drama when he made it home Thursday afternoon. Thursdays were supposed to be his day off since he worked the other six, but he rarely took them. Either someone was very sick in the hospital or some other emergency occurred. ..and he never minded; he knew going in that being a rabbi was a twenty four hour/seven day a week kind of job, and that he would rarely get days off, but the payoff was how much he could help people, how much change and hope he could exact in someone's life. He had not counted on the damn synagogue policies and politics. They didn't teach you about those in rabbinical school.

That afternoon, he had been dusting off all of the parts to the temple's Sukkah. He loved Sukkot. He loved building the Sukkah and adorning it with fruits and vegetables to symbolize the Harvest and then inviting Temple members to join him for a meal in the Sukkah. The days were still warm enough though evenings were cooler, and it felt like one last tip of the hat to summer. Usually he had the high school boys help him gather all the parts and drag them outside to the parking lot where they assembled the Sukkah together, the boys trying to act cool, Mark listening carefully to their conversations, trying not to laugh.

But this year he hadn't been able to find any high school boys who were willing to help him. Last year he had only found two seniors, and they were gone now. It pained him that kids were too busy, or wanted to seem too busy, to help. He had asked Aaron, the fresh air and physical labor would be good for him, he thought. Except for school, Aaron had been staying in the house. But Aaron, too, had said no, something about working on his college applications. He had even asked Mark the other day for his credit card so he could pay some application fees. Mark had been happy to hand it over; just last week he had wondered whether Aaron would have the fortitude, with everything else going on in his life, to apply, and he had worried that Aaron would have nowhere to go once they sorted all of this mess out with Marti because he hadn't been able to get himself to apply anywhere.

This mess. Mark didn't want to refer to Marti's pregnancy this way, but that's what it was. He had called Jewish Family Services the other day, anonymously, and asked them about their birth mother programs. He had thought he could give the pamphlets and web site address to Aaron, see if he could gently press Marti. Things would all come together then, he hoped. Aaron deserved a chance to move forward in his life, no matter how he'd screwed up, and Marti, too, of course. She was a sweet girl and could still go on to live a normal life however she chose. He thought it was the best option, as all of their options dwindled.

While he was assembling and thinking all of this, Anna's heels came clicking up the parking lot. He looked up and tried to form a smile on his face.

"Anna, how nice to see you."

Anna smiled back. "And you. I heard the apples and honey event downtown was a big success." She held herself proudly. It had all been her idea, of course.

"Yes, I think so," he said, and genuinely smiled. It was nice to be complimented, even if Anna was taking some of the credit, and of course, thinking of that afternoon made him think of Robyn and the date he was planning for Saturday night.

"Good. We did get two calls into the office the following week about membership information, and we were quite pleased with that. So we'd like to do another event."

"What did you have in mind?" he asked, and cocked his head. The high holidays were over. He couldn't think of a thing they could ask him to dress up as.

"Free memberships," Anna said.

"Who are we giving free memberships to, and for how long?" Usually the rabbi had no say over financial matters of his synagogue. He didn't determine the cost to join or how to structure the fees or when free or reduced dues memberships were offered, unless a family was truly struggling to make ends meet, and then he might call them and offer help or support.

"We want you to give out free memberships through June."

"Give out?"

"At the gym. I already called and they will be happy to host you. You would go in on a Saturday or Sunday afternoon, and join their children's gym instructor for yoga with the children, and then hand out free memberships at the end."

Mark gritted his teeth. This time they had gone too far. "I don't do yoga," he said, trying to maintain his composure.

"It's not that hard; I do it a couple of times a week. You'll just follow the instructor along. And actually, it might be kind of fun if you're not perfect at it. It might make the kids laugh." She smiled now, again, baring her teeth, not unlike, Mark noticed, the way his childhood German Shepherd, Lance, could when he was feeling a little aggressive. "Just call them and set up your preferred date and time, sometime in the next few weeks would be ideal." She cocked her head. "How is Aaron? What a shock it must have been to you to find out he was dating that, that... Christian... girl." She tsked. Anna was not interested in being supportive. She was interested in gossip. And Mark couldn't help but feel offended on Marti's behalf. Being Christian wasn't bad, it was just not Jewish. The lack of tolerance never ceased to amaze him.

"He's fine; and if you don't mind, I'd like to keep my personal life just that, personal."

"Of course." She had turned then, and headed back to the entrance of the temple. "So good to see you here on a Thursday," she called, waving as she walked inside. "Let me know when you'll be at the gym. Maybe I'll come."

All the way home, he had told himself there was no way he was going to a gym in shorts and a t-shirt or sweat pants and embarrass himself in a yoga class. Nor was he going to hand out free memberships like some kind of salesman on a street corner. He would not stoop that low. And he wasn't going to ask Robyn to help him either. He would face the Board himself, and he would try to talk sense into them.

He was still grumbling when he came in through the garage and went into the kitchen to see what he could scrounge up for dinner. At least he didn't have to go back out tonight. He sighed at the thought. Just him and the remote control.

But Aaron came downstairs as soon as Mark had opened the refrigerator. "Hey, Buddy," Mark said, looking up. Aaron was ghost white. He was ghost white and shaking, and it made Mark sick just to see it. Mark wished Aaron was small enough so he could sit him on his lap, like he would do when Aaron was a child, and stroke his hair and tell him he was going to be okay. But he was a man now, or at least, man-sized.

"What's wrong, Ari?" he asked.

"Dad, uh, I..."

"What?"

Aaron leaned against the counter top and braced his arms. "I've made a decision."

Mark closed the refrigerator door. "Okay, let's hear it." He folded his arms and leaned against it.

"I…I…." Aaron looked down.

"Son, whatever it is, you can say it. You really can."

Aaron stood there for a second, and Mark could hear him breathing deeply.

"So I saw Marti online last night."

Mark knew that Aaron and Marti hadn't been allowed to talk in a couple of weeks, and that Aaron had been desperate to speak to her privately.

"That's good, Son. Did you talk things out?"

"Yes. Yes we did."

"And what did you decide?" Although Mark really thought adoption was the best answer, he wasn't opposed, couldn't be opposed, he knew, to Marti raising the baby while Aaron went to college, maybe came home on weekends and summers to help out. Mark was fully prepared to offer financial assistance. He could see his grandchild that way, get to know him or her, and though it would be difficult, it wasn't completely out of the question, though he had been pretty sure Marti's parents wouldn't go for it. Their unmarried daughter, raising her bastard child? He wondered if anyone even said bastard child anymore. He certainly didn't.

"Dad, we talked for hours last night. Went over our options again and again. She's sixteen weeks now."

"Yes, yes I know."

"And, well, there's no easy way to say this, but Dad…we're going to get married. And there's nothing you can do to stop us."

Chapter 42

Aaron

After Aaron and Marti had talked last night, and gone round and round the subject, he had come to the conclusion that marrying her really was the only option. How could he ask her to raise this baby as a single mother knowing how her parents would torture her, how they would reject her, she'd be left alone, just so he could go to college and live a "normal" life? Or ask her to give the baby up for adoption? She was too invested already for that. What right did he have to alter the lives of so many people, especially Marti and the...baby? He could still go to college. He needed to man up.

He had made this mess and he could clean it up. He didn't want to marry her, at least right now, but he did love her, he thought, and he would grow to love her even more and marrying her was the right thing to do. And she had said he could still go to college and they could live with her parents...she would make sure they didn't force him to become a plumber, like they wanted him to. He could go to the local community college and get a part time job, and they could manage. Marti's cosmetology school program would only take a year, and then she could work part time, opposite hours from him, while he watched the baby. And it would all work out, maybe not the way he had imagined, but definitely, it was doable.

He had deleted his college applications at four in the morning, thrown away the glossy brochures. He was done. Marti and he had agreed to a Thanksgiving weekend wedding, something small, he had begged her. She was sure her parents would pay for at least one night, maybe two, away for a honeymoon.

He'd had all day to get used to the idea, and the wedding was more than four weeks away, even more time to get used to it. Marti's mother had called him this morning, crying, thanking him for doing the right thing, and it made him happy that it had made them so happy. They were already looking at dresses. He wondered if Marti would let his dad marry them, since he was a rabbi, even though she was Christian.

He had paced the upstairs hallway outside his bedroom waiting for his dad to come home. He didn't know where Hannah was, but he was glad she wasn't in the house.

Finally, he heard his father's car in the driveway and the sound of him coming inside. The words he'd planned, the careful words he thought might help, at least a little, fled from his mind. As his father entered the room, he said what came, that they were getting married, that his father couldn't stop them.

His father looked at him like he had three heads. "What are you talking about?" He could see his father's hand clench around the refrigerator door handle, a sure sign that he was furious. A vein in his neck throbbed.

"Dad, I've been thinking about this a lot, and well, it's the best choice out of a lot of not so great choices."

"Sit down, Aaron," his dad said, and they were back on the chairs that'd sat on the night Aaron had told his father that Marti was pregnant. Except that time, his father had held him while he'd cried like a baby. His father had been mad, then, too, but he'd also felt sorry for his son, and Aaron had been relieved. Now, though, they sat far apart, and Aaron could feel his father was out of sympathy.

"Dad, I just...I want to do this."

He could tell his father was making every effort not to yell and he wanted to let his dad know how much he appreciated that, but he didn't know how to say it. So he just continued. "Marti is never going to abort, so that's out."

His father nodded. Aaron knew and his father knew. This baby was coming, no matter what.

"And she's not going to give it up for adoption. I've tried to convince her, but she feels like, or I guess besides her, her parents feel like, it's her responsibility, and you don't just give up your child, and...I don't know that I'm so hot on adoption either. I'd never see the kid, and I kind of would like to. See it. Grow up. And become whoever it's going to become."

"Son," his father interrupted. "I know you want to do the right thing....and in this case it's hard to see what the right thing is, but I don't think marrying her *is* the right thing."

Now Aaron interrupted his father. "She can't raise this baby alone. Her parents would be awful to her. And to the baby. They really do believe all of that unwed mother stuff, and I think, I think she does too. And it *is* my fault. I got careless. I...she...we didn't use protection when we should have." Talking to his father about sex was impossible. But he had to try. "You've always told me to make decisions like a man, to grow up...now I am. This is an adult decision. And I'm making it."

"This is not an adult decision, Aaron! The adult decision would be to give this child to a good home, through adoption. And adoptions aren't what they used to be. You can get pictures and updates..." Mark had a few congregants who had adopted domestically, and they'd said the birth parents could be involved, to an extent, at least.

"You didn't give Hannah that choice," Aaron said quietly.

"That was different. And I don't want to get into it right now."

"Look, Dad, I love Marti. Maybe it's not love like you and Mom had," Aaron couldn't imagine that kind of intensity, his parents had been made for each other, perfect companions who fit together almost like puzzle pieces. "But it's love. And Marti will make an excellent mother." That he knew for sure. Marti babysat her younger siblings all the time, and when her mother had had her eighth child last year, Marti had watched the birth and gotten up at night with the baby for months, happily. She loved babies. And she was more patient than anyone he knew. "And she told me she'd talk to her parents, get them to see that college is the right thing for me."

"Yeah, right," His dad said, short.

"They will! I won't let them talk me into that plumber thing. I can't even use a screw driver!" He laughed a little, and Mark did, too. Aaron had no sense of how to use at any tools. Last year he had hit a nail so hard with the hammer, instead of just tapping it, that the hammer had missed the nail and gone straight through into the wall.

"I promise I will get my college education, okay? Dad, I swear." He wondered if his dad's chuckle just now meant he was giving in, just a little. "So we're going to do it at Thanksgiving. Just something small. And you can do the ceremony, Dad." He actually didn't know if this was true. He hadn't brought it up to Marti yet. Marti and her family would want to use their pastor, some guy with the same first and last names – he couldn't remember it exactly.

"Thanksgiving? That's only a month away!"

"But we have a four day weekend...and we need to be married for a while before the baby comes."

"This is not 1950, Aaron. Everyone already knows that Marti is pregnant, and getting married in a rush won't make a difference."

"I know, it's just, it's important to Marti, and her Mom. And then I'm going to move in with them." That part he wasn't looking forward to. Even though they would have their own space in the basement, he dreaded being surrounded by all of the little kids all the time, and her parents being able to come downstairs anytime they wanted.

"Move in with them?" His dad slapped his thigh. "Are you insane? Do you understand how preposterous this idea is? You don't love the girl, or maybe you think you do, but Ari, it's not love at seventeen. Not the kind of love you need to sustain a lifetime commitment. And trust me, I know about that."

"Maybe it's not what you and Mom had," and again he felt embarrassed. "But it's something. We've been together over a year already," he finished weakly, feeling like an idiot. It did sound crazy. Just a few weeks ago he was trying to figure out how he would cut Marti loose when he left for college, and now he was willing to marry her. "Look, Dad, it's going to happen, whether you like it or not. You can accept it or just be pissed off. Either way, I'm marrying Marti." He sat up straighter in his seat. "I'm marrying her Thanksgiving weekend, and there's nothing you can do to stop me."

"There certainly is something I can do to stop you. You're not eighteen yet. You need my permission. And you know what, Son? You don't have it." Then his Dad stood up, slammed his chair down on the floor, and stalked out of the room.

Chapter 43

Hannah

After school the next day, Hannah headed in the opposite direction from her house.

She walked a long way, at least two miles, she calculated, and with her backpack full of books and homework, it was tough. But she needed to talk to someone, and she knew who that someone was.

She finally made it to the church an hour later, sweaty and out of breath. The door was open, just like the pastor had said it always would be, because they welcomed everyone inside, no matter who they were or what religion they were, what color they were, or what time of day it was. Hannah had really liked that idea, because at her synagogue, the door was always locked, except for services or Hebrew School or an event, and even then, someone stood right inside the door and held it open, watching people as they entered. Her Dad said that was because it was nice to be greeted when you came into a temple, it made people feel more welcome. But Hannah was pretty sure it was because they didn't trust outsiders, wanted to keep non-Jews out, or at least make it hard for them to get in. And that, Hannah realized, meant that if she weren't with her father, *the Rabbi*, she would be one of those people they were trying to keep out. She sure wasn't Jewish, that was clear. You could tell just by looking at her.

She stepped inside the doorway. It was cold out but she had been moving quickly, and she felt pretty gross as her sweat mixed with the cool temperature. It was an odd combination, just like being Chinese and Jewish was. But she wasn't really Jewish. Not anymore. She was unsure how she was going to tell her Dad she wasn't going to have a Bat Mitzvah. She was still going to lessons, but reluctantly, and last week her teacher had sternly told her she was falling behind. She didn't care.

Pastor Jameson appeared in the entranceway of the church building, almost magically. She was sure he hadn't been there when she'd peered through the glass windows. "Hannah, hi!" he said, like he was a game show host.

"Hi, Pastor." He reached out to grip her hand, but she pulled her slick one behind her so he couldn't touch it.

"What can I do for you today?" he asked.

"I was hoping we could talk." She fingered her purity ring nervously. That was the other thing. She wasn't taking it off anymore. It seemed wrong to do that if she was truly going to become a practicing Christian.

Hannah knew there were different denominations. Like Methodist and Catholic and Episcopalian. They were all over town, in their different churches with their steeples. It still seemed weird that this church didn't have a steeple; she'd thought that was a "thing" in all churches. And she didn't quite understand how this church didn't really have a denomination. Maybe the pastor could explain it to her sometime. But not right now. Right now she had bigger things to discuss with him. He hadn't seemed bad, that day they met in town, in fact, she kind of liked him now, and Kristin was always saying how nice and fun he was. Kristin was smart about people. Last year when everyone else liked a new teacher at school, Kristin had said, "She's evil, you'll see," and by the end of the year, the school had fired her for trying to change the standardized test scores.

Her father had always said that talking to a rabbi was one of the best things a person could do if she was struggling, and that he loved when his congregants talked to him about their problems. But she couldn't go to her rabbi – her rabbi was her dad. And she couldn't go to the cantor – she would surely tell her dad, and her dad wouldn't want the cantor to know their personal business anyway. The pastor, though, wasn't he the equivalent of her dad? Surely he would listen and offer advice.

"Of course we can talk!" he boomed again, and she wished he would keep his voice down. It was making her more nervous than she already was. He led her to an office, where two women were hard at work on computers. "Ladies, say hi to Hannah!" They smiled at her and she smiled back. She was glad she didn't know them.

She followed him back to his private office. It was much smaller than her father's, and not nearly as fancy. There was wood paneling on all of the walls, not nice wood paneling, like a study, but cheap wood paneling that she could see was coming detached from the walls. If she touched it, it would probably just be brittle in her hands.

And his desk wasn't fancy, like her father's. It was just a standard cheap desk, like you'd get at Office Depot on a sale day. But he did have a couch, and he told her to join him on it. It was comfy, and she realized when she sat down how tired she was. She could fall asleep right there for a long time.

She supposed she should say something, but nothing would come out of her mouth, not now that she was finally here, like she'd planned. So he folded his hands together, like he was really relaxed, and he started. "I was so happy to see you at our last meeting," he said. "I love when we bring new young people into our mix. You teach us as much as we teach you."

She hated being referred to as "young people," especially by a guy who was not old, like her father was. Jim Jameson was probably around thirty, she supposed, and he was wearing jeans and a regular shirt, nothing that indicated he was a pastor. Then again, her father wore regular clothes, too.

Her silence again enveloped the air. Then he said, "Did you want to talk to me about something?"

"My brother is in trouble."

"Oh, that's too bad. What kind of trouble? Maybe I can help."

"He got his girlfriend pregnant."

"Oh, well, yes, I can see why that would be troubling. Sexual relations outside of marriage are against God's law."

"But now they're going to get married."

"That's good, then, to bring the child into a marriage." She wasn't sure. Getting married at eighteen seemed so stupid. Hannah wanted to go to college and get started on her career first, though she wasn't sure what that would be. But for her, marriage and kids were far in the future, so far ahead she couldn't even see them, really.

"So they are trying to right their wrong," the Pastor was saying. "Of course, only God can decide, on their Day of Judgment, whether they will be forgiven, but He will be happy they decided not to bring a bastard child into the world."

"What's a bastard child?"

Jim Jameson sat up straighter and cleared his throat. "A child born to an unmarried woman. That child would bring great shame upon the woman for not having a husband and of course, that child would not have a father, which each and every child desperately needs. Children need both a mother and a father to do well in this world."

She could be a bastard child, for all she knew. She had no idea where her birth mother was, or if she had been married to her biological father. Maybe that was what was wrong with her, why she felt different, why she *was* different. She was a bastard child. Though she knew a few kids with only a mom, and of course in New York, she had known kids with two moms or two dads and one kid even being raised by an older brother. They all seemed fine.

"I'm adopted," she blurted out, surprising herself.

"I see. Well, that's wonderful that your parents decided to welcome a child not of their flesh and blood into the family, and to give you a chance at a normal life."

Not of their flesh and blood? Oh, she supposed that meant that she wasn't biologically theirs. It used to really bother her that her brother had grown inside their mother, but she hadn't. But now her mother was dead, and she only had a father, and did that mean she didn't stand a chance at being normal? Of God loving and approving of her?

"My mother is dead," she blurted again. Something about this very soft couch and the ugly brown fake paneled walls, and the heat of the room – she pulled her shirt away from her body and fanned it out – made her think about things she never wanted to think about, much less talk about, just come flying out of her mouth.

"I'm sorry to hear that," Jim Jameson murmured. "You're so young to be without a mother."

"I miss her a lot," Hannah said, and then she started crying, which she had promised herself she would not do. She cried harder still from the humiliation.

"I'm sure you do." Jim Jameson rose from the couch, went over to his desk, and plucked off a box of tissues. She wondered if a lot of people cried here, and he needed to be prepared, or whether maybe he just always kept tissues there, coincidentally. Maybe he had allergies or something. She pulled one out of the box and tried to wipe her nose without blowing, because the sound would be embarrassing.

"So does that mean I'm doomed? I just have my dad and my brother."

"What? Oh, no. Your parents were married and they brought you out of a difficult life and gave you a normal one. You can't help that your mom died. I bet your dad loves you very much, and only wants what's best for you."

Now she felt a little better. And a little more courageous. "So what I really wanted to talk about is my brother. I don't think he really wants to marry his girlfriend."

"But she's pregnant. We all sometimes have to do things in life that we don't want to do, for the greater good."

That was true. Her dad said it often enough when she complained, like about the damn Bat Mitzvah she wanted to get out of, or shots.

Still, the whole idea of Aaron getting married seemed far-fetched. "He's only seventeen," she said now. Didn't his age matter?

"The baby doesn't care how old he is. The baby only cares that it has a mother and father, that it has security in its family life, and that its parents are following the ways of God."

Hannah didn't know what the baby would care about. But it did kind of make sense to start it off on as good a foot as possible, with two parents, like her birth mother had done for her. Who knows what would have happened to her if her parents hadn't adopted her? Nothing good.

"My dad doesn't want them to get married."

"Maybe your dad is just scared. I'm sure as the grandfather, he wants what's best for the baby."

It felt so weird to think of her father as a grandfather. She had thought of herself as the aunt, and she enjoyed imagining the baby calling her Aunt Hannah. She would be an awesome aunt. She was just about old enough to babysit, and she could read to it and play with it. She wondered again if it was a boy or a girl and when they would find out what it was before it was born, and she started to get excited, which was the opposite of how she had felt when she had come in here. "My dad is scared," she agreed. "Plus, you know, there's the whole religion thing." Pastor Jim made a weird face, as though he'd suddenly smelled something bad.

"Hannah, who are your brother and his girlfriend?"

"Oh, well, you don't know my brother. We're not members of this church. But his girlfriend is Marti. Marti Engel. She goes here; you probably know who she is." Hannah didn't know how many people were at this church, but her dad made it a point to know all of his congregants, which always amazed her. They had several hundred families, and her dad knew all of their names and their kids' names.

"Your brother is Aaron?" he asked.

"So you *do* know him."

"Your father is Rabbi Mark Friedlander?" Now Pastor Jim looked a little sick, and Hannah hoped he wasn't going to throw up.

She hated thinking about throwing up, and if anyone else did, she always did, too.

"Do you know him?" she asked. She really hoped not. Then Jim Jameson would call her father and tell him she had come to him, and her father would be furious. He had never said so, but she could tell he did not like Jim Jameson. If his name came up, he wrinkled his nose and scrunched his eyes closed.

"Yes, Aaron is my brother, and Rabbi Friedlander is my father. So you can see why this could be a little difficult," she said, trying to sound as grown up as possible. "My father wouldn't be comfortable with me coming here, given his...his...position." She couldn't figure out any other way to say it.

"Hannah, your father and I...we don't see eye to eye on a lot of things." Jim Jameson's eyes were flitting around the room now, as though he thought someone was there who he couldn't see. "And I'm sure he wouldn't approve of you coming here."

"Oh he definitely wouldn't. He wants me to be Jewish. He's making me have a Bat Mitzvah. But I want to be Christian. I feel like I *am* Christian. But my dad insists I'm Jewish, because he is." She wasn't sure, actually, what it meant to feel one way or the other, but she really wanted to know. And there was no way she was Jewish by birth, and the Jews always made such a big deal about being Jewish if your parents were. When she'd asked her dad about it, he'd said whether you were born into the religion or converted, it didn't matter. And he had converted her as soon as she'd arrived from China, so, he'd emphasized, she was definitely Jewish.

But being Christian felt more right. The rules were clear, and they were easy to follow. And Jesus seemed like such a nice person, such a great guy. The Jews just dismissed him, but what if he was really God's son? The Jews would be wrong, then. And there was a Heaven, that she knew. But the Jews didn't talk about that.

She didn't realize that Jim Jameson was staring at her. She forced herself to look back at him now and focus.

"Your father can't make you be any religion, if you don't want to be. You can be Christian. I'll help you." He smiled widely, and she relaxed.

"How can you help me?"

"We'll say The Sinner's Prayer together, which will start you off in Christianity. Then I'll baptize you here and now, but we won't tell anyone. Once you do these things, you'll be an official member of my church. And I'll help you learn about Christ and his wonderful teachings and how you can use them in your own life."

It seemed pretty easy. She didn't actually have to study anything or learn anything. She would just say a simple prayer.

"But we have to lay down a couple of ground rules," the pastor said.

"Okay."

"First of all, when I ask you to come to church, you need to come. And you need to be loyal to me and my teachings. Secondly, you need to support your brother and Marti in marrying, even if your father tries to pull them apart. And lastly, when I ask for a hug, you give me one." He smiled now, and Hannah was relieved. These were all things she could do. She wasn't thrilled about the hugging part, it certainly wasn't the rule at her temple, but maybe they did it differently here.

"I can do all of those things," she said, grinning back. It felt so right to finally have a direction and be able to follow it. Maybe the pastor could figure out a way to get her out of the Bat Mitzvah. And maybe she could become even better friends with Kristin. When her brother married Marti, would they be related? They would have the baby in common. It could all work out. This baby could be the best thing that had ever happened to her.

"I want you to go home, and tell Aaron you're happy he's getting married. Tell him that God approves and that he's doing the right thing. Tell him you support him."

"Sure." She wouldn't say it exactly that way because Aaron would think she was off of her rocker; besides, he spent nearly every waking moment in his room, with the door locked. He didn't care what she thought. But maybe she could think of something positive to say.

The pastor rose, and she rose, too. "Thank you, Pastor Davidson," she said. "I feel so much better already."

"Hannah, out there," and he pointed towards the closed door, "I'm Pastor or Pastor Jameson. But when we're alone, like now, I can just be your friend Jim, okay?"

"Okay." She said. Like Robyn was Robyn instead of Cantor when they were alone. Pretty cool. Then he pulled her to him and hugged her tightly. She hugged him back, but it felt a little weird.

Let's go get you baptized now," he said, "So you can be a true Christian."

Chapter 44

Mark

Mark could not believe that Aaron thought he could go through with this crazy marriage idea. He certainly wasn't going to give him permission to do it. But that would only hold him off until March. When Aaron turned eighteen, he could do anything he wanted. Aaron had not spoken to him since their confrontation Thursday evening, which Mark figured was a good thing, because if they talked about it some more, he might blow a gasket.

It was Saturday afternoon, and he was sitting in his office, staring out into space, instead of working on next Saturday's sermon. He also needed to tack up some of the Hebrew school kids' drawings on the walls of the Sukkah, but it was cold outside, and he wasn't in the mood.

He'd forgotten all about his date with Robyn until this morning, when she'd come into his office before services, a big smile on her face, her eyes bright. "So are we still on for seven o'clock?" she'd asked. He'd almost replied, "For what?" but then he'd remembered and his heart had sunk. The last thing he wanted to do was go out and pretend to have a good time, not when his son's life was falling apart.

But he couldn't do anything for Aaron now, he'd reasoned, and Aaron was not speaking to him anyway. Maybe he could put his troubles aside and enjoy the evening out with this woman. It was just a few hours. It might do him good.

"Seven," he said, pasting a smile on his face. "Come hungry." She'd smiled back gloriously and he'd gone back to his brooding as soon as she'd left the room.

Now he did a quick restaurant search on the computer to see if he could find something a little out of the way, quiet, not too fancy, but not too casual either. It reminded him that he still had not done anything about Hannah's Bat Mitzvah party. He had no idea where to start with that, and though he was sure Robyn could guide him, he wasn't going to put her in that position. It was his job to make a party, though what kind of party it could be, he had no idea. He wished he'd paid more attention when Julie had made Aaron's. That had been a huge affair; this would not be, and he hoped Hannah wouldn't mind. Maybe the restaurant he had picked for tonight would have a back room and he could book that. It was only six months away and he needed to get on it.

Six months. By then, Marti would have had her baby, and if it were up to Aaron, he would be married to her. Mark's stomach sank again just thinking about it. He was going to be a grandfather at the age of forty seven. His son was going to walk into the biggest mess of his life, and not be able to get out for a long time, if ever. And an innocent child, a child who didn't deserve to be put in the middle, was going to be born into a most confusing situation.

He wished he could communicate more with Marti's parents. Her mother had not even called since their "engagement" announcement. He actually liked Marti's parents, and he was surprised about that. Sure, the father was a little overbearing, but he liked how they stuck up for their principles, he liked how much they wanted the best for their daughter (even though what they wanted was the opposite of what he wanted for Aaron), and he liked how warm and homey their house had seemed. Aaron had always told him how much Marti respected her parents and how well they seemed to get along. That must say something.

And Hannah had been acting weirdly, too, ever since Thursday, at least. At first, Mark admitted to himself, he hadn't really noticed. He had been too busy fuming over Anna's ridiculous go-find-members-at-the-gym edict, which he still was not going to do. In fact, he needed to talk to Robyn about that. But maybe not tonight, because tonight was truly supposed to be a date. No work talk, he had promised himself.

Hannah was refusing to go to services, no matter how much Mark had yelled, and then begged and pled about it. She wouldn't say why either. He was almost late Friday night when he finally gave up and left her home. He would need to talk to her about that. There was no way she could keep missing, both because her Bat Mitzvah was in just a few months, and, frankly, because it looked bad for him. He required all of the seventh graders to come to a certain number of services before their Bar or Bat Mitzvah, and he couldn't just let Hannah miss them when he was chasing after so many other families demanding they meet the requirement. Hannah had never been this obstinate before; she'd always been so go-with-the-flow. Julie had called her their "chill" baby. What was this, then? Just normal going-into-her-teens stuff or delayed loss-of-her-mother stuff or neither?

Again, he wanted to talk to Robyn about it, but he would have to resist, at least for tonight.

Neither of the kids was there when he got home and he hated to think it, but he was relieved. He didn't want to face either of his children right now, to deal with whatever was coming next. The relief, those thoughts, made him feel guilty. He was tired, he acknowledged, exhausted, actually. He wished he could talk to Julie right now, to have her deal with all of this. That was how it was supposed to be.

Julie had warned him that Hannah's teen years would be difficult. He knew about all of the physical stuff, of course, and thought he had dealt with that well, bringing Robyn in, who had been fabulous with her. But the emotional stuff – Julie had been concerned that Hannah might struggle with identity issues, with being adopted, and she had wanted him to be on the lookout for those. He didn't know if that was what Hannah was experiencing now, he didn't think so, but even if it were, what was he supposed to do? He realized that Julie had warned him about things to look for, but hadn't given him a way to work on them, to fix them. Why was that? He didn't know.

He quickly showered and put on a pair of khakis and button down shirt, his uniform outside of work, whenever he wasn't in jeans. Julie used to laugh at him; it was always the khakis and button down shirt. He felt safe in them. They didn't require thought.

He hadn't been out on a date in twenty years and wondered if they had changed much. Should he let Robyn pay for herself? He knew some women preferred that. But it felt all wrong to him. He still wanted to pay. And what would they talk about? He had already put on his list of inappropriate topics the kids and the membership at the gym thing. Though he wondered if that was still okay to talk about, if he didn't act like he was complaining. Surely coworkers outside the office discussed concerns like this. He'd have to think about it.

He made sure he had plenty of cash and his credit card in his wallet, grabbed his keys, and left. His first date in twenty years. He had never thought he would date again. He put some Springsteen on and sang along. He felt almost buoyant as he drove towards Robyn's house. He would feel absolutely gleeful if not for Aaron and his problems. Just for tonight, he wanted to forget about them, to just be on his first date with a beautiful, intelligent woman.

His wife had urged him to date again after she was gone. They'd had the conversation late one night just weeks before she'd passed away, when they had given up medical treatment and she had entered Hospice. "I want you to marry again," she'd said, whispering. For some reason, the chemo had made her voice weak, and he often strained to hear her. "To find someone who will love you for you, and love the kids, too."

"Don't say that," he'd said back. "I don't want anyone else but you."

"You're forty-five years old. You're too young to spend the rest of your life alone."

She was right and he knew it. "Let's not talk about it now," he said. "Can I rub your back?" And she'd rolled over slowly so her back was facing him. She'd loved his backrubs, he thought wistfully.

He had not wanted her to give up treatment but she'd insisted. "I'm not me anymore," she'd told him. The doctors had made it clear that no amount of chemo would make her better, that it would merely prolong a life that was already trying to get to the end. She'd gone along with Mark's wishes for another month, but finally she just couldn't do it anymore.

He'd fought her on it, but just for a short while. He could tell she was suffering, and the doctors had been clear with him. She was going to die. Whether it was in two weeks or a month was really up to Julie.

She'd faced it so courageously, so he'd tried to, as well. But every night that last month, he'd waited until she was asleep, and the children were asleep, and he'd take a pillow into the living room and sob into it.

He'd forgotten about their short dating conversation until now, and thinking about Julie gave him courage, strangely. He was going to have a great time tonight, and Julie would have been okay with it, and he was, in fact, now only forty-seven, and still too young to live the rest of his life alone. Plus, he admonished himself, it *was* only one date. He shouldn't get ahead of himself.

It was a brisk evening and as he walked up the path towards Robyn's condo, he wondered if his hair looked all right. He almost laughed out loud at himself. Who cared? He had never thought about it before, unless it was right before a big service, or something. He was starting to bald, anyway. Why would Robyn ever want to go out with him? Balding, widowed, two teenagers, a little paunch creeping over his pants. And Robyn was beautiful, and young, and unattached and had her whole life ahead of her.

He rang the bell and she immediately came outside. "You look nice," he said, an understatement. She had her hair down instead of in the ponytail she nearly always wore, and it was a wavy milk chocolate brown, with some gold undertones. She wore a simple skirt and sweater, and he noted, embarrassing himself, that she had an attractive figure.

"You do, too," she said back, quietly, the first time she'd ever been quiet in front of him.

He drove her to the Italian place two towns over, hoping no one from their synagogue would be there. They were quiet in the car, and he worried that the whole date would go that way. "What are you doing for Thanksgiving?" Robyn asked, finally, as they neared the restaurant, and Mark felt relieved and stupid. He should be the one starting the conversation. "Taking the kids to my mother's," he said, lying. It was too embarrassing to say they would be doing exactly what they had been doing the last two Thanksgivings, staying home while they ate a store-bought, pre-cooked Thanksgiving dinner, nearly silent, in front of a football game.

"Oh I'm visiting family, too! They're all in Massachusetts, and I miss them so much. My sister just had a baby last month, and I haven't had a chance to meet him yet."

Mark felt a pang and yearning for the closeness of family and changed the subject. "I think we're going to get some November snow," he said weakly.

At the restaurant, they continued their small talk through salads, bread, and drinks, and Mark thought it was all going pretty well. He hadn't brought up his children or his dead wife. And he hadn't yet had to use his back up topic of synagogue politics and this idiotic gym idea, though he kept it in his mind for later, if conversation slowed down.

They were just starting their main courses when Robyn brought up Aaron. "If you don't mind me saying so," she said. "You seem so calm, with what's going on with Aaron."

He dropped his fork and took a long drink of water and then he spoke. "I'm anything but. Aaron's been consuming most of my waking hours the last few weeks, and even some sleeping ones, too. But I wanted us to have a nice evening, and I promised myself I wouldn't talk about it."

"It's a major thing going on in your life; of course you can talk about it." She put down her fork, pushed her plate forward, and folded her arms.

"It's a mess," he admitted. "Aaron's insisting on marrying the girl. They want to do it over Thanksgiving weekend."

"And you don't think that's a good idea, obviously."

"It's a terrible idea. They're only seventeen. Too young, even with a baby on the way."

"What do you think they should do?"

"I'm not sure," he replied honestly. "I'd originally hoped she would abort, and," he added quickly. "It's not that I'm cold or callous, but it seemed like the logical thing, they both have their whole lives ahead of them. But she's a strict Christian, and abortion is against their theology. I can understand and respect that. . .so then my hope had been that they would give the baby up for adoption."

"And they don't want to?" she asked gently.

"Aaron wanted it but her family…they think blood should be raised by blood, all of that, and the only way they see is for the two of them to get married…they don't believe in single mothers, either."

"And how does Aaron feel?"

"I'm surprised, but he's all for it…well, maybe not all for it, but totally willing to go along with it. He keeps saying he wants to do the right thing, and that means marrying Marti. It seemed like, at first, he was thinking logically, like the abortion, no matter how difficult, made sense. And then when he realized she would never do that, we talked about adoption. He was okay with that, maybe not all the way, but still, a better option that becoming parents. But, I don't know," Mark stopped and took a sip of water. "If they got to him, or something, but he's convinced now that he should marry her, which is crazy! He even thinks he loves her, and it's so strange because at first he was totally against the marriage idea. He's seventeen; he doesn't get it." His voice got louder on the last sentence than he had meant for it to get, and he told himself to calm down.

She nodded. "I remember being seventeen, and how intense – and confusing -- those feelings could be."

"I told him I wouldn't give him permission, so now at least he has to think about it until March, when he turns eighteen. I'm hoping the idea will burn out before then."

"But then what? How far along is she?"

"Sixteen weeks or so. I'm not sure; I don't know what the answer is. I offered to help support her and the baby while Aaron's at college, though I'm not sure he's even willing to consider going away to college anymore." He had long since dropped his fork. "He's very bright, he could probably go to a top school, and I want him to have that – the college experience. Anyway," he said. "Tonight is not supposed to be about Aaron." He picked up his fork again. "Let's talk about something else. Like how you decided to become a cantor."

"I always loved temple, growing up," she said, almost dreamily. Mark cocked his head at her. Loved temple? Most kids wouldn't describe temple as a place they loved. She smiled. "I know; crazy, right? But I loved the singing and the pomp and circumstance, and I made some of my best friends there. So, anyway, I thought I might become a Rabbi, and I was a Jewish Studies major at Brandeis." Brandeis was considered *the* college for Jews, where many went just to embrace their Judaism. Plus, it was hard to get into. She must be very smart. "While I was there, though, I took a couple of music classes, and I realized, maybe I wasn't the best singer, but I was probably one of the most enthusiastic, and isn't that just what you need to be a cantor? Enthusiasm? For the kids, for the adults…it could be the best of both worlds…plus, sorry to say this, but it seemed like the cantor would get fewer temple politics to deal with." She winked. So she *had* noticed.

He laughed. "I have to agree with you there. They don't teach you how to deal with temple politics in rabbinical school." The conversation flowed throughout the evening, and before Mark knew it, they were back at Robyn's house. He had made it through his first date in twenty years, and more than made it through. He had enjoyed it. He said as much to Robyn as he walked her to her front door.

"I had a wonderful time, too," she said. "You're fun to be with."

"If you call a single dad with a mountain of problems fun…"

"I call *you* fun. I enjoyed it."

They reached her door and she fumbled for her key. "It's in here somewhere," she said, rummaging through her purse. "Take your time," he said. He didn't want the date to end. He didn't want to go home to what faced him—but more than that, he wanted to stay with her. He wanted to talk more.

"Here it is!" she crowed, holding up a large key chain triumphantly. She looked up at him, and he tipped her chin up gently with his hand. He reached down with his other hand, laying it gently on the side of her face and lowered his head. "You're beautiful," he said and then kissed her gently, and she kissed him back.

Chapter 45

Aaron

Aaron sat on the couch in Marti's family room, the same place he had been just weeks ago, trying to figure out a way, they could work this out. But this time Marti sat beside him and they were holding hands. Her hand felt smooth and soft. He could tell her boobs were getting bigger and he could see that her stomach was definitely getting bigger, too. He wanted to touch it, to feel the hardness of it she had described, and he hoped they would have some time alone so he could. He wasn't sure if her parents would allow the alone time before they got married, even though she was already pregnant.

That's what they were talking about now. How his Dad refused to grant permission for them to marry before he turned eighteen. And her parents were not happy about it. "Son," Ken was saying now, (and that was the other thing – suddenly he was on a first name basis with them and they were calling him Son!) "Does your father realize how important it is for you and Marti to have a few months, bonding as husband and wife, before the baby's born?"

"No, Sir, I don't think he does." *And*, Aaron added silently, *he's figuring we'll give up the baby for adoption eventually.*

Marti's mom spoke. "We think it's very important for you to establish yourselves as husband and wife long before a child enters the picture." Aaron nodded. *Best to go along with what they say.*

"I'm not sure what to tell you," he said slowly. "I want to marry Marti as soon as possible. I want us to be a family. But my dad is adamant. . .I'll still be over here as much as I can, and maybe stay here once in a while? I don't think my dad can stop me from doing that." What more did Aaron have to lose anyway? He bet if he did this that his dad would no longer need to pay for some fancy college. Community college would be far cheaper. Aaron tried not to feel depressed as he thought about community college. No dorm. No clubs. No activities. Just a couple of classes with some bozo teachers a few times a week, some crappy job to bring in extra money, though Marti's parents had assured him they would take care of everything, food, clothes, the baby's doctor appointments. He was lucky that way, he reminded himself. This baby would be taken care of. He and Marti did love each other, he was sure now, after waffling, that he did love her, and they would get to be together. And he could still become a doctor or an engineer, or anything he wanted, and eventually be able to provide for his family. It wouldn't be so bad, in fact, it might be pretty good. It would just take a little longer than he'd expected, originally, and would he really miss anything if he didn't spend the next four years getting drunk every weekend?

"No staying over until you two are married," Ken said now. "That's not proper." *Except*, Aaron thought again*, I've already knocked up your daughter*. The worst had already happened. What did it matter anymore?

"Yes, sir," he said, trying to be polite. He had to keep his cool, for Marti and the baby's sake. "Well," he said brightly, "March isn't that far away. We can get married any time after the 13th." He hated the secret feeling of relief he felt, knowing the wedding was going to be postponed for a few months, much like the way he used to feel when his dental appointments were postponed. Momentarily relief, but they would happen anyway.

So he reached out and touched Marti's stomach, felt the hard mound through her sweat shirt. Her mother had taken her shopping for maternity clothes that morning, but they'd gone to a store an hour away, so no one would see them. She would need to start wearing the clothes soon, because she could no longer fit into her jeans, and she only had a few pairs of yoga pants that she'd been rotating. Her mother thought yoga pants were unbecoming outside the house anyway, so she was forbidden to wear them when they went out. It seemed old fashioned to Aaron, who saw kids coming to school in pajama pants every day, but he also liked how caring Marti's mom was, how she wanted the best for her daughter, and in some ways, she reminded him of his own mother. He wondered what his mom would say now. What would she want him to do? He had no idea, but he would think about that and try to figure it out.

Marti interrupted his reverie. "We get to find out the gender next week," she said. "You're coming with me to that appointment, right?"

So far, other than their trip to the clinic, he had not gone to any appointments with her. It grossed him out a little, and he dreaded the birth, which apparently she expected him to attend. When he'd asked, "Don't you want your mom there more?" Marti had informed him that apparently she could have as many people as she wanted in the room, and she wanted both of them – he and his mother.

"Sure, I'll come with you." He was curious about whether it was a girl or a boy. He kind of hoped for a boy– he pictured himself throwing a baseball around a yard with a little boy, taking him to games, explaining football to him. But he knew a girl would make Marti happy; she'd mentioned the hope of a daughter a few times. And he wanted her to be happy, for sure.

Her parents stood up. "We'll give you a little time alone now," her father said. It was the first time they would be alone in a room since they'd told their families she was pregnant. He had almost forgotten what it was like.

Chapter 46

Hannah

Hannah was at a church youth group meeting that night. Pastor Jim smiled at her when she came in, not acting as though they'd had a deep talk or anything last week, and she wondered if she had just imagined it.

They sorted clothes to give to needy children. They did that at her synagogue, too. And they had snacks, just like they did at her temple. It didn't feel any different. Perhaps, she thought, being Jewish and being Christian were more alike than different.

Halfway through the sorting, Pastor Jim called out to her. "Come on with me," he said, and she followed him back to his office.

They sat on his couch. "I just wanted to see how you felt about your baptism," he said once they were settled.

"Fine," she said. What was she supposed to say? It had taken all of ten minutes to convert to Christianity. She kept waiting to feel God more intensely but she didn't. She kept waiting to feel different, but she felt the same. Maybe it was because she had never truly felt Jewish.

"Good, good. Now that you're a Christian, it's important to bring others into the fold."

"What do you mean?" He was looking at her strangely, and she got a weird feeling in her stomach.

"If you see a lost soul, you can invite them to join us. Like Kristin invited you. "

She had only come with Kristin so Kristin would like her more, so the other kids in her class would like her more, and she wanted to say as much now, but she knew he wouldn't like that. So she just nodded. "How will I know if a soul is lost?"

"Good question. Maybe you see a kid sitting alone in the lunchroom. He just wants to be accepted, like we all do. You could invite him here, where everyone is accepting." She wanted to tell him that everyone is actually not accepting, that some of these kids who were finally talking to her a little were only doing so because Kristin made them, that Christian kids could be just as mean at Jewish ones, as Catholic ones, as atheist ones. Religion didn't matter when it came to being mean.

But she supposed she could try to ask some of the kids who sat alone in the cafeteria. She would have liked it if someone had tried with her. So she nodded.

"Or maybe you hear that someone...thinks he is a homosexual. You might want to approach him, tell him there's a place for him, here."

"Most people call it gay now," she said.

"I prefer to use the word homosexual," he said. "And kids your age...they can be confused. They think they are attracted to the same sex, but really, they are just confused. We want to help them, so that they make the right choice, and keep on the path towards God." He had a weird way of speaking.

She didn't know any gay people her age. Her brother had told her there were some in the high school. At the middle school, most people were just playing spin the bottle or five minutes in the closet. She hadn't done either, but if she did, she knew of a couple of boys she might be interested in doing it with. Kristin had done five minutes in the closet, and Hannah had been shocked. It didn't seem to be something that you would do if you were a Christian girl, if you were supposed to wait until marriage for that stuff. Kristin had informed her they were only supposed to wait until marriage for sex. Kissing beforehand was okay. Hannah wondered where it said that in the Bible.

And Hannah had wanted to point out to her that obviously they didn't all wait for marriage, since Kristin's own sister was pregnant. Hannah considered the idea that maybe you should just wait for marriage for everything, even kissing. Because one thing could lead to another.

"I don't know any gay people," she said to the pastor.

"You might know them and not realize it. One way to tell is that gay people can be...very flamboyant."

"Flamboyant?"

"Maybe a boy acts like a girl, or something like that. Or sometimes a girl tries to dress and act like a boy."

She thought but she still couldn't come up with anyone like that. She liked dressing in sweat pants and sports jerseys sometimes but she didn't think she was gay; was she? Even if she did think she could pick out someone who might be gay based on how they dressed, she wasn't sure that she would have the guts to tell that person to come to the church. She was willing to try loners in the cafeteria, though.

"Anyway," Pastor Davidson said now. "I have something for you." He went over to his desk and opened a drawer. He came back with a small box. It wasn't wrapped. He handed it to her. "I wanted to welcome you formally into the church."

She opened the box hesitantly. Inside was a gold chain with a simple gold cross pendant on it. "This is," she gulped. "Wow, this is, thank you."

"Turn around," he said. "And I'll put it on you." How could she explain that she didn't want to wear a cross? Yes, she was Christian now, and she had voluntarily joined their ranks. She liked how Christianity made her feel more like everyone else and how clear it was; there were exact rules for right and wrong and people smiled a lot. But to wear a cross? It didn't feel comfortable.

So she didn't say anything. She turned around and held up her ink-black hair. She could take the necklace off later. Just the purity ring would be fine.

He pulled the necklace around her neck and clasped it gently behind her. It fell perfectly, right under her scoop necked shirt. And then she felt it. His hand grazed the back of her neck, and she could tell it was deliberate. "You're a beautiful girl," he said, and then he smoothed her hair down for her. "Just beautiful."

Chapter 47

Mark

Thanksgiving was going to be odd.

The last few weeks had been odd, too, but in a good way. He was suddenly part of a couple, and he and Robyn had been spending as much time together as they could, which still wasn't much. Every Saturday evening, they went somewhere – to a movie, to dinner, to a play – always out of town, where they wouldn't be noticed or scrutinized. And every date ended with a make out session, though he laughed to himself at the idea of a "make out session" at forty seven, rather than at seventeen.

He didn't find their age difference to be a problem at all. They had so much in common – values and family history and Judaism and other interests. For the first time since his wife had gotten sick, he was feeling more himself. He had Robyn to thank for that.

They couldn't afford to tell anyone. It would be a scandal inside the temple, and they both feared for their jobs. They had talked more about the temple, too. Robyn had confided that she had been looking for jobs elsewhere for about the past year as membership had declined and as the board had made more and more demands. They laughed together at the idea of doing a workout with a bunch of children to drum up business, and they talked more seriously about the idea that as clergy they even had to "drum up business." It used to be that Jews just chose the closest synagogue to their homes and sent their kids there for religious school. Some stayed, after their last child was Bar or Bat Mitzvahed, others left. Nowadays, parents were willing to travel further to find "the right match" and they "Temple shopped" for a good fit. And still, many Jewish parents weren't even sending their kids to Hebrew school anymore, and more than that, so many were marrying outside of the religion that they didn't need or want a synagogue at all.

Mark had been horrified when Robyn said she'd been job searching. In their line of work, a job search most often meant moving to a completely new area. Robyn herself was from Massachusetts, and she had taken the job in New Jersey because that is what had been available when she had graduated from cantorial school. She would like to live in Massachusetts again, where her sister lived, where her parents still lived. Robyn wanted to be involved in her nieces' and nephew's lives. She had gone to Massachusetts for Thanksgiving a couple of days ago, and Mark already missed her terribly.

He and the kids were going to spend their Thanksgiving Day with Marti's family. Aaron had approached Mark two Saturdays ago, right after one of his dates with Robyn. It was one in the morning, and he was still floating on a high when Aaron came into his room as he was getting ready for bed. He was going to pay for his late night the next morning when he had to be a temple at eight to prepare for Hebrew school at nine. He was used to going to bed so much earlier.

"Dad," Aaron had said as Mark brushed his teeth in the attached master bath. He could hardly hear his son through the running water.

"Just a minute, Son," he said through a mouthful of toothpaste.

"What's up?" he said a minute later, coming out of the bathroom in his white t-shirt and a pair of pajama bottoms.

"Thanksgiving," Aaron mumbled, looking away.

"What about it? I already ordered your favorites."

"I, um, I think we should go to Marti's that day."

"Marti's?" The last thing Mark wanted was to spend the holiday with Marti's family, people he hardly knew but was about to know way too well in the next few months. People who were trying to put his son in an untenable position. He felt anger stir in his gut. "I don't think so." He frowned.

"Dad, I know...you're mad at them, and....at me."

"I'm not mad at you, Ari!" Is that what Aaron thought? He supposed, in some way, that he could understand. After all, he had gone pretty ballistic when Aaron had said he wanted to marry the girl. And he had barely spoken of it since. He should have.

He sat down on the bed next to his son. "Ari..." he said, trying not to let his voice crack. "I'm not mad at you. I'm not even mad at them. Not really. I'm frustrated, yes. And you...I am sad for you. For what life will be like for you, if you marry her. I don't think it's a good idea, I'm sorry."

"But I love her, Dad, and you want me to be a man. And I'm trying to be."

"Sometimes being a man is about not doing the obvious thing...the right thing isn't always there, under your nose. And being a man certainly means that sometimes you will need to do something that the majority doesn't want you to do, but is right, anyway."

"So then, why won't you do Thanksgiving? It's not the thing you want to do, but it's the right thing."

Mark started to protest, but then, he realized, his son was right. He smiled and mussed Aaron's hair a little. "Okay," he'd said. "We'll go."

Mark had offered to bring wine, but Aaron had told him Marti's parents didn't drink. Apparently their form of Christianity did not allow alcohol. So Mark decided to provide dessert instead, and he and Hannah had spent time this morning in the kitchen, baking cookies. He had never baked cookies with his daughter before, and had no idea how to do it. But they had muddled through the directions together, and it had been almost fun. He had bought a back-up apple pie from the bakery just in case. It was on Hannah's lap as they drove through the streets to the other side of town.

They parked their car in the long driveway leading up to Marti's house, which was already festooned for Christmas. A large nativity scene took up half of their yard, and dozens of lights had been wrapped around the house. A large fir tree at the front of the property was also festooned in lights.

"Dad," Aaron said as they headed up the icy walk. "Please try not to say anything...controversial."

"What would I say?"

"Just, you know, anything about me not marrying Marti or about adoption or about being Jewish." He could see a few drops of sweat rolling down his son's face, and he reached out to him, tried to touch him, but Aaron shrugged him away.

Hannah was dragging behind them. What was wrong with her anyway, Mark wondered. Hannah should be thrilled that she was spending Thanksgiving with one of her best friends. But since Mark had told her about their plans, she had acted almost frightened about the whole idea.

Mark reached the door first. He rang the bell and put his best smile on. It was easy to do because he was thinking about Robyn.

Chapter 48

Aaron

Aaron felt the sweat dripping down the back of his shirt. He had wanted this, sure, he had been worried his father wouldn't agree to it, yes, but now that it was here, he wanted to turn around and run back to the car.

He dragged himself up the front steps to Marti's house and gave his father the last minute warning. He hoped this would go well, or at least not be a disaster.

As soon as he rang the bell, Marti appeared, looking beautiful in a pink maternity dress dotted in flowers that barely showed off her belly. He hugged her and squeezed her hand as she welcomed them inside. She took all of their coats, but it seemed like a heavy pile, so he grabbed them from her and put them in the front closet himself.

They walked to the back of the house, where Marti's dad and five of her siblings were watching football in the family room. Her mom was nowhere to be seen. "Mom's in the kitchen," Marti said and he nodded.

Marti's dad popped out of his chair. "Rabbi, Aaron, Hannah, welcome!" he said heartily. Too heartily. Fake. Aaron bet that Marti had warned him to be on his best behavior, too. Her dad pointed to the couch. "Why don't you all sit there?" Kristin grabbed Hannah's hand. "Let's go into my room," she said, and they fled. Aaron couldn't blame them.

The room was filled with the sounds of the game. Marti's siblings played on the floor with trucks and puzzles, all dressed to the nines, ties, dress shirts, and dress pants on the boys, even the baby, and frilly dresses on the girls. He was glad he had insisted his dad wear a jacket and tie. Usually their Thanksgivings were jeans and sweat shirts. For a half hour, no one spoke. They all just sat transfixed in front of the game, and it wasn't a particularly exciting one. Marti watched intently, though. "Wow, what a pass, Dad, huh?" she asked at one point. And then a few minutes later, she jumped up and screeched when their team made a touchdown. Who was this girl anyway? Marti didn't even like football. But now she watched as though her life depended on it, and Aaron watched her watching her father, trying to anticipate what to say and when. It made him sad for her. He was relieved when Marti's mom called them to the dining room.

The dining room was set up like a state dinner, with huge candelabras and an enormous display of cornucopia on the table. Fancy china with salad and dinner plates sat at each place, even the children's. There were seating cards. Her mother had thought of everything.

Aaron sat with Marti nearest her parents, with his father across from them. He could see that Hannah had found her place at the other end of the table with the younger children. He bet she was mad. She always liked to sit with the adults better. But when he glanced at her, she was laughing at something, probably some dopey thing Kristin had said. Hannah idolized her.

It was hard to believe he was now considered an adult, he thought, as they said bowed their heads and Marti's father said a prayer. Afterwards, he asked Aaron's father to add something, and Aaron was grateful that Ken had included his father like that. His father kept his head bowed and made a brief statement about God bestowing grace to everyone at the table, to Marti's brothers abroad, and for Marti and the baby's continued good health. Her parents said Amen. Maybe this wouldn't be so bad.

Halfway through a delicious dinner – Marti's mom sure could cook! – Marti squeezed his hand. He clanked on his water glass and waited for the table to silence.

"We have an announcement to make," he said.

Marti was smiling ear to ear, but his dad and her parents looked scared. He couldn't blame them.

"We went to Marti's doctor's appointment this week and we found out some good news. We're having a...girl!" He hoped he sounded excited. Frankly, he had been a little disappointed when the doctor had not said boy. He had no problem with girls, and Marti had been over-the-moon excited, but he had thought he could relate better to a boy, and when he wasn't panicking about the idea of having a baby at the age of eighteen, he had been imagining a little boy. Still, the baby was healthy and he was sure he'd figure out what to do with her, in time. And he already loved her.

Hannah whooped from all the way down at the other end of the table. "A girl!" she cried, and strangely, Aaron felt happy he could make her so happy, even though he had done nothing at all.

Chapter 49

Hannah

Hannah lay on Kristin's pink rug. She was stuffed from dinner. "My mom's pregnant again," Kristin whispered to Hannah. "But don't tell anyone. She hasn't even told me yet."

"Then how do you know?" Hannah picked at the threadbare carpet. It was decorated for a much younger kid, like a princess, and she shared it with her next sister down, Hope.

"I heard her throwing up a couple of times this week. That's always how it starts. Plus she and my father have been making gooey faces at each other, which they always do after they find out." She rolled her eyes and Hannah laughed. "Don't say anything, though. They haven't even told us yet. They'll be some big announcement in a few weeks, I'm sure." She rolled her eyes again.

"But your mom is so old!" Hannah didn't know much about the whole thing, but her mom did seem rather old to have a baby.

"She's only forty three," said Kristin. "That's not old at all. My mom'll probably have a few more, at least. She's friends with this lady at church who's forty four and pregnant right now. You can have them until you're real old, like maybe fifty or so."

Hannah could not imagine that. Her mom had been in her thirties when she had been adopted, and she had always said two kids was the perfect family.

Dinner hadn't been bad either. Marti's mom had made a huge feast, and then Aaron had made their announcement. A girl. Hannah had told Aaron a million times already she wanted a girl. She was going to have a niece! She could dress her up in the cutest dresses and teach her how to use make up (after she learned, maybe Robyn could show her?) and have tea parties...it would be so much fun!

She could tell that Aaron was pretending to be excited about it. She could always tell when he was pretending – he opened his eyes extra wide on purpose and smiled extra big, which was weird because he wasn't much of a smiler in general, and since Marti had announced her pregnancy, even less so. But he was trying, and that was good.

A girl, she thought again, and then her dad called her to go home.

Chapter 50

Mark

It was all so real now to Mark, with the announcement of the gender. He wished Aaron would have warned him before dinner that they were going to say something, he thought, as he climbed into bed, weary from the evening. He would call Robyn in the morning and tell her. At the thought of Robyn, his body relaxed a bit.

The evening had been pleasant on the whole, other than being caught off guard by the announcement, which he reminded himself he shouldn't have been—after all, Marti was about halfway through her pregnancy and of course they could tell the gender at this time. Still, he felt disconcerted. Aaron hadn't told him they were going to an appointment this week. Not that it was Aaron's fault. Mark should have been more on top of the whole situation, asking more questions, listening more. His relationship with Robyn had clouded his thinking.

Marti's parents were good people. Nice people. They were intelligent and seemed to have a loving relationship. They held hands several times throughout the evening and appeared very much in love for two people who had been married more than twenty years and had eight kids. Her mom appeared to be the rock of the household as she guided the children through helping with the dishes, stacking one of the two dishwashers in the kitchen, and then urged the younger ones to get ready for bed. Marti's dad seemed well loved by his kids; each had come to him for a big hug and kiss before they padded off in foot pajamas to sleep. Marti and Aaron had gone upstairs and helped tuck them in, though Aaron had looked like he'd rather be anywhere else. He needed the practice though. He had only been five when Hannah had come over from China, and had no real practical experience with young children.

A girl, he reminded himself, turning out the light and lying in the dark. A granddaughter. He couldn't help but smile a little, though he still felt the whole thing was wrong. A little girl to read to and bring to Temple to show off. He didn't know how the whole religion thing was going to work, and he was afraid to even think it. Clearly, the little girl would not be raised Jewish, but couldn't he, as the grandfather, at least teach her some Jewish customs? He should talk to Aaron about that, though he dreaded the conversation.

And, Aaron had told the whole group, the baby would be named Julia, after his mother, Julie. At least they were following the Jewish tradition of naming for the dead, a similar but not exact name. The middle name would be for Marti's mother, Candace, who was still alive, obviously, but it was just a middle name, after all, and he could understand that Marti wanted to honor her own mother.

Julie would have been thrilled, and touched, though he knew she, too, would be sharing his concerns about how all of this was going to work. Aaron was still insisting he was going to marry Marti as soon as he turned eighteen. The baby was due about a month after that, and there was no way she could be born to a single mother, he kept saying. It was his responsibility.

Mark flipped over on his side and tried to drift off. But he kept seeing Julie, missing her first grandchild, a grandchild who would be raised by her teen parents, and Robyn, smiling, happy Robyn, who he couldn't wait to see again next weekend.

Chapter 51

Aaron

Aaron had kept a really big secret from everyone.

He had applied Early Decision to Columbia, like he'd planned all along, after he'd deleted all of his other college applications. He had told his guidance counselor to tell no one, and he hadn't even told his dad. He'd felt guilty doing it; he was surely not going anywhere next fall, except to community college while he held down a job at the local grocery store.

He was there now, in his dopey store-issued pinafore, mandatory black pants, and black shoes. It was freezing outside, but when he saw a woman leaving the store with a cart full of groceries, he was between bagging jobs, and he called out, "Ma'am, can I help you?" She looked surprised but said yes, took her hands off the full grocery cart, and moved aside so he could take it. He wrestled on the gloves he kept in his pockets and hurried the cart outside. "Where's your car, Ma'am?" She pointed to the far end of the lot, and they took off. Once there, he encouraged her to get in the car. "Just start it up so you can get warm, Ma'am," he said, "And pop the trunk for me." He quickly put the groceries into the trunk, making sure the eggs were in a place that couldn't be broken. The first week, he'd had two customers come back with broken eggs, claiming he'd packed them wrong. He wouldn't make that mistake anymore. "All done," he said, coming around to the woman's window. A trick he'd learned. If you came around to say goodbye, you might get rewarded with a tip. Indeed, the woman handed him a five dollar bill through the crack she'd made in the window. "Thank you, Ma'am. You have a good night now," he said, and rolled the cart back into the store. That five would go into the account he had started for the baby, so he could buy her some things himself. It was mid-December now, and they'd gotten their first snow of the winter earlier this week. Aaron had cleared their sidewalk and also the neighbor's, and the neighbor had insisted on giving him twenty bucks. He had gone around the block with his shovel and made eighty dollars in just a couple of hours. He would use some of it to get Marti a Christmas present, and then the rest would go into his account, too.

After work, he hurried to get home. Today was the day that his Early Decision letter would arrive via email. He'd heard stories from seniors last year that the email came right at three, others had said they hadn't received theirs until later that night. In any event, he wanted to be right at his computer, waiting. He might be in for a long night.

This morning his best friend, Ryan, had come up to his locker. "Hey, Man," he'd said, a huge grin on his face.

"You already heard?" Aaron tried to plaster a smile on his own face, to be happy for his friend.

"Yeah. I got in." Ryan had wanted to go to Tufts, where his parents had met, since forever.

"Congrats, Man," Aaron said, and slapped him on the back. He tried to be happy for Ryan, but his own anxiety covered every other emotion he could possibly feel.

He probably wouldn't get in. His grades had slacked off under all the stress during the first quarter, and he'd had to drop his activities for work and Marti. And, he reminded himself, it didn't even matter if he got in. He was not going to Columbia. He was not going anywhere. Not Duke or Dartmouth or Yale or Cornell. It didn't matter if he got in or not.

Still, he couldn't help but feel a little excited. He just wanted to see. He just wanted to see if he was good enough. If his hard work had paid off. And someday he could tell his little girl that he'd gotten into Columbia, one of the most prestigious colleges in America, early decision no less, and that meant something. Didn't it?

My little girl, he thought as he flipped open his lap top. He'd left it open to Columbia's web site this morning as he'd scrolled through before he'd left for school. He loved the pictures of the campus, remembered how he and his New York City friends, when they were measly high school sophomores who thought they knew everything but knew so little (Sophomore didn't mean wise fool for nothing) had walked through the campus, imagining themselves there in just a few years. They'd pointed out all of the hot girls to each other – and the not-so-hot-ones, at that point none of them had ever had a girlfriend – and they'd visited the cafeteria where it was all-you-can-eat-can-you-imagine? – and they'd even managed to get buzzed into a dorm to peer into a couple of open rooms. Freedom awaited them at Columbia. Freedom and pretty girls and interesting classes.

Now he was about to be a father and he tried to banish his youthful memories from his mind. He had been so stupid and naïve back then. So young. He was a man now, with responsibilities and a lifetime of parenthood ahead of him.

Most of the time, it was overwhelming. He didn't know what kind of parent he would be, and how he would ever get to finish school. He was determined that he was still going to go to college, even if he had to do it a little at a time.

But sometimes, things didn't feel half bad, in fact, he would feel pretty good. He was going to be a dad. Little kids could be pretty cute. Sure, he was young, but he probably had a whole lot more energy than someone who waited until his thirties to have kids. And he was lucky. Both families were committed to helping with the baby and supporting them financially as long as they needed. And college...what was he really going to miss, anyway? Living in a dorm with a bunch of drunk, stoned guys? Eating crappy cafeteria food for four years? Sure, he'd like to go, he'd like to have that experience, but his daughter was so much more important than college. It felt weird to say "my daughter" -- weird and good all at the same time.

He checked his email. Nothing. If he had an iphone like most of the other seniors he knew, he could just keep checking on there and do other things, but he didn't, so he had to wait, tethered to his computer. He could do some homework while he waited.

The last couple of weeks, as everything began feeling at least a little settled, his grades had come back up to almost where they had been before this had all started. His guidance counselor had called him down again to her office, urging him to apply to a few more schools, just in case. But he wasn't going to. What was the point?

Even Marti didn't know he'd still applied to Columbia. It felt wrong, keeping the secret from her. She had made a big deal a few weeks ago about how they needed to be really honest with each other, like God wanted them to. That was one thing that kind of bugged him. Since her parents had accepted him into their family, she was trying to live a "more Christian life," and now nearly everything she said was about how God said this or Jesus wanted that. And, she no longer would have sex with him; not until they were married. At first he thought she was worried about the baby, and he'd even asked the doctor about it at their last appointment, and he had assured them that sex couldn't hurt the baby-- but that wasn't it, she insisted. She wanted to remain abstinent until marriage. He'd laughed out loud at that one and pointed at her growing belly. That had hurt her feelings and he'd quickly apologized. It sucked, but he wouldn't die, or anything. They would be getting married soon enough, and he would move into her place.

It would be weird not living with his father and sister anymore, not that they were like a normal family anyway. His dad was almost never home, and Hannah was almost always hanging with Kristin. He'd heard a strange rumor that Hannah had joined their church, but he'd decided that she wouldn't be so stupid. First of all, Hannah knew their dad would have a fit. Even he had told Marti that no matter what else happened, he was a Jew, and would remain a Jew. They still hadn't decided what religion they were going to raise the baby, and he cringed whenever the conversation came up. Of course Marti was adamant that their daughter would be Christian. Marti even invoked the Jewish law that the baby was whatever the mother's religion was. But he also wanted the baby to know her Jewish roots, and he was hoping Marti would let him plan a Jewish Baby Naming Ceremony for her. Still, though, the religion of the baby didn't seem as big a deal as some of the other obstacles they faced, and since Aaron was eager not to fight about anything, he tried not to bring it up.

He checked his email again. Nothing. He'd finished his math and would work on his physics lab. That would keep him occupied for about an hour.

But he still kept checking his email. Nothing, nothing, nothing. He had known he would be anxious, but he hadn't expected to be this bad. He had to keep reminding himself he wasn't actually going to Columbia. No matter what the email said.

He finished his physics. He'd take a shower. That would kill some time. He turned the music up loud on his ipod and got in.

Fifteen minutes later, he was padding back into his room, towel around his waist, hair wet. Hannah was sitting on his bed, the computer in front of her, looking confused.

"What the hell are you doing in here?" he growled. She had promised after the last time she would no longer go on his computer, and to be sure, he'd been password locking it down in between uses. And to be even *more* sure, he was changing his password every few days to words Hannah would never think of.

She didn't answer him, though. She just looked at him and said, "You got into Columbia."

Chapter 52

Hannah

Hannah hadn't intended to go into Aaron's room or to look at his dumb computer. She'd gotten home late, after Hebrew School. Her father had dropped her off and then he was headed straight back to the synagogue, where he seemed to be spending more and more of his time lately. He'd always been there most of each day, but now it seemed he was always running back there for something, even when he didn't have meetings.

She was just kind of lonely. There was no church meeting tonight and she didn't want to be by herself. Aaron was in the shower, she knew. His music was so loud that she could hear it all the way from the first floor. He might not be the kind of companion she was looking for, but he was better than nothing, she thought as she climbed the stairs. She'd just hang out in his room until he got out.

She hopped up on his bed. She couldn't help it if the computer was right there, in her face. She was just going to play a couple of games, since it was on anyway. What would be the harm in that? She touched the mouse to wake up the computer. It sprang to life. Oh, Aaron's email. She clicked on the in box, knowing she shouldn't. Her dad had punished her after the last time, and she was not eager to go through that again. This weekend the church was having a big Christmas party, they were going to decorate the whole church for Christmas and have a pot luck. Kristin's mom was going to make pork tenderloin, and Hannah was excited about that. As per Jewish custom, she'd never eaten pork before. Tasting it seemed so forbidden, and it would be such an easy rule to break.

But Aaron's email beckoned to her. One message. It was probably junk mail. She would just clean it out for him. She'd want him to clean out her email box for her. It was a sisterly gesture, she told herself, and he wouldn't have to bother doing it later. They could talk instead about the baby. She couldn't wait for her little niece. She was saving her allowance to buy her the cutest clothes, and she wanted to take a babysitting course so Marti would let her sit for her sometimes. Even Aaron seemed to be getting excited about the baby.

The email showed up on the screen. Aaron's music still blared but who knew how long he had been in the shower, when he was coming out. His showers tended to last forever, she reminded herself.

Last month her dad had gone bananas when he had gotten the water bill, and he had put a ten minute limit on showers. She knew Aaron ignored it. She didn't understand what you needed to do in the shower for more than ten minutes anyway. A quick shampoo, soap yourself up. It was pretty boring in there.

But Kristin said that Marti had told her that guys jerked off in the shower. Hannah hadn't known what jerking off meant, but then Kristin explained it to her, and Hannah's stomach had started hurting. Her brother wouldn't do that, would he? Or her...father? That was so gross. So disgusting. Most of the time, she didn't even want to think about how Marti's baby had been formed. Yeah, she knew, her mother had actually explained some of it to her before she'd died, and then they had gone over it in health last year. She couldn't imagine her parents doing that, though she assumed they had, at least for Aaron. Maybe they had realized it was something they didn't want to do anymore, and that's why she had been adopted, though it seemed like most people really liked doing it. But Aaron and Marti doing it? She could not, did not want, to imagine.

But sometimes, and she would never admit this to anyone, she got a warm feeling in her stomach when she thought about kissing a boy, letting him touch her, maybe put his arm around her shoulders. Kissing seemed like it would be okay. At least in the movies, it didn't seem so bad. But all the rest? Being naked in front of someone else...letting a boy...do that to you? She shook her head. No thank you. She would adopt her kids, too.

She opened the email, from Columbia. It would be good to erase it before Aaron saw. He'd just be depressed. Anytime someone brought up college, he kicked in a wall or punched something or stormed up to his room or cursed, at the very least. Dear Mr. Friedlander, the email started. Maybe it was for her father? Asking for money, or something?

Congratulations! You have been accepted into Columbia University for the Fall 2013 term.

What? But Aaron hadn't applied anywhere. His father had begged him to but Aaron had said no, he was going to face his responsibility to Marti like a man. He didn't sound very happy about marrying Marti or having a baby then, but that had been weeks ago, when things were still so tense. Since then, when they'd found out the gender at Thanksgiving, Aaron had seemed almost...happy and excited, at least about the baby.

It must be a mistake. She went to erase it but then she saw Aaron in the doorway with a look of pure hatred on his face. Darn, she had not listened for the shower going off, for the music to stop. She had been too engrossed in her thoughts.

"You got into Columbia?" she asked. "That's what this says."

"Give that to me," he raged, and he grabbed for the laptop, still clutching the towel. She handed it to him. He scanned the email, and his face went from complete anger to uncompromised joy. She hadn't seen *this* look since last spring, when he and Marti had started getting serious.

"I got in," he said. "I got in!" He put the computer down on his dresser, pumped his fist, still clutching the towel around his waist.

He looked back at her. "You are not to say a word," he said, and the cloud came over his face again. "Not one word. To anyone. To Dad. To any of your little friends. No one."

She nodded. "What does this mean, you got in?"

"It means nothing. Nothing at all. Now if you don't want to be punished, don't say a word. Because if you tell Dad, I will kill you. *I'll kill you*. Now get out of here. I need to change." So she scurried out of the room. He hadn't gone completely berserk on her. How weird.

Chapter 53

Mark

Mark and Robyn were in a coffee shop after the yoga event at the gym. They had gone reluctantly, and he'd worn sweats and looked ridiculous doing a simple workout with the kids. Robyn had worn yoga pants that she kept complaining were too tight and not flattering, but all he saw was a curvy body. She always looked beautiful to him. She'd gotten the kids giggling and their parents laughed, too.

It was the middle of a Saturday afternoon, and the coffee shop was practically empty. It was the beginning of January, and freezing out. Mark held onto Robyn's warm hands across the table.

"You're so good with kids," he had said. "Just a natural." She had even taken Hannah out a couple of times over winter break, once to see some girly movie and once to spend the department store gift card she had given Hannah for Chanukah. Hannah had become morose and cranky at home, spending long hours in her room, or off with Kristin somewhere, and she was constantly telling Mark she wasn't going to have a Bat Mitzvah. He had shown her the picture of the restaurant he had finally booked for the party, and asked her for a list of friends she would like to invite. He had even left his computer open to invitation sites so she could look at a few. But though she still went to nearly all of her lessons (a few times he just couldn't find her and well, sometimes he didn't have the heart to battle it out with her) she kept refusing to discuss the actual event, saying she didn't want this and wasn't going to do it. When he had talked to Robyn about it, she had just laughed and said she remembered those times as a young teen, defiant, angry, and she would grow out of it. But Mark had never experienced anything like this, and Hannah wasn't even officially a teenager yet, anyway! She was well on her way, though. Mark could see her body changing in front of him, almost daily, getting taller, curvier. He wanted to ask her if she had gotten her period, but he didn't know how.

"I love kids," Robyn said now, rubbing his thumb with hers. "I hope I get to have a big family, someday."

"How big?" he asked, and he realized that he often forgot her age, that she was seventeen years younger than him – she had recently told him she was thirty, going to be thirty one next August.

"Three kids, maybe four. I always wanted twins." She looked into the air dreamily. "I could dress them in little matching outfits. It would be so cute."

"Trust me, you don't want twins. One at a time is hard enough." He still didn't cherish the memories of babies screaming at one a.m., three a.m., and five a.m. Hundreds of diapers and then hours of bribery to get two year olds to sit on the potty. His wife had done most of that, but he still remembered. He couldn't imagine trying to do it with more than one baby at a time.

Still, there was that feeling he had for her, wanting her to be happy, to have anything she wanted. He recognized it from when he and his wife were at the heaviest of their dating. Love, it was love. He loved Robyn. Why hadn't he realized this before?

If he told Robyn he loved her, where would it go? Where *could* it go? He didn't want any more children, and he couldn't if he wanted to. He'd had a vasectomy a few years back, after a pregnancy scare following Hannah. It was ironic that after years of trying for a second child on their own, and then going through the long, often stressful process of adopting Hannah, that they would find themselves possibly pregnant. It turned out his wife wasn't, but that had led to a serious discussion about more children, and both had agreed they weren't willing to take that chance. A month later, Mark had the simple procedure done in the doctor's office.

He had not thought of it since. Until now.

Chapter 54

Aaron

Aaron felt guilty. Last week, without telling anyone, he had withdrawn enough money out of his account to pay his deposit at Columbia. He was not going to Columbia, he kept telling himself, and thinking about it wasn't going to help any. He sat on the couch next to Marti, trying not to think of what he had done. Marti was getting bigger by the day, and now he put his hand on her growing belly, feeling the baby kick. He couldn't believe how strong she was for how little she was. Marti pulled up a picture on her laptop. "Look, see?" she asked, putting her head on his shoulder. "This is how big the baby is right now." He was going to as many doctor's appointments as he could and had grown accustomed to looking at her huge, swollen belly there, her top pulled up so the doctor could check the baby's heartbeat. But the idea of going through the birth still made him queasy. They had signed up for birthing classes, which freaked him out, because Marti had told him they would see films of births there. He didn't want to look. What did you need a class for anyway? It seemed to Aaron that it was just hours of pain followed by the baby being born. What was there to learn? And why would Marti want to know so much about it?

Columbia was emailing him stuff all the time, forms and information and dates for orientation and ways to apply for work/study jobs. At first, he had not even looked at the emails, just deleted them as fast as they had come onto his computer. But after the third or fourth, he had begun opening them. The pictures of people hanging out on the front lawn, the fully stocked labs, the dorms...and all of the opportunities, just there for the taking. He'd won a decent scholarship, too, and he knew his parents had been saving for college forever. He could go. It was right there in front of him.

But he couldn't go. Not with Marti having the baby in three months. He was turning eighteen March 13th, and Marti's parents had scheduled their wedding for the following Saturday, the 16th. They had even paid for an overnight down the shore, at a Bed and Breakfast afterwards, like Marti had wanted. It would be a small wedding, just immediate families, and they had agreed that his dad could officiate along with their pastor. His dad had groaned at that.

He had met Pastor Jim and didn't like him. Aaron had not met him, so far, but apparently he and Marti would start pre-marital counseling sessions next month. He had no idea how *that* would be. In fact, their first session would be on one of the Columbia Early Decision visiting days, he was going to have to miss that, although, he reminded himself, it didn't matter, because he wasn't going to Columbia anyway. Still, it was like he couldn't help himself, and he had sent in an RSVP saying yes, he would attend. Both the Dean of the Engineering School and the Dean of the Pre-Med program were going to be there. Aaron hadn't decided which one he was going to major in, but he wanted to hear them both speak. He sighed.

He wasn't even going to get his deposit money back. It was nonrefundable. How stupid was he. That five hundred dollars could have gone to a crib or clothes or diapers. Still, he opened the next email. Housing choices. Because he had been early decision, he was allowed first picks of housing. He scrolled through all of the choices. Dorms, suites, and even a few single rooms. A single room might be nice, he thought. No roommate to answer to, to consult on things like cleanliness and study hours. Plus, and now he knew he was crazy for thinking it, if he went to Columbia and got his own room, he could have Marti and the baby come stay with him sometimes. It would be tight, but maybe just an overnight or two a week. And Columbia was so close by that he could come home every weekend, and he would, if she agreed to it. He could just hop on the bus out of Port Authority and be back in an hour, hour and a half. He wouldn't be missing out on Julia's growing up that way. Lots of fathers had to travel during the week for work. Most of his friends' parents back in New York traveled every week, and were home only on weekends. It was just part of life. And he could get such a good education there, and ultimately make more money for them to live on. They wouldn't have to rely on her parents and his dad for so many years. It actually made sense. Maybe he should talk to Marti. Bring it up some way. Meanwhile, just to make sure, in case she did agree, he checked off a single and emailed the housing form back in.

Chapter 55

Hannah

Pastor Jameson was taking a bunch of the teenagers to a rally just an hour away, and Hannah was going with them. She had told her dad she would be at Kristin's—but Kristin, with her parents' blessing, was going, too. It was going to be a long day, starting at eight in the morning, and not getting back until late. They would spend a couple of hours making signs, and then they would head out.

For not the first time, Hannah wished she were part of Kristin's family. Her parents were so nice, and they were warm and loving. They kissed and hugged Kristin every night before she went to bed, and they said a prayer together. Her mom always had meals ready on time, and even with as many kids as they had, Kristin could talk to her anytime. Sure, Kristin complained about them, she hated sharing her room and her parents were really strict, but Hannah thought it would be so nice to have that kind of family.

The pastor explained what they should write on the signs. "We want to make sure that people know Jesus loves them no matter what," he said. "But we also want to let them know that they can change their ways, that there is a path to redemption; that if they want to get into Heaven, they must do everything they can to get there." It was about being gay again, Hannah knew. The pastor was very into to stopping gays from being gay, to making them turn straight. She didn't know why it was such a big deal. She wanted to ask him, but she felt strange butterflies in her stomach every time she thought about it.

She didn't actually want to make a sign. She thought it was wrong to try to convince people to change like that, though when she said that to Kristin, she had just shrugged and said, "We're just trying to help them get into Heaven. What's wrong with that?" Nothing, as far as Hannah could figure, but still, it didn't seem right. She wanted to go to Heaven, though, and be with her mother. It sounded like such a great place.

So she picked up a paintbrush. If she didn't write the actual words, but maybe contributed some artwork, would that be okay? She didn't want to offend God, or even Pastor Jameson, she thought, but she didn't want to write words that might offend other people, either. She sat with a group of girls for a while, first sketching out a sun and then painting it a bright yellow, while the other girls worked on the wording. How could Kristin's parents be okay with this? They were always saying you should love and accept people and ask them to join you, not push them away. This seemed like pushing away. But Kristin admitted that she didn't know if her parents knew exactly what they were doing. If it was church sanctioned, they normally just let her do it and they had no problem with the rallies against abortion. So why would they have a problem with this? It was just another way of getting God's word out.

The pastor came by. "Excellent, girls!" he said. "You're getting the true meaning of Jesus." He stood by them for a few minutes, and Hannah felt awkward as she added blue sky to the poster board. She wished he would move on to the next group.

"Hannah," he finally asked quietly. "Please come with me." She wondered if she could say no. She wanted to stay with her friends. Kristin's other good friend, Meghan, had sounded like she was just about to ask everyone in the group to sleep over tonight, after they got back. Hannah was desperate to be invited to Meghan's. She was even more popular than Kristin, and if you got invited to her house, you were set for the rest of the school year.

Plus, the pastor sometimes looked at her strangely. It made her skin crawl. She supposed she should think better thoughts about a man of God, someone who had sacrificed his entire life to serve God and this church. Kristin had explained to her that it was very hard to be a pastor, and of course, Hannah knew her father had a hard time as a rabbi. People judged you constantly. She shouldn't be so rude to Pastor, so she got up and followed him into his office.

He shut the door after they went inside. She sat down on the couch, and he sat down next to her. "How are things going with your brother and Marti?" he asked. He seemed almost obsessed with this subject, Kristin thought, and he was always asking about them, even though she knew they were coming to the pastor for pre-marital counseling and he was going to help marry them. If he was going to see them himself anyway, why did he always need to be asking her?

"Fine," she said. "The baby's a girl. I'm so excited."

"I heard. That's wonderful. Perhaps the next baby will be a boy, to pass on the family name, but girls are wonderful, too. I see you're wearing your cross today."

She hadn't wanted to but she knew Pastor would ask, because he asked every, single time she was there. She had said she was Christian now, she knew that, but she didn't want to wear the cross. To make things fair, she also never wore the Jewish Star necklace a relative had given her when she'd been converted to Judaism after her parents had adopted her. She had always loved that necklace, and had worn it often, but she thought about it differently now. She had never really been Jewish. But was she really Christian? And if she wasn't sure, should she really be wearing the cross?

But she had made sure she was carrying the cross necklace in her coat pocket when she came this morning, and she'd gone into the girls' bathroom to put it on just as soon as she'd gotten there. She had also made sure she was wearing her purity ring.

"Yes," she said. He moved closer to her on the couch and stared at it; then turned her to one side. "It looks a bit knotted back there. Can I fix it?" And before she could reply, he was sweeping her hair to the side with a very gentle touch and unhooking the necklace.

"So," she said nervously. "When are we leaving for the rally?"

"In an hour or so," he said, now caressing her neck. It felt good and bad all at once. She had never felt a touch like this, and she didn't think he should be touching her this way. But she couldn't tell him to stop. He was the pastor. She shouldn't have come in here, but she didn't want to be rude and tell him no. For a while, she had thought he was pretty cool, but she was starting to have weird feelings about him, again.

He hooked the necklace back and brought her hair back down. "That's better," he said. See, it was nothing, she told herself, relieved. He was just trying to help.

He touched her shoulders gently and again she felt her stomach drop. "I have to help the other girls," she said. "It's not right for them to do all of the work without me."

"Oh they'll be fine. Let me look at how the necklace falls on you now." He turned her to him and she felt his eyes boring down on her chest. "Perfect!" He grabbed the cross and held onto it for a minute. He was too close, and she could smell his aftershave, like pine trees, and it didn't smell bad, but she still didn't want him this close to her.

"I really should go," she said, jumping up, almost ripping the necklace in her haste.

"Of course." He blinked and stood up with her. She could see the outline of his penis straining his pants.

Chapter 56

Mark

Mark was going to spend a cold winter Saturday afternoon at Robyn's. It was the first time she was going to let him into her condo. Until now, she'd only allowed him to walk her to her doorway. He'd always kissed her good night at the door, but Robyn had never suggested he come in. He wasn't sure, until now, that he had been ready, either. Part of him still felt like Julie's, but now that he knew he was in love with Robyn, he wanted to tell her, in private. He thought if she invited him into her condo, that she might be feeling ready to hear it. He hoped she would say it back.

They were going to watch a movie – a documentary she wanted to share with him about Israel's fight against the Arabs. It was not a romantic choice, and he wondered if she was sending some kind of signal. *You're overthinking it, Mark,* he thought to himself. Still, he brought flowers with him, and had stopped at the bakery to pick up cupcakes. She had told him once how much she loved cupcakes; what a perfect treat they were, just the right size, piled high with chocolate frosting. He'd gotten a half dozen.

She answered the door wearing jeans and a loose sweater. "Hi," she said, reaching up to peck his cheek. He thrust the bakery box at her. "Oohh, what's this?" That was another thing he loved; how happy she seemed when he gave her anything at all, even something small, like this. He wondered momentarily how she would react when – make that if, he cautioned himself – he ever presented her with an engagement ring.

"I'll give you the quick tour." She showed him through a spacious but spare living room, just a large sectional and one chair, a few prints adorning the walls, a scratched up coffee table with a few family pictures on it as well as a bowl of chips and another of pretzels. The kitchen was off the living room. It was tiny, galley style, and, Mark noted, exceptionally clean. She pointed to three pictures on her refrigerator. "Emma, Kayla, Jacob," said, pointing to two toddlers and a newborn. Her nieces and nephew. She had talked about them often before, her eyes lighting up each time.

They went back into the living room. "That's about it," she said. "No dining room, so I eat my meals on the couch." She waved to a hallway he hadn't noticed before, just beyond the condo's front door. "Bedroom and bathroom down that way." Maybe she wasn't ready yet to take the next step. He didn't know whether to be relieved or disappointed.

"Have a seat." She plopped down on the couch and curled one leg under the other. She wore her hair loose today, instead of in her usual ponytail. He liked it this way.

He sat down next to her. "You can take off your shoes, if you want," she said, starting the DVD with the remote. She got up once again to turn the lights down and the show began.

An hour later, he wasn't quite sure what he had seen. He had taken her hand midway through, and he had been rubbing her thumb and forefinger. All he could think about was telling her he loved her, and then maybe showing her.

So he picked up the remote and put the movie on pause. He turned to Robyn. "I've been wanting to talk to you about something," he said, and he felt his hands go sweaty, like he was a kid in high school or something. That made him think briefly of Aaron, but he blinked to rid himself of the image of his son. "The last few months have been really special to me."

She started to answer. "Me…" He took one hand out of hers and put his finger to her lips. "I need to say something." She looked at him and he could feel a zap all the way to his toes.

"I love you," he said simply. "I fell in love with you early on, and the feelings have just grown deeper over time. I love your smile and your upbeat attitude. I love that your zest for life and I love…everything. I love everything about you."

She smiled then. "I love you, too." Tears formed in the corners of her eyes.

"Don't cry," he said, wiping them away.

He reached for her, and they kissed for a long time. "I want to show you how much I love you," he croaked. "But I don't know how you feel about that."

"I want you to show me. I want to be that close to you." She stood up and grabbed his hand. They walked toward the bedroom.

Chapter 57

Aaron

By the end of January, Aaron was feeling like a trapped animal. He'd been fine with the whole wedding and marriage thing, he'd felt it was the right thing to do. He'd even thought fatherhood might not be so bad, in fact, it could be good. He was going to do all the fun things with his daughter; building snowmen in the winter, like he saw all the little kids outside his window today doing with their parents, t-ball in the spring, soccer in the fall. (He *really* hoped she turned out athletic.) He loved Marti in his own way, she loved him for sure. Her parents, once he had really gotten to know them, were supportive, even nice to him. His father wasn't thrilled, but he would come around. Aaron's own dad had been so busy lately anyway that it didn't matter. And Aaron would have left home eventually anyway, though admittedly he should have been going to college. Still, he was just becoming independent in a different way.

But this morning had been tough. A guy, Joseph, in his AP Calc class, who didn't even get As like Aaron, he got A minuses, or B plusses even sometimes, had sauntered over to his locker. He had never liked Joseph, who was always bragging about something, who always wanted to compare test grades. "Hey, Aar," he said as Aaron grabbed his history book out of his locker.

Aaron nodded. "What's up?"

"Nothing....hey, by the way, just wanted to tell you...in case you hadn't heard, I got into Duke, early, scholarship even." Aaron could see Joseph actually standing a little taller.

"That's great, Man."

"Yeah, with the scholarship money, my dad said we have enough for a car, too. So we're going out after school to look for one."

"Great," Aaron said, feeling like he was going to throw up. This guy? Duke? He would fail out in first semester. And then he felt the depression he had been trying so hard to shake climb back over him, like a huge, weighted blanket holding him down.

As soon as Joseph had walked away, he'd gone outside to the Senior courtyard and taken out his phone. He called Marti.

"Hey, Hon, what's up?" she asked, sounding rushed.

Joseph, you know, that asshole from my Calc class? Got into Duke, scholarship."

"Oh?"

"Yeah, can you believe that? Why would they take him early? Or even, you know, at all?" He scoffed.

"Yeah Babe, I know, that's so…anyway, my mom and I are out looking at strollers. Can I call you back later?"

"Yeah, of…course. I love you, you know."

"I love you, too. And our baby is going to be a whole lot better than college." She'd hung up and he'd wondered *really*? And then, feeling guilty, he had run to class, late.

Their first pre-marital counseling session with Pastor Jim would be at ten on Saturday. He had wound up sending Columbia a quick "Sorry, I can't make the Orientation, I'll come to the next one" note, even though it had killed him. He knew he was doing the right thing.

It had snowed the night before, and Aaron carefully held onto Marti as they walked in, making sure she didn't slip on the ice. Her belly protruded all the time now, and in fact, she could no longer button her coat up against the winter wind. But she didn't mind, she'd said. She was always warm with the pregnancy. The pastor motioned to two chairs across from his desk. "So," he said after they were settled. "You'll do three sessions with me before the wedding, every other Saturday for the next six weeks, and then it will be time for your nuptials. I hope you are as excited as I am about the big day." He smiled and leaned back.

"Yes, Pastor," Marti said. "We can't wait." Aaron, for his part, remained silent.

"One of the things we do in pre martial counseling is talk about concerns either of you might have about marriage. We talk about the man's role and the woman's role in marriage, in accordance with Jesus' teachings. Aaron, I know you come from a Jewish home. How do you feel about following the Christian model of marriage?"

"I don't know if we're exactly following it…"

"Of course we are, Ar! We already agreed." Marti smiled sheepishly at the pastor. "I don't know what he's talking about. Of course, we'll have a Christian marriage and raise our children," she patted her stomach lovingly "in the faith."

"We didn't agree to it, actually," Aaron cut in, suddenly feeling he had to say something. "We agreed that we would be married by both your pastor and my dad. And that we would live with your parents. But that's about it. I didn't promise you the baby would only be Christian. Why can't we do both?" He didn't know why he was pushing so hard for this. It was true that he hadn't agreed, but he hadn't made an issue of the two religions before, either. He'd sort of gone along with whatever Marti and her parents wanted.

But now he didn't just want to go along.

Marti stared at him. "Don't be silly." She touched his leg slightly and he jumped. He wanted to push her hand away but he willed himself not to. "The baby will be Christian, mother's religion, and all of that. We're naming her under the Jewish tradition, after your mother. I thought that was good?" She looked at him questioningly and he felt bad.

"That *is* good," he said, appeasing. But then he thought again that he wasn't going to take this anymore. It was his life, too.

The Pastor interrupted. "Aaron, I think if you look at our religion, you'll find there are a lot of positives. Men have a great responsibility, to Jesus Christ himself, and their wives know it. Marti will recognize that you are the head of the household, and that ultimately, you make the decisions for the family. She will honor your choices and decisions. But you must accept the religion in order to have that privilege. We take Jesus' word seriously." He smiled, and Aaron felt a shudder in his back.

Marti cut in before he could say anything. "My father is the head of our household and it works beautifully. My mother, of course, she makes most of the decisions about the kids, and stuff like that, but he has to answer to Jesus, and that's a big responsibility, one that I don't want. You'll have that." She beamed.

What was all this talk about answering to Jesus? Aaron had already made it clear, at least he thought he had, that he wasn't converting. They hadn't decided which religion they were going to raise their baby in – he'd thought they would sort of piecemeal it together as they went. He could see now that he had been stupid.

"I don't want to answer to Jesus. I'm Jewish. And we'll figure out Julia's religion as we go."

"Another good thing about our religion," the Pastor continued, as though he hadn't heard Aaron, "is that the wife is never to say no to her husband." When Aaron looked at him, confused, he said, "Sexually, that is. Marti will recognize that you have needs as a man, and that your needs being met are essential to household harmony."

What? He had never heard of such a thing before. It sounded so...old fashioned. Not that he had given sex a whole lot of thought, but it was how they'd gotten into this mess.

Marti blushed. "Sex in marriage is a beautiful thing."

Pastor nodded. "I agree. I wish you two young people had waited."

Marti's blush deepened. "I do, too. I have prayed for Jesus to forgive me."

"He will. God always forgives. Now, about birth control..." Aaron had already given that one serious thought. He was going to insist that Marti go on the Pill or get the shot, or something, and then he was going to use condoms, too, as a backup. They couldn't afford another mistake, and he didn't want another child at least until he was out of college, maybe longer, maybe never.

"God says 'Be fruitful and multiply,' and that means you should accept as many blessings as God gives you," the pastor quipped.

"Of course, Pastor." Marti bowed her head.

"What does that mean?" Aaron's heart started beating wildly. It had better not mean what he thought it meant.

Marti touched his hand. "Just that God will determine the size of our family."

"Are you kidding me?" He felt the sweat drop down his back. He had never, and he knew never, agreed to this! And yeah, they had only used that natural planning method, that stupid idea of Marti's, but it was still a form of birth control, wasn't it? He turned to her his voice raising. "We could wind up with a dozen kids!"

"A dozen would be nice." She looked at him dreamily. *Who is Marti, anyway?* Yeah, she was religious, but she also always seemed so practical, wanting to get a cosmetology degree so she could go to work sooner rather than later, helping her mother with the kids, understanding that he wanted to go to college, figuring out ways he could still do that...

"A dozen? Are you crazy?" Now he was really yelling. "I'm not having a dozen kids! I'd never be able to finish my degree."

"Of course you would. My parents will let us stay downstairs until we're ready. You should see it, Aaron," and she rushed her words. "My mom's been helping me fix it up. We've got a new big screen t.v. down there now, and I picked out bedding and..."

I'm not having a dozen kids. We're using birth control."

The pastor cut in, leaning back in his chair. "See, that's what these counseling sessions are for, to discuss these issues so they can be worked out before the wedding." Aaron thought he looked almost smug. This guy wasn't even married! How would he know what it was like? What a pompous ass to be advising them how they should live their lives when he hadn't even done it, himself, yet!

He tried to calm down. He commanded his heart to slow. "It is good to discuss the issues, you're right," he said. "But the birth control thing is a nonissue for me. We're going to use it."

"I'm trying to live my life the way the Bible says. And the Bible says we should let God decide the number of children. It's very clear. And God wouldn't give us any more than we can handle. Look at my parents. There are eight of us kids so far, and my father manages to take care of us just fine. When they first got married, he was just a plumber's apprentice – he was *paying* another plumber to teach him to become one. My parents were around our age. And they moved in with my mom's parents and had my brothers and then me. My mother jokes that I didn't even have a crib the first couple of months – couldn't afford one. So we're starting off with more than they did, and they did fine. We have everything we need."

The pastor looked at his watch. "We need to move onto other subjects to get everything in this time. Clearly this is something you two will need to continue working on. Aaron, I urge you to come to me – man to man – to discuss this issue. We can read the Bible passages together, talk about your needs, make sure Marti knows to how to meet them. Sometimes one-on-one counseling is needed and it all works out." He winked at Marti. "Don't worry. A lot of young husbands panic about taking care of a sizeable family. But we can work on it."

No way, thought Aaron. *No frickin' way.*

Chapter 58

Hannah

Hannah managed to get through the rally the church had attended, but she made sure to stay far away from the pastor. She couldn't stop thinking about the outline in his pants and how he had smiled at her and touched her neck. And she didn't understand why his touch on her neck had felt a little good, but mostly bad, and she knew it was wrong. But now she was just so uncomfortable that she didn't want to be around him, not unless someone was with her.

She was still pretty sure that she wanted to be Christian. She liked the rules that Christianity set. They were clear. She liked praying to God whenever she was in a bind. Like now. She was going to talk to her dad and she needed to feel like God was with her. She knew he was with her all the time, but it helped to pray. It made that deep anxiety go away, it helped her focus, it made her feel more powerful, like she was capable of doing and being so much more than she thought she had been.

Her dad had barely been home the last few weeks, and with Aaron at Marti's all the time, she felt lonelier than ever. She had thought about talking to Robyn about how she was feeling, but Robyn didn't seem to be around much either.

Today, though, her dad was going to be home. He told her they could have dinner together and then watch a movie or whatever she wanted. He seemed like he was in a really good mood, and she felt somewhat bad that she was about to ruin it. But not too bad. Because how she felt was important. And he had to listen to her.

He called her to the table. For a change, he had cooked; baked ziti, one of her favorites. And she could smell garlic bread browning in the oven and there was a salad on the table. She gulped. This was going to be hard. Her Dad was making it harder, and he didn't even know it. He was just trying to be nice.

She sat down, poured some Italian dressing on her salad, started munching on a piece of lettuce. Her dad came to the table with the steaming ziti and a jar of parmesan cheese. They talked for a while, about nothing. School, temple, a new movie that she wanted to see, softball team tryouts next month, when it would snow again. And she knew she was putting it off, but she couldn't, not any longer.

"Dad," she said. "I need to tell you something."

"Sure, Honey." He looked so concerned, his eyes full of sympathy, that she felt even worse. He hadn't looked at her like that in she didn't know how long. Not with all of Aaron's problems and temple problems and everything else.

She gulped, took a long drink of water.

"I..." She put her fork down. Looked in her lap.

"What?" He gently pulled up her face to meet his. "You can tell me anything Hann-y Banan-y." Her eyes filled with tears. Her mom had called her that stupid nickname. Aaron used it, too.

"I don't think I can."

"Sure you can. I was a kid once, too. And I know all about problems girls can have." He looked at her knowingly. He thought it was a "girl" problem? She wasn't going to tell him about boys, or her period, or anything like that. Giving him the Health Class form, which stated they were going to learn about boys' and girls' anatomy, had been humiliating enough. She'd almost forged his signature for that one.

"It's not like that."

"Okay, what then? School? Your brother? I know it's going to be hard, with the baby and all but..."

"Dad, just stop. Okay? Stop."

He looked hurt. "Stop what? I'm just trying to help you."

"Just be quiet then, okay? Look, this isn't easy for me to say. You're going to be really mad."

He looked scared then. Maybe it hadn't been a good idea to start with that.

"Dad, it's just...Okay, I'll just say it. I don't...I'm not going to have a Bat Mitzvah."

"Let's not start in with that again, Hannah, okay?" His tone shifted from gentle to hostile. "We've been over it before. I know you're worried about not having friends there; it'll be fine. It doesn't have to be big. Every kid is nervous about the service; I know it's scary, and I know you sometimes skip lessons, but if you put some effort in, you'll be caught up by then."

"I'm not going to do it."

"You're doing it. There's just no way around it."

"Dad, I'm not Jewish."

"What? Of course you're Jewish." He leaned back, puzzled. "And Jewish kids have a Bat or Bar Mitzvah at age thirteen."

"I'm only Jewish because you made me Jewish."

"You're Jewish because you *are.* You're Jewish because you're being raised in a Jewish household, with a Jewish family. Because I personally converted you. You can't get out of it." Now he smiled a little, like he was trying to make a big joke out of it, and he speared a cucumber onto his fork.

"I don't feel Jewish," she said sadly and he put his fork down again.

"Hannah, lots of kids get to this point and they...question it. That's normal. But I promise you'll look back on this one day and be glad you did it."

"Yeah, you refused to get dressed for your Bar Mitzvah, saying you'd never do it. You told that story a million times, Dad." She rolled her eyes and she could tell he was trying hard not to laugh. Like he had won. But she wasn't going to let him.

"And then your dad told you if you didn't get dressed he was going to take you over his lap and spank you like a baby and he'd never said anything like that before and at first you laughed but then you realized he was serious, and you were scared, so you got dressed. And it turned out to be the best day of your life."

"See? You already know how this is going to end," her dad said, smiling again. "So why fight it?"

"You're going to put me over your lap and spank me? Because you can try to, but I won't let you. And I'm not doing it!"

"What I'm saying is that it's not worth it to fight me because you're doing it. The invitations are ordered. The caterer is ready. People are excited! We have relatives coming from all over." That wasn't exactly true. Her mom's father was coming from Chicago; her dad's parents weren't well enough to travel anymore. And they barely had any the relatives. But that was beside the point anyway, and she told him as much now.

"Dad," she said, trying to look in his eyes with complete seriousness, to let him know. "I'm not being Bat Mitzvahed, and the reason why I'm not is because I'm...Christian." And then she pulled the cross necklace out of her pocket and handed it to him.

Chapter 59

Mark

Mark had not been able to sleep. He had spent the night alternately staring at the clock and getting up and pacing his room. He had been unable to maintain his calmness after Hannah showed him the necklace, after she had defiantly clasped it around her neck and then pointed to her purity ring and told him what it meant. And then she told him about her baptism and how much time she'd been spending at the church. She told him about her friends there and marching in that rally, and he couldn't believe it. How had he not noticed? How had he been so...unaware of his own daughter's needs? His wife would be furious at him. He was furious at himself.

Sure, she had seemed different, but happier, and he thought maybe she had found some new friends. Her grades were perfect, like usual; he had checked the Parent Portal a few weeks ago. And she had been fine at home. But then he realized that he hadn't been spending much time at home, himself. He'd been too caught up in Robyn. And Aaron's problems were constantly hanging over him.

He'd yelled at his daughter, told her she was to stop going to that church immediately, that he was personally going to go see the pastor and talk to him, that she could not see Kristin anymore, that she was on restriction until further notice. And she'd cried. She's told him he couldn't stop her from being any religion she wanted, that she would always believe in Jesus Christ, that she prayed to him all the time.

He'd really gone berserk then. "Hannah," he'd pled. Pleading with a twelve year old. He'd stooped to a new low. He was supposed to be in charge, and he was anything but. "This is my *life* you're talking about. Who I am, what I stand for, what has meaning for *me*."

And she'd looked at him through flashing eyes and said, "This has nothing to do with you."

But it did. Sure, some kids went through the whole "I don't want to be my parents' religion" thing. He'd counseled dozens of families over the years, weepy eyed mothers and weary fathers and their defiant teenaged kids saying they weren't going to be Jewish anymore. And he had talked to them calmly and softly and they'd eventually agreed to the Bat or Bar Mitzvah, to continuing with

Hebrew School. Some of those kids had gone on to have careers in Jewish life, Rabbis, Cantors, Jewish Educators. He'd been proud.

But this was his own kid and now he felt like a huge failure. He'd been a terrible father, one of those fathers he never thought he would be – unaware, and then, unyielding. But it was different, different with your own kid. Hannah had to become a Bat Mitzvah. Not just because it was the right thing – and it *was* the right thing, but also because, and he hated to even think this because it was true, because if she didn't, if she dropped out, if she refused to go through it, there was no way the synagogue would renew his contract at this end of this year. It would almost be comical if it weren't so overwhelming – the rabbi whose own kid rejected Judaism.

He was going to see that pastor. That damn Jim Jameson. What right did he have, converting his child without telling him? Did Mark go around trying to convert the church's children to become Jews? None of the other clergy had ever done anything like this.

Now it was nine in the morning, an hour or two before church services, perhaps the pastor was preparing his sermon. Mark started his car, and he felt his anger growing as he gripped the wheel with determination. If he had to confront him in front of arriving parishioners, he would. Let them see who their pastor was. A man who stole children from their rightful communities. He would tell the pastor exactly what he thought, and tell him to release Hannah. He would make sure the pastor never had another chance at a Jewish kid in this town again.

Chapter 60

Aaron

Aaron's Sunday was not starting out any better than his Dad's. He was up and out of the house early, headed over to Marti's. They had to pick out wedding rings today, and it felt all too surreal. He wanted to pay for them, buy cheap bands over the Internet – he'd found a couple for a hundred bucks, plain, gold, simple. What else did you need?

But Marti had wanted something nicer and her dad had taken him aside and told him they would front him the money. When he'd protested, her dad had clapped him on the shoulder, said, "Son, don't worry about it. You can pay me back after you start making some real money." He'd thanked her dad, tried to sound grateful, but it felt wrong.

As it was, Marti's mother had bought her a fake engagement ring, telling her to wear it so "people wouldn't talk." At first they had been furious with Mark's father for not granting him permission to marry at seventeen, but after just a few weeks, they had come around, saying this gave them time to plan a "proper" wedding. So now Marti wore this fake engagement ring, and kids around town commented on it. "Where did you get the money for that?" they'd asked him at school, even though Marti was no longer there. She was being homeschooled now, and her parents had taken her brothers and sisters out of the public schools, too, soon after she had announced her pregnancy. They were concerned about the morals there. So now her mother was homeschooling all these kids besides helping her father run his plumbing business and maintaining the household, and, Marti had told him, she was pregnant again, due in August. Aaron was impressed by her, though he had no idea what kind of education they were all getting. Hannah had been furious when Kristin got ripped out of school, but then Hannah seemed so busy, maybe she had made other friends at school. He didn't know. Kind of hadn't had time to care.

But anyway, he hated that stupid fake engagement ring, he thought, as he went to pick Marti up. And he hated that they had to rely on Marti's dad to pay for their wedding rings, which seemed like something he should be doing. And he hated that he was so reliant on her family for everything right now, and he hated that his dad was not helping with anything. Though if his father helped, if he paid for things, would it make Aaron feel any better? He doubted it.

He went up to the door to get Marti. Her parents would not let her go out with him unless he came to the door and rang the bell, no matter that they knew who he was, that things couldn't get any worse than they already were, that it wasted time to go up there and collect her. He just did it. Easier than to argue about it, which would be futile anyway.

She came out of the house. Her winter coat, as usual, was unbuttoned and her stomach was prominent. "Hey," she said, kissing him chastely on the cheek. He put his hand on her belly and the baby moved for him. Nice and strong, like always. Maybe she would be the first major league female baseball player, he had told Marti once. She'd smiled, and he had, too.

"She kicked the remote off of me last night!" Marti said. "I was just sitting in my room, watching t.v., and she knocked it right off!" She laughed. Aaron laughed, too. Maybe a soccer star then, he thought, not baseball.

They drove to the jewelry store, found easy parking. Inside, it was like a warehouse, with dozens and dozens of glass cases lining the walls, more forming an octagon in the middle of the room. Sales people stood inside the octagon, cheap, vinyl-like suits on the men, gaudy polyester dresses on the women.

Marti pointed to one case. "Let's start here," she said, and they walked slowly down the aisle. Aaron wasn't really looking at any of them. He would choose a plain gold band and be done with it. It would be weird to go to school wearing a wedding ring. Weird and wrong. He thought about taking it off the minute he left in the mornings, wondering if anyone would tell Marti. He didn't want to wear one.

Every now and then, she would squeal at a diamond set. They couldn't afford a diamond set. Her father had given them a five hundred dollar allowance. Finally, she settled on one case with a number of rings she liked, all heavily ornate, with complicated etchings and a few with diamonds, smaller than the ones she had initially seen.

"Can I help you?" a woman asked, coming up to the from behind the counter. She smelled like bad perfume, and Aaron almost gagged.

"We're looking for wedding rings," Marti said and Aaron tried to smile. "We want to match."

"When's the big day?" the sales woman asked, smiling knowingly at them. Aaron hated that, how everyone must realize how young they were, how they "had" to get married. He was still mad at himself for not using a condom, and at the same time, somehow very excited to meet his little girl, already proud of her, already loving her. She was why he was doing all of this, he reminded himself. So she could have everything, a Mom, a Dad, a family. So she would feel secure in her life. It would be worth it.

Marti pointed to a few sets. "We'd like to see these, and these, and these..."

Aaron cut in. "We have a strict budget. No more than five hundred for both."

"Oh, Aar, Daddy won't care if we go a little over."

He hissed. "Five hundred." And she grew quiet.

"Most of these are five hundred just for the ladies' ring," the woman said. "I'm Janice, by the way. Nice to meet you." She held out her hand to shake and both Aaron and Marti obliged.

"Oh," Marti said, her mouth turning downward. "I really love these."

"Let me show you some things in your price range." She led them further down the row of cases until they came to a section with simple gold bands, some filigreed. "You can do nice white gold – that's the trend right now – or yellow, if you prefer – matching, engraved with your names and wedding date if you would like – for five hundred, tax included. When is the big day?"

"March 16."

"So you still have about six weeks. That's plenty of time. If you pick them out today, we can have them ready for you in two."

Marti again pointed to a few and Janice pulled them out. Marti frowned. "They're fine, but they're all so, I don't know, bland."

"Let's see your engagement ring. Maybe we can do something to match that."

"It's not real," Marti whispered. "I'm going to get a real one later."

Aaron looked around. Many couples were shopping for rings today, was the entire world getting married in a few weeks, like he was? They were definitely the youngest ones there. They should have been planning for the prom, which was only six weeks after their wedding. Marti's dad had said maybe they could go, but Aaron, who once had been saving money to rent a limo and a tux that night, whose friends had decided a year ago they were going to rent a beach house the weekend after the prom together, no longer cared. How ridiculous they would be, going to a stupid prom, when they would already be married, parents even? He had told Marti he didn't want to go. But in the end, he would do whatever she wanted.

He wished now that she would just decide on rings. He didn't care anymore. *This is boring*, he thought, as he tried on one band after another. They all looked similar to him. But she was adamant that they find the right ones.

Half an hour later, she picked. He had to go to the bathroom by then, and while Marti would decide what the rings should be engraved with, he would use the restroom. Janice pointed to it on the other side of the store, and he had never been so happy for a full bladder. Anything to get out of there.

He found the bathroom, chose a urinal, shook his head again at how crazy all of this was. As he was washing his hands, his phone buzzed. It was Jake. The text read, "Get over to Marti's church. Now."

Chapter 61

Hannah

Hannah sat on her bed, clenching her fists. She was so sick of her father thinking he knew everything. He knew nothing. *Nothing*. He didn't know what religion was best for her; what she wanted, what she felt. God. He was just some small town rabbi who couldn't even keep his own congregants. He kept pretending they were normal, but they weren't. They were so messed up, it wasn't even funny. A Jewish father with a converted daughter who didn't even want to be Jewish. A Jewish son with a pregnant Christian girlfriend. They were the opposite of normal.

She was going to move into Kristin's house. Her parents had said she was always welcome, and it would be cool, living with a lot of kids in that big house. Soon, Marti would be moving down to the basement with Aaron and the baby would be born, and if Hannah lived there, she would see the baby every day. She could babysit while Aaron was at school and Marti and Kristin were being homeschooled. She could be homeschooled, too, actually instead of going to the stupid public school that didn't even allow prayer. She bet Kristin's mother would be happy to have her.

She dropped to her knees right then and there, in front of her bed and prayed. She prayed for God to understand she didn't want to hurt her father, but she was sick of not living life the way she wanted. She prayed for God to understand she needed to move on. Surely, God and Jesus were on her side. They wanted this for her. They wanted her to be Christian.

She would pack all of her stuff, as much as she could fit anyway, into some suitcases they had in the basement. After her father and Aaron were quiet for the night – it was already one a.m., and she could barely keep her own eyes open, it had been such a long week – she had crept downstairs to the basement to dig them out. She didn't like going down there. It was dark and it smelled bad. But that's where they kept the boxes they'd never unpacked and the suitcases from their move. She had to get them.

She had to make sure the door was propped open before she went down stairs. She dragged a chair to hold it ajar and then ran to get the suitcases and bring them up. She had to go down three different times. They were heavy and bulky. How would she get them all to Kristin's? She couldn't do it herself.

Oh, well, she thought. *I'll just pack now and worry about that tomorrow*. She brought them up to her room and started throwing clothes and underwear and shoes and boots into them. They filled up pretty fast. She wasn't going to be able to take a lot of stuff. Like some of her stuffed animals. She'd like to take her stuffed horse, from when she was a baby. She remembered carrying it around, tucked under her arm, whenever she and her mother went out do to do errands. It was nearly threadbare now, worn under on the underside, the soft brown fur she used to twirl in her fingers matted at its neck. She still slept with it every night.

And the picture of her mother she kept by her bed. The one of her mother and her in the airport right after they had flown in from China. Her dad and Aaron had stayed behind in the United States. She'd been eighteen months old, and she didn't remember any of it. But she could tell how happy her mother was in the picture. She was glowing. And Hannah herself didn't look scared or anything. She was smiling as her mother beamed into the camera, looking comfortable, as though Hannah had already been hers forever. Her mom had said her dad was the one taking the picture, but what if it that wasn't true? Maybe he just wasn't that interested in her. Maybe he hadn't even come to the airport to get her! No, that wasn't right, she reminded herself. Aaron remembered the trip to the airport, getting there at eight at night. He hadn't been used to being out that late, and had been fascinated by the planes against the night sky.

But still, her dad couldn't bother getting someone else to take the picture so he could be in it, too? Just to prove he cared? No, of course not. Whatever. She shoved the picture into her bag, cramming it against her socks, and wiped away a tear. Her dad didn't want her around. Everyone would be better off this way.

The other picture she wasn't sure she wanted to take. It was of her and her mother in her parents' bed. Her mom didn't have hair anymore; she just wore bandanas and her head seemed to have shrunk. Her skull was lily-white, the color of milk. Hannah used to trace the blue veins running across her head, wondering if she had them, too. Her mother had her arm around Hannah, and Hannah was leaning into her mother. Her mother had a brave smile on her face, but Hannah still knew that look. Even though her mother had been smiling in the picture, she hadn't been happy at all. She had been resigned.

Hannah kept that picture under her bed, with her slippers and some balled up socks and the dust bunnies. She blew the dust off of it now, wondering if she should take it. At least here, in her own house, she could pull it out every now and again and remember. There, at Kristin's, there would be a lot of questions. A lot of "Poor yous." She didn't need it. She put it back under her bed, where it would be safe from prying eyes. She could come back and look at it whenever she wanted.

Her bags were packed and she was ready to go. It was three a.m. She dropped to her knees again, pulled out her cross, said her prayers. She even prayed for her father this time. He was going to need it.

Chapter 62

Mark

The streets were quiet as Mark made his way over to the church. It gave him a chance to think about what he would say, how he would say it, what Jim Jameson could possibly say back. Oh he'd probably claim that he hadn't influenced Hannah, that she had come on her own. He would probably say, "You know how teens are, you can't convince them to do anything. I merely gave her a safe place."

Except Hannah wasn't a teenager, not yet anyway. She was twelve. Sure, she would be thirteen in just a week, but even then, she wasn't old enough to make these kinds of decisions. Ironic, Mark thought, since that's exactly when the Jewish people considered a child to be entering adulthood, when the child made Bar or Bat Mitzvah. He had always counseled the families about this – your teen will throw this at you numerous times in the next year – I was a Bar Mitzvah, Jewish law makes me an adult. . .He would always have to explain to the kid that the Jews consider him *on his way to being a Jewish adult* – and that until he was eighteen, American law still said he was a minor. Inevitably, some kids tried to do some stupid things anyway, and he'd have to remind them again.

He was nearing the church now. He could just go around back and knock on the parsonage door. It would be best to do this without Pastor Jim expecting him. But first he would try the church, just in case. He parked the car, climbed out, walked to the front door of the church. It was low and wide, except for the big hump of the auditorium sticking out the back. This used to be a small church, from what Robyn had told him, but they had been trying to make it "mega" the last few years, so they had tacked on the auditorium to accommodate larger crowds. He supposed their efforts had paid off. While his own membership was slowly decreasing, this church was expanding. They'd added a side parking lot and a wing of classrooms for Sunday School.

Surprisingly, the front door was open. He let himself in. The front entry way was dingy and drafty. Again, a surprise. At the synagogue, they wanted to make it as comfortable and beautiful as possible as soon as strangers came through the door, to make them want to be there. He walked through an airless, pitch black hallway. The secretary's office was empty, of course, as were all the other rooms he passed as he walked down the long hallway. At the end was the auditorium, and he peeked in. It was dark, too, but he felt for the light switch and the light flooded in with full force. He was in a huge room with stadium seating surrounding a pulpit in the center. He walked around it slowly. This is where the congregation had put its money.

Back at the door, he shut off the light, closed the door quietly, and continued on down the hall. The pastor's office must be here somewhere. He walked stealthily, passing restrooms, a coat closet.

Finally, he saw a light coming out from under a doorway. It was muted, like weak sunshine on a mostly-cloudy day, and he wondered if the pastor was there with someone. The door was cracked open, but barely, and muffled sounds came from the room. He thought he heard the pastor's voice. On the phone, maybe?

He couldn't see anyone or anything in that tiny crack. What was he really going to prove, barging in here and then doing exactly what to the pastor? He wasn't going to hit the guy. He wasn't even going to tell him off. He couldn't demand the pastor leave town. Now that he was here, it seemed like he'd made a mistake. Maybe he should go home, go home and deal rationally with Hannah. She was just a little girl, despite what she thought. Not quite thirteen and was sure she knew so much. Well, Mark knew more, way more, and he wasn't going to let his daughter make these kinds of decisions. She would be Jewish because in their family, everyone was Jewish. She would become a Bat Mitzvah because in their family, that's what the kids did. Maybe Robyn could talk some sense into her, though, he thought, he couldn't keep relying on her for this kind of thing. Robyn wasn't Hannah's mother, not even her stepmother...yet.

No, it was up to him to deal with this mess. To talk to the pastor, man-to-man, a father trying to save his daughter, to direct her appropriately, surely the pastor would back off then. Hell, he thought, the anger rising again in his throat, it wasn't up to the pastor to try to help him, just to know his place, and Mark would damn well sure get the message across.

He opened the door a crack more, thinking that the polite thing to do would be to knock first. But he wasn't going to be polite. Wasn't going to give this guy the chance. So he pushed the door open with a shove this time, and in front of him was the pastor, sitting on the couch, a young girl, maybe around Hannah's age, next to him. Her top was off so that all Mark could see was a small, naked back, a thin bra strap hanging down over a hunched shoulder.

"What the hell are you doing?" Mark asked incredulously. And the pastor jumped up.

Chapter 63

Aaron

Aaron turned to Marti, showed her the text. "What does this mean?" he asked. He really hoped it wasn't some stupid surprise bridal or baby shower, something he had heard her mother talk about on and off, that he'd already told Marti he wanted no part of. They should be getting married quietly, without fanfare, it was not exactly the happiest of times. And the baby shower – he didn't want anything to do with that. Jewish tradition forbade baby showers – something about waiting until the baby was born to see if it was healthy. It was a whole superstitious thing, and he recognized that, he had told Marti when she had brought it up. Still, even if she wanted these things, he didn't want to be involved. He knew Marti's mother would ultimately decide, and probably make a shower for her anyway. But he wasn't going, no matter what they said.

"I don't know!" she said, squinting at the text. The saleswoman was writing up a receipt for the rings, and they still needed to get fitted so they could be sized appropriately.

"Are you sure it's not a shower?" he asked, his eyebrow rising. "A surprise thing?"

"If it was a surprise, how would I know?" she asked, her head cocked to one side. Aaron couldn't decide whether she was telling the truth. She was a pretty good liar.

"Then we won't go," he said, testing. "We'll just stay here and finish with these, and then we still need to go over to the suit store." She and her mother had wanted him to wear a tux, but he had again insisted that was not appropriate. They'd finally agreed on a new suit, and his father had actually said he would pay for that. "Fine with me if we don't go." Marti shrugged.

Aaron had been surprised by his dad's offer to buy his suit. His father was only doing this whole thing on protest, and Aaron knew how hard it was for him. His father would never get to see him marry a Jewish woman, in a synagogue, maybe ten or fifteen years from now, after he'd gone to college and then grad school, started a career. Marrying at eighteen, to a shiksa – his father never said the derogatory term some Jews still used for non-Jewish women -- but Aaron was sure his father thought it – when she was pregnant, this was humiliation for his father. Aaron knew the whole thing was killing his dad, as it would have killed his mother, and he burned with shame when he thought about the embarrassment he was bringing them. Still, his father had tried to rise to the occasion. He was nice to Marti, and was excited they were naming the baby after Aaron's mother, and had even asked if they might want to live with him for a while, though their house was not equipped to deal with a newly married couple and their newborn baby, and there would be no mother there to help them. Still, Aaron had been touched.

The woman came over to measure their fingers.

Chapter 64

Hannah

Hannah slept late Sunday morning after her night of packing. She had almost forgotten everything that had happened when she first woke up. But then she looked around her room and saw the suitcases, still lying open, filled with clothes and stuffed animals, pictures, and some of her favorite books. Her floor was a mess and her desk was covered with stuff she still hadn't decided on whether to bring.

She burrowed under the covers. It was a cold February day, and she wondered if it had snowed last night. She looked at her clock. Eleven thirty. She would need to hurry and finish packing and get out of here. She strained an ear. It was quiet downstairs. Her father had let her sleep through Hebrew School. That was a first. Maybe, finally, he was listening to her.

She would finish packing, but there was no way she could carry all of this stuff to Kristin's house. How could she get it there? Maybe she bring some to the church. Pastor Jim had said to come anytime, for anything, and she knew he would help her with this. He wanted her to be Christian, to live in a Christian home. They could move it all when her father was out. But she tried not to be around him alone too much anymore. Still, if she was going to leave, she was going to have to rely on him, just this one time.

She pulled the covers off and got out of bed. She would just get dressed now, and maybe eat a granola bar on the way to the church. She could see him right away, and they could make a plan.

Chapter 65

Mark

Mark blinked a few times to make sure the scene in front of him was real. He went over to the girl. Her shirt was lying on the ground. "Put this on, Honey."

Shaking, she flipped her shirt right side out and put it on.

"It's not what it looks like," Jim stammered. "I was just praying with this young woman..."

"Without her shirt on?

"Prayer can...require touch sometimes."

"It does not....I want you to call your parents," Mark said. He threw her his cell phone.

"And you," he looked at the pastor in disgust. "You will stay with me while we wait for the police to come."

"And then, in a flash, the pastor ran out of his office. "Stay here!" Mark called to the girl. "Call 911!" and he dashed off after the man.

Chapter 66

Aaron

After Marti and Aaron had picked out a simple gray suit, and they had both agreed on a pink tie to honor their daughter, Aaron's phone buzzed again. It was his friend Jake, again. "Where the hell are you? I said get over to the church. Too late for that. Go over to the police station instead."

He showed the text to Marti. "The police station? What the hell is going on?"

The salesman heard him. "Some big doings over there. Seems that pastor – you know, of that big church down at the edge of town – seems he was touching some girl or something, molestation, I don't know, and he got caught and he's being held there."

"What the hell?" Aaron said. Marti stared at him, her hand to mouth, her voice nowhere to be found. He texted Jake back. "I heard about the Pastor and the girl. Why do I have to go to the police station?"

Just a minute later, as Aaron was paying the balance for the suit and the salesman was handing him his receipt, Jake texted back. "Because your Dad is there. He's the one who caught him."

Jake and Marti made it to the police station quickly, but they couldn't get in. It was blocked by mobs of people, all shouting and trying to go up the stairs to the main entranceway, which was being blocked by two burly policemen in their blue uniforms. Reporters lined the sidewalks and grassy area in front of the station, and Jake recognized some of them from the New York news stations. He even thought he saw someone from CNN.

"This is nuts!" he shouted to Marti, who still wasn't saying a word, just rocking back and forth, her big belly swaying in front of her. "I am so stupid," he said, hitting his hand to his head. "You shouldn't be here." He walked her quickly back to his car, which he'd had to park a couple of blocks down the road. He kept his arm protectively around her, and made sure no one jostled her as they went by. He put her in the car, turned to her. "I need to try to get back in there," he said. "Can you wait here? Will you be okay?" She nodded. He touched her belly. "It'll be okay. I'll get to the bottom of this," he told her.

Just as he was getting out of the car to walk back to the station, his phone rang again. It was his home number. Was his dad already home again? He answered and before he could say hello, a tiny voice said, “Aaron, I need you.”

Chapter 67

Hannah

Hannah had been just about to leave the house when she heard the phone ring. She almost didn't answer it. It wasn't going to be for her anyway, just probably some stupid salesperson or something. But as soon as it stopped ringing, it started again, so she figured, maybe it was important. Her Grandma did that sometimes – called and hung up and then kept calling again until someone picked up. It drove her dad crazy.

"Grandma?" she asked as she answered. She walked into the kitchen and figured she could at least make herself some breakfast while she talked to her grandmother, who was known for going on and on about nothing. She shouldn't have answered; she wanted to get to Kristin's as soon as possible, get settled into her new life, certainly before her dad got home.

"Is Rabbi Mark Friedlander there?" the unfamiliar voice asked.

"No…can I take a message?" Where was her dad, anyway? Hebrew School would be over by now. She rifled through the junk drawer, searching for pen and paper. Why couldn't they keep anything clean in this house? Her mother would be horrified to see how disorganized they were. She hoped Kristin's mom kept the house better, though with all those kids, how could you? She could help with that. She loved organizing things. *See*, she thought, *I'm going to be helpful.*

"This is Bill Ritter at ABC-TV. Is this Hannah?"

Bill Ritter? Why did that name sound familiar? And why was someone from television calling? And how did he know Hannah's name? Had Hannah heard right?

"This is Hannah."

"Hannah, I would like to talk to your dad about the…situation in your town today. Is he home?"

She was never supposed to say whether she was home alone. She was supposed to say her dad wasn't available or give the phone to Aaron. But she wasn't even supposed to be home alone at all. Yet she was, all the time, it seemed.

Who cared, anyway? Soon she would never be alone, with all of those people at Kristin's. She was getting out of here. But she was kind of curious about this t.v. thing and what was going on in her town. She pulled a banana off the counter. It was a little too ripe; if she cut out the bad parts, it should be okay.

"What's going on in town today?" The town paper had interviewed her dad and Robyn – the cantor – after their apple dress up thing at the book store last fall. That had been so stupid. She hoped no one there realized she was related to him. But t.v.? Why would t.v. want to talk to him? She peeled the skin off the banana.

"It's just...I really need to talk to your dad, okay? So can you get in touch with him for me, maybe tell him that I want to talk to him? I bet he wants to talk to me, too. Can you write down the number for me?" She put down the banana and jotted down the number, repeated it back to him. This was all so strange.

He said goodbye and she hung up. She cut all the bruises off her banana and ate the rest, which was like mush in her hands.

The doorbell rang. She wiped her hands on her jeans and headed towards the front of the house. No one ever came to their house; she couldn't remember the last time she'd even heard the bell ring.

She ran to the living room window to see who it was. The bell rang again before she could get there. *Geez*, she thought. *People are so impatient*. She was impatient, too. She was desperate to get out the door, finally, to start her new life.

She pulled back the curtain, stared outside. Her front lawn was covered. The driveway was covered. The street was covered. There were police cars and news vans and neighbors...her heart pounded wildly and she ran back to the kitchen to get the phone off the counter. She dialed the first number she thought of.

And Aaron answered.

Chapter 68

Mark

Mark had been at the police station for two hours already, being interviewed, writing out his statement, and having his few bruises and stiff shoulder looked at by a doctor who had appeared at the station out of nowhere.

He'd had to chase the pastor through the building and out into the parking lot. Mark had not moved that fast since he had been in high school. He chased the pastor down the long, dark hallway. The man was agile, and he knew the building well. All Mark could do was follow the sound of his steps.

"Stop!" Mark yelled, but of course Jim Jameson was not going to do that. He heard a door open and light filled the end of the hall. The pastor lurched outside and Mark followed, just a few steps behind, the icy coldness of the winter morning hitting him. He chased the pastor up a long hill behind the church and he felt his chest constrict. The pastor was fast, and also about twenty years younger than him, and he didn't know if he would be able to catch him. Finally, the pastor slid on a wet stick, and Mark had been able to jump on him and pin him down with his shoulder, which ached now, even though the doctor said it was just sore, not broken, and would heal. The girl had run out of the building by then. "The police will be here soon!" she called, and Mark, over his shoulder, had urged her to stay inside until they came.

They had arrived just a few minutes later, the pastor still wriggling underneath him to get free. Any longer and Mark wasn't sure he would have been able to hold him. The pastor had been kicking him in the back, and Mark knew he was going to be sore from that.

He relayed his story to the police, and one had helped him off the pastor while two more turned Jim Jameson over onto his stomach and handcuffed him. The girl's parents arrived just moments later, and they ran to their daughter. All three of them were crying.

The police had taken the pastor to a squad car and led Mark in the other direction, asking him question after question. He asked if he should get a lawyer. "You're not a suspect," the cop said. "We can't advise you either way, but based on what you're telling me, it sounds like the other guy's the one who has the problem."

The girl was here, too, with her parents. She was still crying on and off, and Mark had wanted to go over to her, talk to her, tell her it would be okay, that her parents were here now, that no one was going to let anything bad happen to her. But the police had kept them separate, said it was to make sure the investigation didn't have any blemishes, and Mark understood. There would be a defense lawyer, and he or she would look at any way to get the pastor out of this. But Mark knew what he had seen. He was not mistaken.

He asked when he could go home. He was worried about Hannah. Word traveled quickly in this town, and he didn't want her to hear the news from anyone but him. And he felt bad. He had not left things with her in a good place last night. She had needed him, even though she had acted like she hadn't. She didn't realize she needed him, more than ever, and it had been his job to make it clear to her that she did, and that he wasn't going anywhere. His gut ached with remorse. But instead, he had pushed her further away. He shook his head at himself. He had essentially dropped the ball with Hannah, and Aaron, too. Both kids were going through major events in their lives, and Mark had stepped aside, he had thought to let them work things out on their own, but now he saw it was because he had been a coward. He hadn't wanted to deal with the hard stuff. Hadn't felt capable of dealing with the hard stuff. *But that's too bad,* he admonished himself now. *You decided to have two children, and that is a commitment forever. And whatever else is going on in your life – Robyn, the synagogue, your job, it doesn't matter. And with your wife gone, your kids need you even more.* Aaron might be nearly eighteen, a grown man according to the law, but that didn't mean he was. He was going to be a father. And he was nowhere near ready to be a father. And he was going to get married. And he was nowhere near ready to be a husband. And what had Mark done? Pretended it wasn't happening. Stupid.

Just then, a commotion erupted at the doorway of the station. From his vantage point, towards the back, sitting on a plastic bucket sat, he could hear police officers. "We're not letting anyone in now," he heard one say. "We're still interviewing the subject, and the witnesses, and the victim." But he could hear a voice, a strong, adult male voice among the cacophony. "I have a victim here with me, too. She needs to make a statement."

It was Aaron, and when Mark rose to get a look at him, he could see he had his arm around Hannah.

Chapter 69

Aaron

Aaron had driven as fast as he possibly could back to his house, Marti clutching the seat but urging him on.

"She sounded so scared," he said as he zipped down side streets to avoid the zoo of the main thoroughfare. The adrenaline rushed through his veins and he felt like he might come right out of the driver's seat.

"We'll help her, don't worry, Sweetheart," Marti said. Marti had never called him Sweetheart before. And he never called her anything besides Marti.Two blocks from his house, the traffic was dead stopped, news trucks, vans, and cars all jamming the narrow streets. Neighbors were standing on their lawns and in the roads, talking, pointing in the general direction of his house, and many other people, strangers, were marching that way.

He couldn't bring the car any closer to home.

"I'll wait here," Marti said. "You go."

"It's not safe," he said, looking around helplessly. "Especially with you..."

"I can take care of myself, she said. "I'm a big girl." She smiled, took his hand. "You need to get there, to your sister."

So he hopped out of the car, using backyards to wind his way to his house. He jumped a couple of fences and jogged through lawns until, a few minutes later, he got to the back door of his house. It was locked. Good, he thought. Hannah had known enough to do that. He knocked. "Hannah," he called. "It's me. Let me in." People had started floating through from the front to the backyard, and now they were jamming up against the door. He pushed them back, trying to puff up his chest. "Get away," he grumbled. "There's a little girl in there and you're scaring the hell out of her."

"We just want her side of the story," one reporter said, shoving a microphone in his face. "Are you the brother? Aaron, right? Do you want to say anything?"

"I said get the hell away. That's it."

He heard Hannah at the door, saw her face scoot behind the cheap curtains the last owner had left on the glass pane. He was happy now that they had.

Another reporter with a note pad asked, "Is it true your father wrestled the perp to the ground? That he walked in on him in a compromising position with a minor?"

Aaron didn't know the details, but he sure wouldn't tell these guys even if he did. "I don't know anything and I have no comment," he said, using the phrase he had heard on police shows time and again. "I just want to get into the house, talk to my sister. Okay, guys?"

They looked disappointed. "Can you give us anything? Anything at all?"

"No, I can't. Now back off." He elbowed the one closest to him, and he took a step back. A female reporter tried to shove another microphone into his face, but he grabbed it. "I will rip this right out of your hands," he said. "If you don't back away." Hannah was still peeking through the door, her features too fuzzy, he hoped, to get a clear shot of her on t.v.

"Open the door, Sweetie," he said, and he realized he sounded like his father, back in the day that his father had time and energy to protect his kids. "Let me in." He heard the sound of the door unlocking and the pull of the handle.

"It's okay, I won't let them in with me," he said, hoping what he was saying was true. They couldn't actually come in his house without asking, could they? More were flocking to the back yard every second. They must have heard the ruckus.

He turned around, shouted, "Leave us alone," and then the door opened a crack. He shoved his way in and slammed the door on all the people, locking it shut.

Hannah flung herself into his arms. "I was so scared," she sobbed.

He rubbed her head gently. "It's okay. I'm here now."

They moved towards the kitchen. He texted Marti. "Inside the house. Everything okay. You?"

"Neighbor brought me inside, told me she would bring me home. You do what you have to. We're fine." He smiled at the *we're*. She was talking about their daughter. Julia.

He sat Hannah down at the table. "Do you want a drink?" he said, talking as though it was just a normal Sunday afternoon, them hanging at the house while their dad was at temple or out doing other stuff. Except when had it last been a simple Sunday afternoon? He'd been far too caught up in his own crazy life lately to pay attention to

Hannah. In fact, he had found her downright annoying. He had been sick of her snooping, sick of her acting like she knew everything. He'd had far too much going on, important stuff, to worry about his little sister, to find her little more than an annoyance.

"Yeah," she said, and he got her a glass of apple juice. She drank it quickly, as though she had been parched. "What's going on?" she asked. "Some reporter said something about Daddy and the pastor? Daddy tackled him? Why would he do that?"

"Hannah Banana," he said as lovingly as he could. "They say the pastor was..." This was going to be hard. Hannah was so innocent. She had no idea about this stuff. Thought everyone was a good person.

"Hans," he tried again. "They say he was kind of...touching this girl wrong, and Dad saw him and held him until the police got there."

"Touched her wrong how?" she asked and he couldn't read her face.

"I don't know, like, I guess...maybe in ways he wasn't supposed to. You know." *Don't make me say the words* he begged her in his mind. *Please don't make me say the words.*

"He touched me, too," she said.

"What do you mean?" She couldn't know what she was saying. *She can't know.* When was she even alone with the pastor?

"I was in his office, sort of...talking about Christianity, and, well, he rubbed my neck and my shoulders sort of...not the right way." She finished and gulped.

That didn't mean anything, did it? And why the hell had she been in his office? He felt his heart speed up. He remembered then, the rumors that she had gotten involved with the church. How he had ignored them.

"It felt wrong," she said, and now he could see that she looked relieved to tell it. "I thought it was normal, that he didn't mean anything by it, even though it made me feel...weird. I think I...I have to tell. The police. And Dad. If he did this to this girl..."

"Are you sure?" he asked slowly. The pastor had touched his sister this way? Even if it was just her neck or her shoulders? He shuddered.

He had to get her out of the house, get her to the police station. How was he going to do that without all these reporters on their tail? He called Marti, told her what to do. A few minutes later, she was only a block away. Aaron and Hannah tried to open the back door as quietly as possible. They closed it quickly behind them, and dashed through the yard. They climbed over the fence through the adjoining neighbor's back yard, and ran through that one, and then through another onto a back street until they reached Marti. She dropped them a block from the station, as close as she could get, and turned around and driven home.

When they got in the front door of the station, his dad had come pushing forward. "What are you talking about?" he asked, looking confused, much like the night Aaron had told him about the pregnancy. But a policewoman came up and stopped him, walled him off away from them. "Sir, you need to step aside."

"Dad," Aaron called. "It's Hannah, too. It happened to Hannah." The police woman put her arm around Hannah's gently, and, after Mark confirmed she was his daughter, led them both to a side room. "I need to come too!" Aaron said. "This is my sister!"

"Only the minor and parent," the police woman said, not unkindly. "I'll have someone come get you after she gives her statement." So he was left in the hard chair his dad had just occupied, waiting.

Chapter 70

Hannah

It had been unbearably stuffy in the police station, despite the cold, windy February day, and Hannah was so happy when they were able to leave. A policeman drove them home in a dark car hours after the sun had set, so no one would see them. A few reporters were still on their lawn, but the policeman made them wait to the side and quickly shuttled them into the house. "What you did today was very brave," he told Hannah once they got inside. "You helped your dad, and you helped this girl, and most of all, you're helping Jim Jameson stay away from other young children, so this never happens again."

Hannah knew she should be proud of what she had said, yet she had only told the truth, and she still wasn't sure that the pastor touching her neck and shoulders like that – creepy as it was, wrong as she admitted to herself now that it felt – was so bad. By the end of the day, the pastor had been officially charged and would remain in jail until his trial, most likely, they said, unless he could come up with some big bail money. And it turned out she and the other girl – they wouldn't release her name because she was a minor, and Hannah would be known in public as Child Jane Doe 2—weren't the only ones.

The next day, another girl around eleven had also gone to the police station and made a statement against the pastor. And once they started digging into his past, they discovered that he had a similar pattern of behavior at two other churches where he had worked. A week later, his defense attorney shared on Good Morning America – the story had grown so big that the national news was covering it – that the pastor had a history of mental instability, that he, in fact, had been abused as a child, and that they would be seeking psychiatric treatment to help him. Hannah was glad for that. She didn't want to think about the pastor, but she had to. She was glad he was getting help, but his name made her stomach hurt all over again. She had misjudged him, and she was embarrassed. And mad, too. He had hurt a bunch of girls, worse than he had hurt her. She supposed she was lucky that it hadn't been worse, that her dad had saved that girl, saved her.

Now, Hannah stood in a beautiful light blue dress with a tiered skirt. It had spaghetti straps and a wrap dyed to match. She loved how the skirt swished at her knees when she moved. Robyn had helped her pick it out for Aaron's wedding, which was only two weeks away. She couldn't wait. Soon she would be a sister-in-law, which sounded so old, and then an aunt, which was way cooler than being a sister-in-law, even.

Her dad had been different since "the incident" as he referred to it. He was home by seven every night, and he came into her room before she went to bed and asked about her day, and listened like he really wanted to know. He had instituted an interfaith panel across all the churches in town to discuss these issues, and they were going to hold a bunch of conferences for all of the people in town to teach the warning signs. He told Hannah he felt terrible that he hadn't known, but how could he have? She had kept it to herself. But he had insisted he should have known, that he had been caught up in his own problems, his own life, too busy to really focus on her, and he felt terribly guilty. He even had said she didn't have to have a Bat Mitzvah, if she didn't want to. That it was her choice, as it should have been all along. That he wanted her to choose Judaism, and to him, she was already one hundred per cent Jewish, but that she was growing up, and it had to be her decision. She was still thinking about it. She might think about it for a long time. He said that was fine with him.

The best part of everything that had happened over the last few weeks was that it turned out cantor – Robyn, she reminded herself, which was what she was supposed to call the cantor now – and her Dad were *going out*. Only her dad didn't call it going out. He called it *seeing each other*. When they were together now, you could sort of tell. Her dad would look at Robyn like he used to look at her mom, and they were always holding hands or sitting really close together. Her dad had explained they couldn't act that way at temple, which is why no one had known. But now they had told everyone there, too, and the congregation was happy for them, all except that Anna who was on the board. She said their relationship opened up the possibility for a law suit, and one of them should step down. Hannah was worried when she heard law suit, but her dad assured her that Anna wasn't important and not to worry. He could always find a job somewhere else.

She took the dress off, hung it carefully on the padded hanger. She smoothed it down, and kept her closet open so she could look at it whenever she wanted. She lay on her bed, and reached to finger her cross necklace. But then she remembered that she had taken it off and put it in her jewelry box. She wasn't ready to declare her religion yet.

Chapter 71

Mark

Mark and Robyn were alone for the first time in two weeks. Aaron and Marti had taken Hannah to help shop for baby clothes and gear. Before they left, Hannah had brought Mark's lap top over to him on the couch, gone on a baby clothes web site and showed him the outfits she would be looking for today, the ones she thought were the cutest. She had picked a lot of pink and frills. He had stifled a laugh. He doubted that Aaron would want his daughter dressed like that, but Aaron would humor her and bring her along for the shopping trip. Hannah just wanted to be included and he had failed at that for the last few months, maybe even since his wife had died two years ago. But he would do better now. He wanted to, he had to.

So he had invited Robyn over to his house. They had never been alone at his house before, and it felt a little strange. But good. They were sitting on the couch in the den, and he had his arm around her. They had watched a movie, and a now empty bowl sat in front of them. Robyn had brought popcorn with her, something he hadn't thought of.

They were both in good moods. Last week, Anna had resigned as the president of the temple after it came out that she had been hoping to remove Mark as rabbi so her sister's son, a rabbi who had been bouncing from job to job, could come in his place. After Mark had exposed the pastor, synagogue support was stronger than it ever had been for him, and she couldn't tolerate it anymore. The temple had offered him a new three year contract, and he had accepted. Robyn was slated to continue to work there another two years under her contract. It was nice to feel at home. Settled.

He had decided to ask her to marry him, but there was something they had to talk about first. Something that had to be worked out before he could get to *that* topic.

She snuggled into him. "Hannah seems good, after all she's been through," she said. Mark loved that she thought about Hannah, seemed to really love his girl. Hannah desperately needed a mother figure, he realized now, and he had not worked hard enough to provide her with one. If Robyn said yes, she would have one. But that's not why he wanted to ask Robyn to marry him. He simply couldn't imagine life without her in it.

"She's doing well," he agreed. "But I wanted to talk to you about a couple of things."

"Of course," she moved slightly away. "Are you okay? You sound so serious."

He took a deep breath. "I love you," he said, taking both her hands in his.

"I love you, too." She snuggled back against him.

"But..."

"Uh oh, but isn't a good sign." He could hear she tried to sound playful, but underneath the playfulness was worry.

"You want kids," he said. "Right?"

"Yes..."

"Robyn, I had a vasectomy. Years ago. I can't have any more children."

For a minute, she didn't say anything, and he could tell by the look on her face that she was processing. What would she say? She was young yet, and she was entitled to have her own children, something he couldn't give her. She could easily go off and find a husband who could. And, oh, she would be fabulous with her kids. He could already tell that she would be gentle, and patient, and kind, and love doing all of those tedious things some parents hated, like going to recitals and concerts and t-ball games. He could see how she would give her children a sense of security, and how beautiful her kids would be.

She continued to stare into space. "Say something," he urged. "Anything."

"It's true," she said slowly. "I do want kids. I've pictured myself with children forever, just been waiting for the right man to share them with."

He hung his head, and he felt tears smart his eyes. He would not cry, he said to himself, if she ended it right here and now.

"Do you want more kids, though?" she asked in such a small voice he wasn't sure he heard her right.

"I never thought I did, until you." He had been thinking a lot about this the last few weeks, and he thought it would be nice to have little kids running around again. He had been fondly replaying memories from when his kids had been little, and remembering not the hard stuff, like the potty training and lack of sleep, but the fun times – Sesame Street and children's museums and their first true understanding that Chanukah was actually eight days long, which meant eight presents, one for each day.

"You've made me want them again. I totally see you with children, *your* children, and I know you'll be the best mom, and it would be a privilege to share that with you. Even as I am about to become a grandfather." They both chuckled. It wouldn't have been what he had picked for his son, but he was impressed that Aaron was making the best of it, even as his friends had started making plans for college. He was doing what was right. And he would learn to be a good father. Mark was still learning, and he was forty-seven.

"Mark I'll be honest with you. I had a feeling about the vasectomy."

"What? How, but…"

"You didn't offer to use a condom the first time we…or any time after. And you're so responsible, but you never even asked about birth control. At first I was surprised, but then I wondered…of course I didn't know for sure, but you never even brought it up. But just in case…things…worked out for us, I did some research. Did you know there's vasectomy reversal?"

"No."

"It's not a guarantee, but sometimes they can put your…you back together, and you can conceive that way. And if that doesn't work, we can do in vitro. They only need a few sperm for that. And if that didn't work….I would be okay with adopting. Look at how well it turned out for you." She smiled. He knew how much she loved Hannah. "It doesn't matter to me how we get the kids," she said. "I would just like to raise them with you, if you're interested, of course."

"So you're not disappointed?" He couldn't believe it. She'd really thought this through. Done research. Considered the life he had to offer her.

"Of course I would like biological kids, but…after seeing you with Hannah, I think adoption would be great. It wouldn't matter if they weren't from us. And to do some good…maybe adopt a child from abroad, give it a chance at a life it could never have otherwise…that feels good to me. And right."

"Then we have to talk about something else." He was grinning wildly now, and jumped up, ran to the hallway coat closet. He opened the door, fiddled through his overcoat, resettled himself on the couch, the small velvet box soft in his hand.

Then he decided he might as well be all in. He got down on one knee, and he felt the faint crackle of sore joints. A little arthritis had started to settle in, and here he was, proposing to a thirty year old in top physical condition.

"Robyn Strauss," he said. "It would be an honor and a privilege to make you my wife. Will you marry me?" He opened the box with a flash and showed her the two carat, pear shaped diamond in a platinum setting.

"I will!" She hugged him, pulling him tight, and he could smell her perfume. He pulled the ring out of the box and slipped it onto her finger. It fit perfectly.

Chapter 72

Aaron

Aaron was sitting on his bed, his computer turned to the web site he couldn't stop looking at. He was turning eighteen in just a week. He would have to register for the service, and he would be able to vote in the next election. He had ordered his cap and gown for graduation, and he already knew Marti would be his prom date in June. Her mother had promised to watch the baby so they could attend.

He also knew something else that he was going to do. He was going to Columbia. He smiled as he read, for the millionth time it seemed, the class of 2017 web page. And he wasn't going as a married man. He just couldn't. When he was out of college, maybe in graduate school, he could see marrying Marti. When they were established; when he felt ready. But right now, he just didn't feel ready. He was barely able to cope with becoming a father, and he wanted to be the best father he could. But being a husband when he wasn't sure he wanted to be one...that would not be good. It wouldn't be fair to Marti, or her family, or especially, his daughter. She deserved a happy family, and a happy dad. Columbia, at least, was close enough so he could come home to see her on weekends, for vacations, and he would be as actively involved in her life as he could. And he was going not only because *he* wanted to, but because it was best for her. His daughter deserved a life of not hearing her parents worrying about paying the bills, or giving her the best schools, the best of everything. Without that college education, he knew, it would be much harder. And an education from Columbia? He would be ahead of the game.

He just had to tell Marti.

It would kill her.

They were already so far into the process. His father had been working on the ceremony, and the church was ready. Since the pastor went to jail, the church members had interviewed several other candidates, and they had found an older guy, Lee, to substitute until they decided what direction they were headed in. The congregation had been horrified at what they'd learned about Jim Jameson, and embarrassed that he had not been vetted better. While the congregation did not support gay marriage, they believed that Jesus loved everyone, and that included gays. They held a prayer vigil for Jim Jameson's victims, and brought in an expert to speak on child molestation. Marti's parents had been actively involved in recruiting the new pastor, and they had acted on the church's behalf at news conferences. Marti and Aaron had met with the new pastor last week, and Aaron had immediately liked him. He was sympathetic to their position, and he had worked with them on the pros and cons of marrying so young. He had applauded their decision not to abort, and he had told them he would support them through their rocky times. And that's who Aaron had gone to, himself, a few days later, to tell him he didn't want to get married. Not right now. And he wasn't sure how to tell Marti.

Lee had listened to him, really listened. And then he'd asked him a bunch of questions. And he had helped Aaron think. And in the end, Aaron was still sure he didn't want to marry Marti, not right now, and Lee had supported him. Lee had said teen marriages almost always turned out badly, and that he always encouraged young people to wait until after college to make these big kinds of decisions. He said that their daughter would be lucky to have such well-meaning and thoughtful parents, and that Aaron should not enter the marriage if he wasn't a hundred percent sure that he thought it would last through eternity.

Then he'd offered to counsel them. They'd made a plan. Aaron would bring Marti to the church, tell her there was something he wanted to discuss with her that Pastor Lee would help them with. And then they would tell her, together.

So that's what he had done, and they'd made an appointment for today, exactly one week before his eighteenth birthday. They were sitting on the couch in the pastor's office – a new one – the old one had been given away, too many bad memories resided there, the congregation felt – and Marti was nervously jiggling her leg up and down. Aaron's stomach was in knots. He was about to break her heart.

"So why are we here, really," she asked after they had made "It's-very-cold-and-windy-even-for-March" talk. "Because I know something's up."

Aaron opened his mouth but couldn't think of the right words to say. Even though he'd practiced them.

Pastor Lee looked at him and nodded. He had gray hair that was still blonde on the sides, and a warm, open smile. "I love you so much, Mart," Aaron said, grabbing her hand. "And I love Julia, so, so much. I want to be the best father. I want to give her everything. And despite where we started in all of this, I'm really looking forward to her. I'm excited to meet her and even for late nights and, if you can believe it, dirty diapers." She smiled and he grinned, just for a moment.

But then he turned serious again and her face clouded over. "Mart, I have to tell you something. And it's going to be hard. But I have to."

"Just tell me, whatever it is."

So he blurted it out. "I'm going to Columbia. I got in; I never told you. I didn't tell anyone. I got in Early Decision, even got some scholarship money…and I know this is the right thing to do. I'll come home weekends and holidays and summers…and I'll do whatever I can, and I know this seems shitty – sorry Pastor –my bad – but I want Julia to have everything in her life, and that means I have to get a college education. And a good one, not just from anywhere. And I – this is selfish – I really want the college experience. And…I think if I don't at least try it, see what it's like, I'll resent you." Marti's eyes grew moist. "And I never want to resent you, or her, or…my situation. So I'm going. There's really nothing you can do to change my mind. I've thought this through."

"Did you know about this?" she asked, looking right at Pastor Lee.

"Yes, Aaron…is a very brave young man. He came to me, and we talked about it. Even prayed about it, right Aaron?" Aaron nodded. He'd never been much for prayer, but it had helped…to center him. It had helped him feel he was making the right decision.

"I don't want you not with me," she cried.

"Columbia's not that far away. Like I said, I'll come home weekends, holidays…"

The Pastor looked at Aaron again and Aaron gulped but continued. "I don't want to get married," he said. "Not now anyway. We're too young, and when we marry, I want to do it because it's right, not because we feel like we have to."

Marti cried harder and Aaron thought he would break in two, listening to her choked sobs. The pastor handed him a box of tissues, and Aaron unpeeled them, one by one, and handed them to her. He put his hand on her knee, but she pushed it away.

"If you don't marry me, you won't be able to see Julia. You're either all in or all out."

Aaron was about to answer but Pastor Lee put up his hand to stop him. They'd talked about this very point, that Marti might refuse him access to Julia. Aaron had been afraid of that. Pastor Lee had assured him that he wouldn't let that happen. "Marti," the pastor said. "You're very upset right now, and rightfully so. Let's pray about this, let's spend some time really thinking about it, and if, at the end of that time, you feel that Aaron shouldn't be around Julia for now, he'll give you space. But I hope you'll see what I've come to know about Aaron. He's a caring, loving young man who wants to do what's right." Aaron had known the pastor would say that, and he tried not to add, "I've already talked to a lawyer, and I know my rights." No one, not even Marti, would keep him from his daughter.

"This isn't right!" she cried, and then she stood up and stomped out of the office. Aaron didn't know if he'd even get to see his daughter come into the world.

Chapter 73

Hannah

It was sweltering out, more like the dog days of August than early-June summer. Earlier this week, Aaron had graduated from high school as salutatorian, and they'd had a small family get together, with Robyn of course, to celebrate. Next week they would go into the city for Aaron's college orientation. Hannah had thought it sounded horribly boring, but then Robyn had said that while her dad attended, she and Hannah could go to lunch and see a Broadway show, any show Hannah wanted. She had picked Wicked, and she couldn't wait. Robyn was so cool.

Today, though, was another celebration. Her Dad looked handsome in his new suit and tie. Robyn was wearing a light, cream colored dress, and the highest heels Hannah had ever seen. She had no idea how Robyn walked in them. Hannah and Robyn had picked out Hannah's dress together -- a sundress that made her feel beautiful and set off her tan skin.

The temple was bustling. It was Sunday afternoon, and Hebrew School had been out for a couple of weeks. Hannah wasn't used to seeing so many people there on a regular Sunday afternoon. Except for Rosh Hashanah and Yom Kippur, attendance at any extra event was rather small.

Robyn's family had come from Massachusetts yesterday. They'd all had dinner together at the Italian restaurant a few towns over. Apparently it had been the place Robyn and her Dad had their first date. Hannah had gotten to know Robyn's family last night. She liked them a lot. Robyn was just like her mom, all smiley and full of energy. Robyn had introduced her as Mrs. Strauss, but her mom had told Hannah to call her Nana, like Robyn's sister's children called her. It felt weird, but Hannah was sure she could get over that in time. Robyn's mom was really easy to talk to, and she'd given Hannah a beautiful locket and asked if she would like to put her mother's picture in there.

Aaron and Marti hadn't been able to come to the dinner. Julia was a colicky baby, and she cried a lot at night. But during the day she was so sweet, she was already smiling and sometimes she held her mouth like she really wanted to say something. Hannah was already calling herself Aunt Hannah in front of the baby. She couldn't wait until Julia called her that. They were here today, Julia all dressed up in a white dress for the occasion.

The baby had come on Marti's birthday. She and Aaron had had a big fight in March, when Aaron had canceled (though Marti kept saying postponed) their wedding. At first, he had been scared that Marti wouldn't see him, that she wouldn't let him near the baby, but Pastor Lee and her dad had worked with both of them, and Marti had come around. Last week, Hannah had gone over to Marti's to help. Julia was so soft and squishy, with plump legs and arms, and she was already smiling a lot. While they gave the baby a bath, Hannah had gotten up the courage to ask Marti about all of it. "Are you still mad at Aaron?" she'd asked. Marti had hesitated. "Sometimes," she said. "But Aaron's really an excellent father, and that's the most important thing."

"Your mom and dad are probably still mad, aren't they?"

"Yeah, I guess they are. But...I think they know they needed to be a little more flexible. Pastor Lee talked to them about it, and that helped. And they know Aaron isn't ignoring his responsibility, which I think is what they were really worried about." And although he was going to start classes at Columbia over the summer so he could try to graduate early, Marti was no longer worried she wouldn't see him. He was crazy about their daughter.

The rabbi who had ordained her father was here today, officiating. He had talked with all of them this morning to make sure he understood how they wanted the ceremony to go. Aaron was her father's best man, and she was the maid of honor. She'd never been in a wedding before.

The music started, Pachibel's Cannon, and her father walked down the aisle, smiling. Aaron and Hannah would go down next. Robyn was in the back, a veil covering her face, but Hannah could tell she was smiling, anyway.

Hannah smiled, too. Her family had come back, and, as she made her way up the aisle, her father winked at her. She had everything she wanted, for now.

Readers' Discussion Questions

Consider contacting Judy if you would like to share your book club experience with her. She's happy to Skype, Facetime, or even join your book club (depending on distance!) for an in-person visit. Meanwhile, here are some questions to consider:

Is Hannah's issue really about her religion, or is it about something else entirely?

Do you think Rabbi Mark is a good father?

How can you reconcile Aaron's choice not to use birth control but be a responsible young man otherwise?

Are religions all more similar or more different?

None of the characters ever questions the existence of God, though they do question their religions or the religions of others. Why do you think that is?

How did you feel when you were beginning adolescence? Could you relate to Hannah or did you find her view something you couldn't relate to?

How can a congregation become so unaware of what its leader is teaching its children? Is that possible? Do we give our religious leaders too much power?

What do you think happened to Aaron and Marti?

Acknowledgments

Thank you to my amazing editor, Laura Garwood Meehan, who made this a better book, and is a joy to work with!

Thank you Sherwin Soy, my cover artist, who always does a fantastic job!

Thank you to my early readers, who gave me great feedback as always: Nancy Chirlin, Jenny Milchman, Rosemary Gohd, Anita LeBeau, Molly Couto, and Dielle Courtright. A special shout out to Dielle for coming up with the title of this book even if she didn't mean to, and for helping me understand Christianity. (Any inaccuracies in the book are solely mine, however.)

Thank you to family and friends alike who encourage me to keep going even when I really don't want to....and especially to Rich, who puts up with a lot, and our girls, Rebecca and Lauren, who are everything.

Author Biography

Judy Mollen Walters' first book, *Child of Mine*, was published in March, 2013. *The Opposite of Normal* is her second novel. She lives in New Jersey with her husband and two daughters where she is at work on her next manuscript.

Made in the USA
San Bernardino, CA
19 April 2014